# STALK THE SKY

# STALK THE SKY

## WAR OF THE ALLIANCE

2

TARA GRAYCE

STALK THE SKY



Published by Sword & Cross Publishing

Grand Rapids, MI



Cover Illustration by Sara Morello

www.deviantart.com/samo-art

Dust Jacket Cover by Sword & Cross Publishing

Map by Md Shah Alam on Fiverr



To God, my King and Father. Soli Deo Gloria

LCCN: 2024918620

ISBN: 978-1-943442-61-4

DWARVEN MOUNTAINS
MT. DETMUK
AFRISTANI PLAINS
Milnissi River

OSMANA
KOSTARIA
TINENRESH
DAR GORANTH
DROGENVROH ISLAND
BRENZUK ISLAND
URIXIDOR ISLAND
PEACE BRIDGE
Gulmorth River
TARENHIEL
NINTHALOR
LETHOREL
ESTYRA
PERSATRA AERODROME
SYLMARE
DANORBIC OCEAN
BRIDGETOWN
FORT LINDER
Hydalla River
FORT DEFENSE
CHIBO RIVER
AYRE
FYNE RIVER
ALDON
TREEHAVEN
FORT CHARIBERT
WHITEHURST MOUNTAINS
WINDERDON LAKE
LANDRI
ESCARLAND
MONGAVARIAN EMPIRE
Frogg's Hollow
GROYRIA
N
W
E
S
THE WORLD OF THE
ALLIANCE KINGDOMS

# Fieran's Family Tree - Dacha's Side

Ellarin* — Leyleira

Vianola* — Lorsan* - - - Filauria*

*Deceased

Weylind — Rheva

Ryfon
Brina
Emmyth

Melantha — Rharreth

Rhohen
Sontar

Jalissa — Edmund

Jayna

Farrendel — Elspeth

Fieran
Adriana
Louise
Elliana
Tryndar

# Fieran's Family Tree - Mama's Side

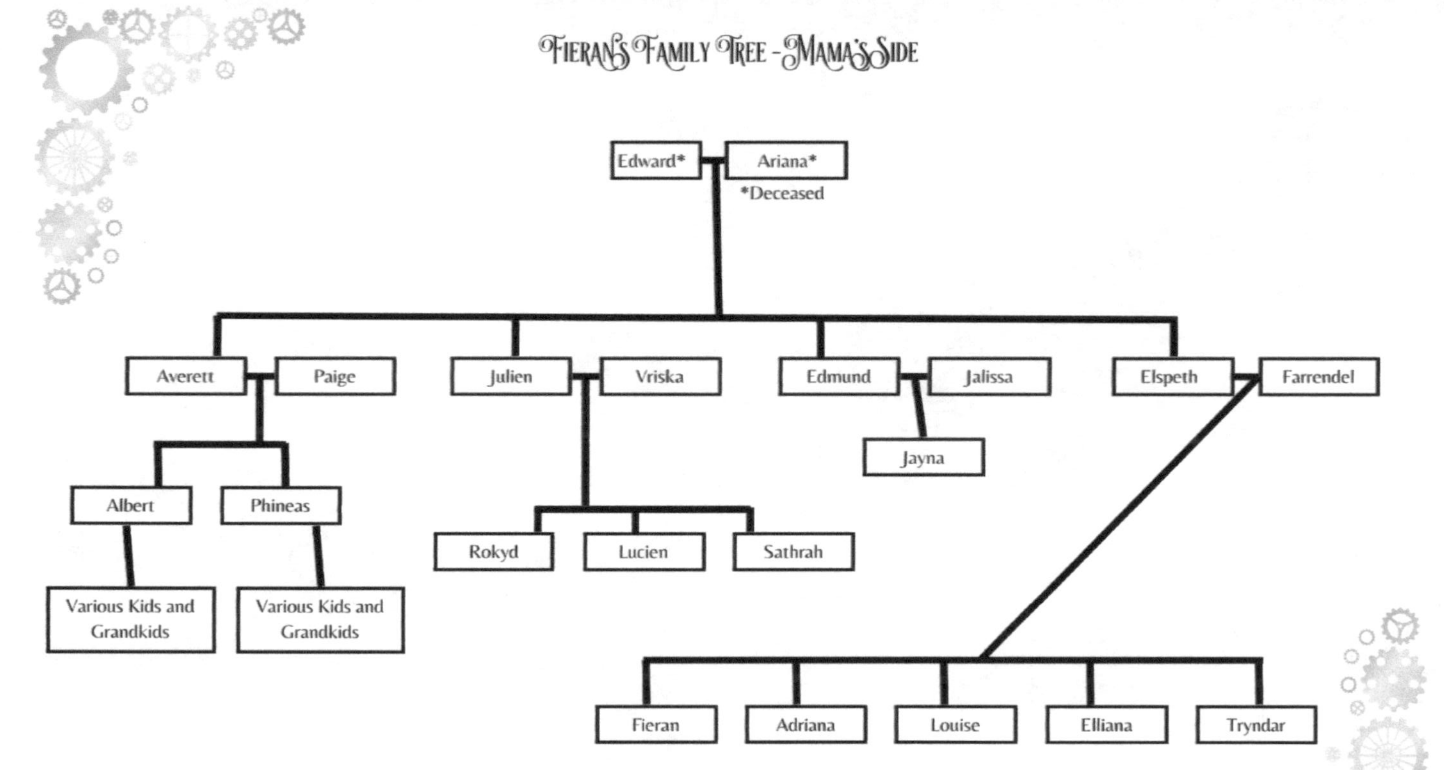

# CHAPTER ONE

Fieran Laesornysh threw himself into a front flip, landing lightly on the iron walkway that ran along the spine of the Escarlish airship. This high up, his lungs burned with the exertion of breathing the thin air, and he'd ditched his uniform jacket and PT shirt long ago, letting the cold air blast his bare skin.

The ocean spread in a blue-green ink broken only by the white slashes of the foaming waves. A cargo ship plying the waters appeared as nothing but a slim speck, visible due to the white wake stretching behind it.

A faint vibration and gentle thuds came from behind him as his best friend and fellow half-elf Merrik landed his own flip.

Fieran spun to face Merrik again. Merrik, too, had ditched his shirt here in the privacy of the top of the airship. Merrik's short chestnut hair—more a brown with red highlights rather than Fieran's brilliant red—glinted in the morning sunlight.

Holding his hands before him as if he gripped the hilts of the swords he'd left at home when he'd joined the

Escarlish Flying Corps, Fieran spun and parried an invisible enemy, dodging and ducking. Hints of his magic curled over his fingers, and he didn't try to fully hold it back. There was no one around but Merrik to see, and he held tightly enough to his control that he was in no danger of incinerating the airship beneath their feet.

Not that Fieran was likely to get into trouble for using his magic here. This particular airship captain had a case of hero-worship for Fieran's family—his dacha and Uncle Julien in particular—that could rival Pip's, if that was possible.

Merrik copied his movements, and for several minutes the two of them pantomimed a sword fight, slashing and parrying with their invisible swords.

Despite the crisp wind whipping past Fieran's face, the stench of smoke still clogged his nose and the taste of ash coated his tongue. No matter how hard he pushed himself in training, he couldn't quite seem to hold the memories at bay.

Memories of a nighttime attack and bombs falling on the innocent city of Bridgetown. The bodies he'd pulled from the rubble. The flag-draped coffins loaded onto the train with an accompanying honor guard as Fieran, his squadron, and the rest of Fort Linder stood by, saluting the fallen.

The feel of his magic crackling over Mongavarian airships and airmen moments before he let his magic consume canvas and iron, blood and bone, without discrimination. Without mercy.

*Today you are Laesornysh.*

That was what Fieran's dacha had stated, naming him not just with the last name he'd inherited but with the elven warrior title he'd now earned. A title meaning *Death on the Wind* in elvish.

Fieran felt the weight of those words now, five days later, just as much as he had the morning after the attack when his dacha had said them.

Thus the reason he was up here on the top of the airship, pushing his muscles, reflexes, and lung capacity to the brink. Growing up, he hadn't fully understood why his dacha, the famous elven warrior Prince Farrendel Laesornysh, would often exercise on top of the train as the family traveled from Treehaven, their estate in Escarland, to Ellonahshinel, the elven treetop palace in Tarenhiel.

Now Fieran understood all too well.

The nearly four days of travel had given him all too much time for contemplation. After riding across the Alliance Bridge in army trucks, Fieran, Merrik, the thirty-odd men of their squadron, Pip, and the other mechanics who had been sent with them had boarded an elven train at the station in Calafaren, which hadn't been damaged in the bombing. The nearly thirty-six-hour train trip took them north through Estyra, then east until they reached the port city of Ninthalor, where they boarded the Escarlish airship.

During their two-day flight after boarding the airship, Fieran had been afforded the run of the airship and courtesy well above what he should have, given that he was a newly minted first lieutenant. The airship's captain had even offered him a cabin in the officers' quarters, but Fieran had refused, instead bunking in a hammock among the gas balloons with his men. Both so that he wasn't quite so smothered by the captain and because sleeping among the balloons made it easier to sneak onto the top of the airship each morning.

Merrik dodged one of Fieran's imaginary swords just as a shaft of brilliant sunlight broke through the clouds along the horizon, shining so brightly off the metal walkway that Fieran had to squint. The next moment, Merrik grasped his wrist, pinning his arm between their chests as Merrik held his other hand poised as if holding the blade of a sword to Fieran's neck.

Fieran huffed a breath and held up his free hand in surrender. "I yield. But just so you know, the sun was in my eyes."

"I still won." Merrik stepped back, releasing him. "I always win when you are distracted. And you are rather distractable."

Fieran didn't have an argument for that. It was far too true.

Shading his eyes, he faced forward, the sun slightly off to his right as the airship traveled northeast. The cold breeze as the airship plied the sky prickled against his sweaty skin.

The coast of Kostaria was nothing but a smudge to their west while nothing but the ocean lay as far as they could see to the east.

Down below, the shapes of two islands came into view. Waves crashed into their rocky coasts while tall white lighthouses marked their highest points. On either side of the channel between them, gun emplacements guarded the vital waterway.

Beyond the islands, icebergs dotted the waters, forming a perilous maze. Despite this, the channel between the islands and the waters on either side were choked with fishing trawlers, cargo ships, and gray-painted iron warships. All the ships easily maneuvered between the icebergs, likely thanks to having a troll on board with ice magic.

Something any Mongavarian ships on their way to attack Dar Goranth wouldn't have.

Their airship continued on for long minutes more, the islands disappearing behind them.

"We are dropping lower." Merrik halted next to Fieran at the bow of the dirigible.

"Coming in toward Dar Goranth." Fieran pointed, squinting with the rays of the rising sun beaming warm against the right side of his face. "I think that smudge is Drogenvroh Island up ahead. Remember the last time we were here? That was a fun trip."

Merrik crossed his arms over his bare chest and eyed Fieran. "You gave your cousin Prince Rhohen a black eye."

"In my defense, he started with the insults and threw the first punch." Fieran gestured from himself toward the island ahead. "What else was I supposed to do but punch back?"

"Be the more mature cousin and not fight him?" Merrik waved with one of his hands without uncrossing his arms. "Just a suggestion."

Fieran shrugged, not fighting too hard against his grin. "We were in Kostaria. Not fighting is more insulting to Rhohen than fighting him."

"Uh-huh." Merrik's disapproving frown didn't waver. "You cannot claim complete innocence in that incident. You made faces at him all through the formal treaty signing ceremony."

Well, there was that. Fieran *might* have done a bit of the provoking. But silly faces trying to make his cousin stop scowling so darkly was a far cry from insulting one's mother and father.

Not that Rhohen had truly meant what he'd said. Nor had he gotten off easy once his parents had heard what he'd said and done.

"I probably should have paid more attention to that

treaty ceremony." Fieran shrugged, peering into the morning mists to make out the craggy cliffs of Drogenvroh Island's southern point coming into view. "It's the reason we're going to be stationed here, after all."

About forty years ago when the naval base at Dar Goranth was coming into more importance, Escarland and Kostaria had signed a treaty giving Escarland not just access to the Kostarian base, but also the ability to treat it as their own—for a certain amount of funding.

While the Hydalla River was deep enough for ocean-going vessels, and Escarland had a naval base outside of the river city of Ayre, it was a long treacherous trip up the river past miles of Mongavarian shoreline. That treaty forty years ago made Dar Goranth the primary station for Escarland's seaborne navy.

The other part of that treaty had been a deeper integration of the various branches of the armed forces of the Alliance Kingdoms. Escarlish citizens could serve in the Kostarian navy, something that was necessary since Escarland had the population and Kostaria had the fleet in need of sailors. While Kostaria had a few airships, Escarland and Tarenhiel had far more, so Kostarian citizens could serve on one of Escarland's airships.

Since Kostaria's army had so far forgone starting a Flying Corps in favor of focusing on their navy, Escarland's and Tarenhiel's Flying Corps would need to protect the skies and airships of all three kingdoms.

Merrik gave a grunt of assent, leaning back slightly to balance as the airship drifted more steeply downward. "If Prince Rhohen is there now, you will need to be more polite. Your dacha will not be there for me to fetch."

"Do you think Rhohen will be at Dar Goranth? I haven't heard if he's left Osmana or not." Fieran planted his feet wider against the downward trajectory of the airship. He and Merrik weren't supposed to be up there, especially without safety ropes, while the airship was coming in for a landing.

The island looming on the horizon was a gray-and-green mass rising from the crashing waves of the ocean. A white lighthouse perched on the point while piles of slushy snow coated the shadows in the crags and hollows.

"Since joining the army, you have had to get your information from the press instead of your parents." Merrik rolled his shoulders and finally uncrossed his arms enough to gesture ahead of them. "Prince Rhohen is the only warrior with a form of the magic of the ancient kings that Kostaria has. They aren't going to advertise his whereabouts any more than Escarland tries to advertise yours."

Good point. Fieran had assumed Rhohen would be at Osmana, shielding that city from attack.

Now that he thought about it, Osmana was in little danger, protected by the craggy peaks and buffeting winds of the Kostarian mountains.

But Dar Goranth lay outside of the magical Wall Fieran's dacha had created with help from Uncle Rharreth and Uncle Weylind. For months, everyone had assumed it would be the location of Mongavaria's first strike in this war. Uncle Rharreth and Rhohen had probably been camped out here for the past few months, preparing to ward off an attack if it came.

But Uncle Rharreth couldn't stay in Dar Goranth for long. He had a kingdom to run. Yet he couldn't leave Rhohen here alone. While Rhohen was numerically the same age as Fieran—eight months younger, if one wanted to be technical about it—Fieran had aged faster thanks to having a short-lived human for a parent instead of two longer-lived parents as Rhohen had. Rhohen was an adult, barely, still coming into the full strength and control of his power. He couldn't be turned loose to protect Dar Goranth on his own.

While Mongavaria had chosen to strike a symbolic blow by attacking Fort Linder, Bridgetown, and Calafaren as their opening move of the war, the hammer blow would likely fall on Dar Goranth next. Rhohen might be good enough for a just-in-case measure, but they needed someone trained to defend the naval base now that the war had begun.

Fieran heaved a sigh, his breath misting slightly before his face. "Fine. I'll do my best not to antagonize Rhohen. But I can't promise more than that. My very presence seems to rile him."

"True. Then again, his presence riles you, so it is mutual." Merrik eyed Fieran in that way that had Fieran squirming. "Keep in mind, you could be court-martialed now for fighting outside of a structured fighting bout, even here on a Kostarian base where their rules about fists flying are laxer than Escarland's. Not to mention, both you and Rhohen have come into your magic since then. You could level the base if either of you lose control."

Another good point. Merrik was annoyingly skilled at those. There could be actual consequences this time if Fieran gave in to the temptation to wipe the pouty smirk off Rhohen's face.

"Like I said, I'll do my best." Fieran turned away from the sight before them to reach for his shirt where he'd left it tucked into the dogging wheel for the hatch to enter the dirigible. "I can't make promises for what Rhohen will do."

"That is what worries me." Merrik claimed his own shirt, tugging it over his head.

Once they were both dressed in their drab olive-green uniform shirts—identical except that the bar on each of Fieran's shoulders glinted silver instead of bronze, as did the wings pinned to his chest—Fieran stepped toward the side of the airship instead of the hatch.

There, a long metal ladder clung to the side of the dirigible, curving to fit the shape. The ladder was supposed to be used for maintenance of the dirigible's outer skin while at dock.

But it seemed like a far faster way down than taking the network of ladders and catwalks inside the dirigible that wove around and between the inner balloons, which held the helium keeping the airship aloft.

Merrik heaved yet another sigh. "Really?"

"Yep." Fieran grabbed either side of the ladder as if to climb down, then pressed his boots on either side of the ladder as well. With one last smirk at Merrik, Fieran loosened his fingers just enough that gravity sent him sliding down the ladder rather than climbing it.

The cold wind raked through his hair and tugged at his clothes. The rush of falling and the exhilaration of the sea spreading out so far below bubbled up inside him so that he couldn't help but give a whoop. The endless ocean was a bit like the trackless sky. Dangerous. Beautiful. Something to be both loved and feared in equal measures.

Soon he would get back in a flyer and feel this same heady thrill each time he took to the sky. Five days without flying was far too long.

All too soon, he had to tighten his grip with both hands and feet, slowing himself just enough that he landed lightly on the metal platform at the top of the gondola. He stepped aside, giving Merrik room to land just as easily, their footfalls so light that one of the

Escarlish airmen bustling farther along the catwalk didn't even glance their way.

Fieran led the way through a hatch onto the walk that surrounded the outside of the gondola, not quite ready to give up the fresh air for the narrow passages inside.

As he dropped down another level onto a lower walk, he found Tiny, the half-troll, half-human pilot, hunched over the rail near the stern. Despite being perfectly fine while flying an aeroplane, Tiny got horribly airsick on airships. He'd learned the hard way to vomit over the stern instead of into the wind on the bow.

Tiny pushed away from the rail, making a valiant effort to straighten and give Fieran a proper salute, despite the green cast to his gray skin.

Fieran suppressed his sigh and quickly saluted back. Was it bad that he was already regretting his promotion? For those golden weeks of training, he had been just one of the guys for the first time in his life. Not a prince. Not the son of famous parents. Not someone to be treated as anything special.

Now he was back to the way things had always been. The weight of a title—or of command in this case—rested on his shoulders and separated him from others.

At least the gulf between a first lieutenant and second lieutenant wasn't that wide. They were all officers. He could maintain his friendships, even if his friends had to salute him occasionally.

As soon as his salute was acknowledged, Tiny returned to his spot gripping the rail.

Fieran gave him a pat on the back as he edged by. "Hang in there, Tiny. We're almost to Dar Goranth and solid ground."

Tiny just gave a miserable nod in return.

Merrik hurried past Tiny as well, giving him a sympathetic look but staying well clear.

A few yards past Tiny, Fieran and Merrik reached the door to the officers' mess, which was on the other side of the airship's kitchens from the mess for the noncommissioned airmen.

Inside, the thirty-odd men remaining in his squadron after training and the battle in the skies over Bridgetown had gathered around the various tables. A few plates were piled in the center of some of the tables while several flyboys were finishing the last bites of their breakfasts.

At least the mess was considered neutral territory. No saluting of officers or coming to attention required. Meals would be chaos if everyone had to spring to their feet and salute every time a superior officer walked in.

Fieran headed for the table near the bank of portholes where his friends had gathered. Pretty Face—the disgraced seventh son of an equally disgraced Escarlish nobleman—lounged on the bench, his legs stretched out underneath the table. Across the table from him, blond-haired, beanpole-thin Elijah Lake scowled and tried to find a spot to stick his own equally long legs without bumping into Pretty Face.

Beside him, Stickyfingers, their resident ex-thief, had a set of lockpicks and a padlock in his hands, and he appeared to be teaching Pip—their half-dwarf, half-elf female mechanic—how to pick locks. She had a second padlock and another pair of picks in her hands as she followed Sticky's instructions.

"Why are you learning to pick locks?" Fieran halted beside the table, peering over Pip's shoulder. "You can just move the metal with your magic and unlock any lock that way."

"Because it's fascinating." Her dark brown curls tumbling over her shoulders, Pip gave a shrug, swiveling and craning her neck to glance up at him. "You never know when you might want to be more subtle than just tearing apart a lock with magic."

Fieran raised his eyebrows at Stickyfingers. "You're a bad influence on the squadron."

"Says the elf who was wandering about on top of the airship a moment ago." Stickyfingers shrugged, then held up a lockpick and padlock. "I can always teach you after Pip is done."

Fieran shook his head, waving the offer away. "No need. I already know."

Stickyfingers squinted up at him, his brow furrowing beneath his shock of brown hair. "You do? But you're a prince. And...not..."

"Delinquent? Felonious?" Pretty Face supplied.

Sticky flexed his fingers on the padlock like he was contemplating chucking it at Pretty Face's head.

"My Uncle Edmund taught me." Fieran needed to get the focus back on the conversation before things devolved.

"Ah." Stickyfingers nodded.

That was all the explanation needed. Fieran's uncle Edmund was the top spymaster of Escarland. He was well-versed in the more shady side of life.

Fieran's dacha and mama had made the mistake of letting Uncle Edmund and Aunt Jalissa watch Fieran, Adry, and Louise when Ellie was born. The three of them had gotten an education Dacha hadn't been expecting. Mama had just laughed.

Pip's padlock clicked open. She grimaced down at it. "Simple locks are ridiculously easy to pick. It's worrisome."

Stickyfingers grinned, showing off his crooked and stained teeth. "Told you."

"Anyway, if the lesson in the more dubious arts is over, we're nearing Dar Goranth." Fieran gestured toward a door set between two of the portholes, which led onto the lower catwalk around the gondola. "You'll get a good look at it from the catwalk."

Chairs scraped, then a stampede rushed for the door. For many of the men in the squadron, this was their first time ever leaving Escarland, except for brief visits to Calafaren across the Alliance Bridge, much less their first time seeing Kostaria.

Fieran stayed at Pip's back, protecting her from being jostled in the rush for the door. Merrik also waited, though Lije, Pretty Face, and Stickyfingers joined the chaos headed for the door, the latter stuffing padlocks and lockpicks back into his pockets as he went.

Once the others were outside and shoving for positions along the rail, Fieran held out a hand to Pip. "Ready for your first look at Dar Goranth?"

"Yep. I'm sure it's impressive." Pip took his hand and let him pull her to her feet, releasing his fingers as soon as she was standing. Her head didn't even come up to Fieran's shoulder, and he found himself looking down at her dark brown hair. She tilted her head to grin up at him as she stepped past him. "I need to take lots of notes to describe it in my next letter home. My muka has a great interest in troll architecture."

That made sense, given that Pip's mother was a dwarf. While both trolls and dwarves had the ability to manipulate stone with their magic, the trolls used their magic directly on the stone while the dwarves used their magic in conjunction with tools to craft the stone.

"Hopefully you'll be able to see Osmana someday."

Fieran followed her with Merrik trailing after them. "Even I find Khagniorth Stronghold quite impressive, and I'm not normally one to note architecture."

"Perhaps someday." Pip shrugged. "It's hard to imagine I'd travel that far. Until now, I've never been to Kostaria."

"Well, I've never been to the dwarven mountains." Fieran hurried a step ahead and opened the door for her. A blast of frigid air slammed into him, cutting even colder than it had when he'd been on top of the airship and exercising away his fidgets.

As Pip stepped outside, she rubbed her arms. "Brr. It's cold."

"It's still winter in Kostaria." Fieran strolled next to her along the catwalk to the end of the line of flyboys, heading for the bow.

"I might have to stock up on warmer gear at whatever Dar Goranth has for a commissary." Pip shivered again as she claimed a spot free of flyboys against the railing. She wore the shirt and coveralls the army provided, but no thick overcoat.

Fieran had a green, army-issue wool overcoat in his rucksack, but he hadn't bothered bringing it with him that morning. He'd pull off his shirt and give that to her, but he wasn't sure if she'd laugh or get embarrassed by that. Besides, his shirt was just a hint sticky with his sweat, even though he'd taken the time to let the wind dry his sweat before putting it on. It was too gross to give to her.

He leaned against the rail beside her. "I guess I'll just have to provide a windbreak."

"That works." Pip tucked herself closer to him, not quite touching but nearly so.

Merrik took the spot on Pip's other side, creating even

more of a buffer from the wind, though Merrik left more space between himself and Pip than Fieran had.

As they stood there, chilled in the sea breezes, the airship drifted past the long, green island with stretches of rocky cliffs bordering the crashing waves. A small sandy cove came into view far to the left, and a few wooden docks reached into the waters while what looked like a small collection of stone buildings were tucked into the rolling green hills rising from the water.

The airship eased to starboard, paralleling the coast for several minutes before it worked its way around a jutting, rocky headland with a squat, stone lighthouse perched on the point.

The headland opened to a large bay with long sea grass rolling down to the white-capped waves. The points on either side sported gun emplacements and bristling fortifications overlooking both the harbor and the ocean.

Two airships, one flying Kostaria's flag, the other Escarland's, hovered over the gun emplacements.

At the bow of their airship, a signal corpsman waved a series of flags. He must be sending out today's recognition code and their airship's information for a few moments later, their airship was allowed to proceed into the harbor.

To one side of the harbor, the commercial port bustled with large ironclad merchant vessels. Some had both smokestacks and masts for sails rising from the deck while others lacked smokestacks entirely and must be magically powered. Both troll and human workers toiled along the quays, unloading and loading the various ships carrying vital supplies for the war.

Filling the rest of the vast harbor, the Dar Goranth Naval Base stretched into all the fingers of the bay. The water was filled with gray ships of all sizes—from smaller cruisers to the mighty dreadnoughts bristling with turrets sporting guns as long and wide as trees. The ships flew a variety of the three flags of the Alliance, though Kostaria's flag dominated.

As the elves hadn't taken to iron ships all that well and Escarland was essentially landlocked except for the Hydalla River seaway, Kostaria had to be the Alliance Kingdom to rule the waves and protect the trade routes, and they had taken to the role with alacrity.

Airships drifted over the harbor, casting long black shadows on the water and the teeming wharves below. On the airships, Tarenhiel's flag was better represented, though plenty flew the insignia for Kostaria or Escarland.

Fieran leaned farther over the rail, but at this angle he couldn't make out the names painted on the sides of either the surface ships or airships.

"Do you think your cousins are in port?" Merrik's murmur was too low for the others to hear, except for Pip huddled between them.

"I don't know. It's possible." Fieran shrugged, still searching the warships below. "It would be nice to have a few cousins who actually like me here."

"It would be nice to have some backup in case you get in a brawl with your other cousin," Merrik grumbled as he, too, peered down at the ships below.

"That sounds ominous." Pip stopped gawking at the harbor long enough to eye Fieran.

"Nothing to worry about." Fieran shot her a grin.

Merrik snorted but he didn't comment as they studied the harbor stretching below them.

The sound of pipes trilled from the various ships along with the shouts of orders. The whole harbor rang with the clangs from the shipyard where crews swarmed over three unfinished hulls in dry docks. More warships in various stages of construction floated at their slips.

As the airship passed over the dry docks, Pip straightened, then leaned farther over the rail. "I sense dwarven magic. I think there are dwarf work crews building those dreadnoughts."

Fieran let a little trickle of his own magic wind around his fingers, and his magical senses heightened.

There was so much magic present in Dar Goranth, from troll magic laced all through the cliffs ahead of them to the magical power cells fueling the airships and the dreadnoughts in the harbor that Fieran struggled to pick out the faint, foreign magic emanating from below. It didn't feel exactly like Pip's. Then again, Pip might have dwarven iron magic, but she used her magic the way an elf would.

Stickyfingers leaned farther out, squinting. "Real dwarves? I'd like to see them! Not that you aren't a real dwarf, Pip. But…you know what I mean."

Pip rolled her eyes. "Lije, give Sticky a smack upside the head for me."

Lije grinned and did as asked, smacking the back of Sticky's head lightly.

"For once it wasn't me saying something inappropriate." Pretty Face smirked, lounging more languidly against the railing.

Lije reached over and gave him a smack on the back of the head too.

Pretty Face tried to duck but not fast enough. He gave an exaggerated wince. "What was that for?"

"A preemptive smack. I'm sure you'll deserve one eventually."

"Preemptive. That's a rather big word. I didn't know you knew that kind of vocabulary."

Lije huffed. "There you go. And yes, I've been working to expand my vocabulary. I'm a lieutenant now. I need to sound like one."

Fieran shook his head and tuned them out as he tipped his head to Pip. "Are the dwarves from your muka's kingdom or one of the others?"

"I don't know. I'll find out when I have the chance to speak with them." Pip's gaze remained locked on the working dwarves until the dry docks passed from sight beneath the airship.

Ahead, tall, craggy cliffs formed the back wall of the Dar Goranth base, its face pockmarked with windows and doors that opened onto balconies formed out of the cliff. The entire cliff was a warren of passages and rooms in true troll fashion. Why live on a mountain when one could live in it?

Three flagpoles stood in a circle of cleared space among the buildings just before the cliffs. Here the Kostarian gray-and-white banner flapped higher and in the center while the Tarenhieli and Escarlish flags were relegated to either side.

One side of the cliffs had a series of staggered protrusions of stone, and two airships were already at dock, tied in the shelter of the cliffs where they were protected from the buffeting winds.

At the top of the cliffs, a grassy field spread out long and straight. The base's airfield. A few knolls rose from the otherwise flat top, with dark mouths of openings leading into the cliffs.

Dar Goranth. The mighty bastion of the Kostarian Navy amid the storm-tossed northern ocean. Fieran's first post and first command. Time to prove himself all over again.

# CHAPTER TWO

Fieran waited with his squadron of flyboys and mechanics as the airship settled into place alongside one of the docking stones jutting from the cliff. The various human airmen threw lines to the troll ground crew, who tied the ropes to the large stone bollards.

After a bit more rigmarole of docking, the gangplank was extended, connecting the airship to the stone.

Finally, a gray-skinned, white-haired troll in a white naval uniform with a commander's insignia marched up the gangplank. He was tall and well-built as most trolls were with arms bulging with enough muscles that he looked like he could bend metal with his bare hands. After a glance around, he faced Fieran and the others. "Are you the Escarlish pilots?"

"Yes." Fieran strode forward and saluted the troll. "First Lieutenant Fieran Laesornysh reporting in."

The troll blinked at Fieran's name, something flashing through his blue eyes. No surprise that he'd recognize the

Laesornysh name. Hopefully Fieran's dacha hadn't killed someone this troll knew, back in the wars between the elves and the trolls.

"You and your men, follow me." The troll spun on his heel.

Fieran set out after him, and his column fell into step as well. They strode down the metal gangplank, then along the stone pier. At the end of the pier, the troll commander gripped the handle of a stone door and yanked it open as easily as one might a gauzy curtain.

He didn't hold it open for them, and Fieran rushed forward to grab it before it swung closed. As Fieran stepped inside, he held the door long enough for Merrik to take it from him, who then passed it to the next man in line.

Inside the mountain, glowing stones set into the rock walls of the passageway lit the way, casting a white glow. The troll commander waited at the end of the passageway where it branched into a large hallway as the rest of them piled inside.

As soon as they were all inside, the troll glanced both ways, then led the way across the intersection with the main hallway to a staircase that spiraled around a pair of lifts. He marched up the stairs without looking back to see if Fieran and the others were following.

They climbed for several levels before the stairs opened into a large cavern at what must be the top of the cliffs. Stone pillars set at intervals held up the slightly domed ceiling while the very far end of the room gaped open, giving a view of sunlight shining on the green of the airstrip.

Inside the expansive stone space, aeroplanes lined up between the stone pillars, though there seemed only a handful of flyers compared to what this space could hold. Different carts and stations held tools for the mechanics.

In the center of the cavern, a female troll warrior in a white naval uniform stood waiting, her hands clasped behind her back. Her white hair was half-pulled back, though the parts that had been left free were wound with leather and a few stone decorations in the traditional fashion of troll warriors.

About thirty elves—mostly male but with a few females—in the darker, evergreen Tarenhieli army uniform assembled before her. All of them were second lieutenants except for the first lieutenant standing in front of them.

The elf first lieutenant had long honey-blond hair darker than Dacha's silver-blond. He carried himself with his slim nose tipped slightly high in the air.

As he swung his gaze to Fieran, his nose flared, his eyes narrowed, and his pouty mouth curled in obvious disdain.

Fieran didn't like him.

Something sparked in the elf's eyes. At least the dislike was mutual.

Worse, there was something familiar about this elf lieutenant. Fieran was pretty sure he was some kind of elf nobility, though Fieran couldn't place him. He didn't attend many of the elven social events, as elven nobility tended toward snobbery.

Fieran halted his column, and they assembled in military formation. They then proceeded with a salute fest as all the lower ranked officers saluted all the higher ranked ones of all the various armies assembled there.

At last, the female troll warrior stepped forward, the insignia of a captain glinting on her shoulders. "I'm

Captain Gradrah of the Kostarian Navy, in charge of all flight operations here at Dar Goranth."

Fieran straightened his shoulders. Captain in the navy was much higher ranked than captain in the army.

For the past seventy years, the Kostarian and Tarenhieli armies and navies had re-structured so that their ranks matched that of Escarland, making it easier for the three armies to deploy together or even have units assigned under each other. The elven warriors had already begun adding ranks such as generals back in the wars with the trolls, and the trolls had eventually adapted their shield bands into a military structure matching Escarland's, though vestiges of the shield bands still remained in Kostaria's military.

Captain Gradrah swept a hard gaze over Fieran's assembled flyboys and the elven pilots. "TFC and EFC pilots, you have both been placed under my command by your respective militaries, and I have been authorized to combine you into one squadron, the Alliance Flying Corps Squadron D. Lt. Rothilion, you and your elves will be Flight A. Lt. Laesornysh, you and your men will be Flight B."

Rothilion. Now Fieran remembered him. Saranthyr Rothilion. He was a nephew of an elf who had been briefly engaged to Fieran's aunt Melantha back in the day. The ending of that betrothal hadn't been a pleasant one, and that particular elven noble family hadn't gotten along with Fieran's family and extended family ever since.

As if completely oblivious to the tension crackling between Fieran and Lt. Rothilion, Captain Gradrah continued, "Lt. Rothilion, as you gained your rank two weeks before Lt. Laesornysh, you will be acting commander of the entire squadron."

This was bad. So very bad. Fieran gritted his teeth, keeping his eyes forward and resisting the urge to glare at Lt. Rothilion. He had joined the Escarlish Army specifically so he wouldn't have to answer to elven commanders.

Looked like he was going to have to do just that anyway. Worse, it wasn't just any elf commander, but one with a snobby attitude just dripping off him.

At least Captain Gradrah hadn't promoted the other lieutenant, just made him acting commander. So he and Fieran were still the same rank, and Fieran didn't have to salute him. That was some consolation.

"Yes, ma'am." Lt. Rothilion took the news of his new command with a nod.

"I trust that there will be no issues with combining your units." Captain Gradrah glanced from Lt. Rothilion to Fieran and back. Perhaps she wasn't so oblivious to their instant dislike of each other.

"No, ma'am," Lt. Rothilion stated in that gratingly smooth tenor of his.

"Not at all, ma'am." Fieran would have to make sure of it. He could be professional. As long as Lt. Rothilion was the same.

"Your immediate commander will be Commander Druindar." Captain Gradrah gestured to the troll commander who had led them from the airship. "Commander?"

Holding a clipboard he must have grabbed, Commander Druindar joined Captain Gradrah at the front, sweeping his gaze over Fieran's men, his gaze lingering on Fieran and Merrik. "Lt. Laesornysh, do any of your men suffer the elven weakness for stone and troll magic?"

Across the way, Lt. Rothilion's elves shifted, as if uncomfortable at this conversation. Elves not only hated being underground, but being surrounded by a lot of stone could give some elves physical symptoms, like headaches. Enough stone and troll magic could make it difficult for an elf, especially younger elves, to use their magic.

It was how the trolls had kept Fieran's dacha imprisoned twice during the wars between the trolls and the elves.

Fieran glanced over his shoulder at Pip. She gave a slight shake of her head. He hadn't thought she was affected by stone, based on the stories she'd told about visiting her dwarven grandparents, but he'd wanted to be sure before he spoke.

Facing the troll commander again, Fieran shook his head. "No, sir."

Neither he nor Merrik, the only other half-elves in the squadron, experienced any side effects from stone.

Much to Dacha's relief.

"Very well. If any of you should develop symptoms caused by all the stone, do not hesitate to report to sick bay, where healing stones will be issued to you." Commander Druindar flicked a glance at Lt. Rothilion's elves.

A few of the elves had shifted, some reaching as if to touch something tucked beneath their shirts. They must have already been issued healing stones, which counteracted the symptoms of the elven weakness.

How long had Lt. Rothilion and the elven pilots been here? Perhaps they'd come straight here after their training had finished two weeks ago. The Escarlish and Tarenhieli training programs were staggered so that a group of new pilots would be graduating every month.

But Fieran's group had been sent on their way two weeks early.

Commander Druindar consulted his clipboard. "Lt. Laesornysh, you and your men will be housed on Level 23 in sections A-D with the male mechanics for both Flights in Section E. Your female mechanic will bunk on Level 24 in section E with the female elven pilots and mechanics. Lt. Rothilion's male pilots have been assigned sections A-D of Level 24."

Lt. Rothilion's mouth pressed into a thin line that had that disdainful curl again. It seemed he didn't enjoy his underground accommodations, even with the healing stones negating the physical discomfort.

Though from what Fieran had seen from the airship as they were coming in, Dar Goranth didn't have much for accommodations that weren't underground. In the event of a bombing attack like the one on Fort Linder and Bridgetown, living underground would be preferable.

"Level 1 is comprised of the command rooms, communications, and the parade ground. The mess halls and kitchens are Level 2. Sick bay is Level 3. The commissary is Level 4. Levels 5-8 are officer quarters while Levels 9-20 are quarters for enlisted men and women and other assorted personnel. Levels 21-22 are storage. The training arena deeper inside the island can be accessed via several passageways connecting to Levels 1-3. The schedule for the arena is posted on the wall of the parade ground, and you must check with one of the base's clerks to request a slot on the schedule."

Fieran made a mental note of that as much as he could. It would take some exploring to learn his way around, though it sounded like he would mostly need to know how to get from his rooms to this hangar bay—Level 25 according to the large number painted on the wall by the stairs behind Captain Gradrah—and down to Level 2 for food.

While using what was likely a spacious training arena for practicing his magic would have been nice, signing up for a time on what was likely a packed schedule—knowing how trolls liked their fighting bouts—would be a hassle. Far easier to just find a secluded spot on the island somewhere.

"As you can see, we currently don't have enough aeroplanes for the full squadron." Commander Druindar's heavy gaze landed on Fieran. "Lt. Laesornysh, the Escarlish Army assures me that they will be shipping your aeroplanes shortly, and they should arrive in the next few weeks."

Wait. What? There weren't even aeroplanes here for them? Fieran's stomach plummeted. So much for getting back in an aeroplane anytime soon.

He probably should have expected this. After all, aeroplanes would need pilots to deliver them.

Which begged the question of how the army was shipping them. Perhaps parked on the deck of a barge?

Grounded. After everything Fieran had done to get into a flyer, he was once again trapped on the earth. Or under it, in this case.

Lt. Rothilion gave another nod, an even more self-satisfied curve to his mouth. "Flight A will be more than capable of handling the patrols, as we have for the past two weeks."

Fieran was going to grind his teeth to nubs if he kept gritting them like this.

Commander Druindar shot a glance at Lt. Rothilion that had the other lieutenant snapping his mouth shut. At least the troll commander wasn't the type to appreciate such flagrant butt-kissing. "In the meantime, Lt.

Laesornysh, I'd like you and your men to work with the mechanics to come up with a viable way to arm the aeroplanes. I want a working solution by the time your flyers get here, understood?"

"Yes, sir." Fieran gave his own sharp nod at this.

At least arming the aeroplanes would be something productive to do while they were grounded. And it would involve some shooting and experimenting. A few things might get destroyed. That might be kind of fun.

And he'd get to spend the time with Pip. That might be worth being grounded for a week or two.

"We also have a few two-seater scout planes. Lt. Laesornysh, Lt. Rothilion, put together a schedule for Flight B pilots to ride with Flight A pilots." Commander Druindar gestured from Fieran to the elven half of the squadron. "I'd like any movement of Mongavarian warships to be documented and photographed. We all know Mongavaria needs another decisive strike, and that strike will likely be here. We need to be ready."

"Yes, sir." Fieran spoke at the same time as Lt. Rothilion, and it grated on him.

After going through a few more rules of the base—and specifying the all-important meal times for their unit—Commander Druindar dismissed them.

Fieran dismissed his flyboys to get settled into their rooms. Pip and the other mechanics scattered to find their own rooms and check in with the head mechanic.

Instead of leaving, Fieran squared his shoulders and faced Lt. Rothilion, his new commanding officer. Merrik remained at Fieran's back, as if he doubted Fieran's ability to stay calm.

Fieran was perfectly calm. He wasn't about to go starting trouble. Instead, he plastered on that perfectly pleasant smile he'd learned from his mother and stuck out his hand. "I look forward to working with you, Lt. Rothilion."

His words were as sugared as spoiled milk laced with honey to attempt to make it palatable.

Lt. Rothilion stared down his nose at Fieran's hand and didn't shake. He didn't even offer the elven forehead to mouth greeting gesture. His mouth curled as if he did indeed taste the spoiled milk in Fieran's words.

Still giving them that nose-in-the-air look, complete with the faintest disdainful sniff, Lt. Rothilion glanced from Fieran to Merrik and back. "You do realize that as an Alliance Flying Corps unit, long hair is now permitted."

Behind Fieran, Merrik stiffened, going so still Fieran could sense it without having to turn around to look.

That hadn't occurred to him yet, nor, it seemed, had it dawned on Merrik either.

As Alliance units would be made up of a mix of trolls, elves, and humans, certain Escarlish military regulations no longer applied. Such as the rule on keeping one's hair a regulation length.

Merrik could re-grow his hair. Well, Fieran could too, but he wouldn't. He supposed even the humans in his unit could grow their hair long if they liked, but he doubted any of them would let it get too shaggy. Some of them might opt for facial hair, which would also now be allowed. A concession specifically added so that Fieran's Uncle Julien could keep his beard once beards were no longer allowed in the Escarlish Army.

"No proper elf would allow his honor to be stripped away in such a fashion." Lt. Rothilion somehow managed to stare even more down his nose at them. "But I suppose neither of you are true elves."

With that, Lt. Rothilion spun on his heel and strode briskly away.

For elves, long hair was a symbol of honor. When elves committed crimes, their hair was often shorn as a sign of dishonor. For that reason, when the trolls had wanted to humiliate Fieran's dacha when they'd captured him during the wars, they'd cut his hair.

Fieran clenched his fists at his side, his magic burning in his chest and down into his hands. But he didn't let so much as a single bolt curl around his fingers. It would be too tempting to zap Lt. Rothilion's posterior as he sauntered away in that self-satisfied manner.

That had been a dig not only at Fieran and Merrik, but also their human mothers. Probably even Fieran's father, given what the trolls had done to him back then.

Merrik joined Fieran, his own fists clenched, his jaw hard. "I almost want to keep my hair short just to protest."

"Don't. The only one that would hurt would be you." Fieran lightly bumped Merrik's shoulder, forcing a grin back onto his face. "I'll be the improper elf for both of us. I'm good at that."

Merrik's shoulders relaxed a fraction, and he sighed. "And here I thought Prince Rhohen was the most likely one to drive you to brawling. Just keep in mind, punching our acting commanding officer is just as bad as punching a prince. Probably worse. King Rharreth would let you off lightly. The military will not be so forgiving."

All too true. Fieran wasn't quite sure how he was going to get through his time stationed here at Dar Goranth without punching that pouty smirk off Lt. Rothilion's face.

He wasn't normally the type of person to resort to punching as a way to solve problems. But there was just something about an attitude like Lt. Rothilion's—or his cousin Rhohen's, for that matter—that just brought out the temper Fieran was supposed to have because of his red hair.

Or maybe it was Dar Goranth and the more punchy culture of the trolls that made Fieran want to throw a few punches of his own.

## CHAPTER THREE

Pip wound her way through the underground hangar until she found the corner that seemed to be the mechanics' headquarters. A male troll with broad shoulders, white hair, and grease-smeared coveralls was fussing over a partially disassembled engine on a stand, his back to her.

Beyond him, six elves—two females and four males—cleaned tools, talking in elvish among themselves. They must be the mechanics who had come with the elven half of the squadron.

Pip adjusted the straps of her bag where they were digging into her shoulders. Perhaps she should have settled into her quarters first before finding the head mechanic. But most of the weight in her bag was her tools, and she'd rather unload those first before climbing back down the steps to find her room. "Excuse me. Are you the head mechanic for the aerodrome?"

The troll turned around, then his face split in a wide grin. "Pippak! You've arrived! It's great to see you again."

Pip blinked at the troll before her, craning her neck to

look up into his face as he strode toward her. "Baragh! I haven't seen you since we graduated. How have you been?"

Baragh had been in her magical engineering class at Hanford University, and they'd graduated together. He'd been a friend, though they hadn't kept in touch after they went their separate ways.

"Good. Got a job here at Dar Goranth right after university, and I've been here ever since." Baragh gestured at the expansive hangar. "I'm the chief mechanic for all airships and aeroplanes that stop here at Dar Goranth."

Making him her boss. That was convenient. She'd been worried she'd get stuck with some gruff and grumpy troll.

"That's great." Pip grinned. She was always happy when she heard about someone she knew from university succeeding.

"What about you?" Baragh grabbed a nearby metal cart and pushed it toward her.

Pip took her bag off her shoulder, opened it, and dug out the tools she'd brought from home. "I returned home to the western rail terminal and went back to wrenching on trains. Until I joined the Mechanics Auxiliary a few months ago."

"Huh. I was sure you'd get a job at the Alliance Magical Power Company." Baragh shrugged, his gaze narrowing as he studied her. "You had the mind and magic for it."

Pip stilled at the mention of the AMPC, the company in Escarland run by the famous inventor Lance Marion, Merrik's dacha Iyrinder Loiatir, and Fieran's dacha, the famous Prince Farrendel Laesornysh. *Internal hero worship squeal*. Her face grew hot as she tried to breathe normally.

When she finally swallowed and spoke, she struggled to sound casual rather than squealy. "I thought about it, but I missed home too much to move away."

At least back then. It had taken a few decades, but she'd gotten restless again. Restless enough to join the army mechanics.

"Well, we're glad to have you here at Dar Goranth." Baragh glanced up as footsteps came in their direction.

The other four mechanics from Fort Linder wove their way between the aeroplanes before halting a few feet away from Pip.

Baragh grabbed a slightly grimy clipboard. "I'm Baragh Garr, head mechanic for all airborne vessels here at Dar Goranth. Since you already have a good working relationship with the pilots you trained with, I'm assigning you to Flight B."

Pip breathed a slight sigh of relief. Not that she wasn't used to working with elves. Her home was in Tarenhiel, after all, and she'd worked with elves all her life.

But she much preferred to stick with Fieran and her flyboys. She didn't trust anyone else to keep her boys safe.

"Pippak Detmuk-Inawenys, you'll be the head mechanic for Flight B."

Pip stiffened, nearly dropping her favorite wrench on her foot. "Pardon?"

The other four male human mechanics who had been at Fort Linder with her shifted, glancing between each other. While she had gained their respect enough that they didn't hassle her, she had mostly kept to herself during training, hanging out with the flyboys more than her fellow mechanics when off duty.

"You're by far the most qualified with the most years

of experience." Baragh glared past her at the other mechanics. "Any of you have a problem with that?"

One man opened his mouth, like he was going to say something, before he snapped his mouth shut and shook his head.

"I didn't think so." Baragh faced her again. "Get your men settled, then organize what you'll need for arming the aeroplanes. We have two older-model flyers there in the back that you can use for testing various designs."

Pip nodded, her words stuck in her throat. She'd never been in charge before. At the western rail terminal, her mother and brother bossed the other workers around. Pip could just go and do her own thing.

She glanced over her shoulder at the four mechanics put under her charge. Two of them were in their thirties or forties, physically older than her, even if she had more years of experience by virtue of being a slow-aging half-elf, half-dwarf.

The four men stared back at her with looks varying from dubious to resentful.

What had Baragh been thinking, putting her in charge?

After organizing her personal tools, inventorying the provided tools, seeing to it that her men had their own carts and tools, and inspecting the two aeroplanes, Pip was more than ready to retreat to her room.

With her pack considerably lighter now that she'd unloaded her tools, Pip made her way down the flight of stairs to Level 24. At the landing, arrows and labels pointed into the labyrinth of tunnels, showing where

Sections A-E could be found on this level of the mountain.

Pip followed the arrows, the tension in her shoulders easing at being surrounded by so much stone. While she'd grown up in the light, airy, and very wooden buildings of the western rail terminal, there was something about the dark and deep places of the earth that called to her. Her muka would love it here.

As she reached Section E, she found a small corridor with only ten doors, five to each side. The hall ended in a door to the outside, which led onto a tiny balcony. Four of the female elf pilots were already crammed onto that balcony with a fifth hovering in the doorway.

A few of the doors stood open, lilting elvish floating out.

Pip froze at the entrance of the corridor for a moment. How many female pilots had there been? There had been two female mechanics, and she had seen quite a few females among the pilots. Were there enough rooms here for everyone? Was she going to have to share?

Forcing herself to move, Pip checked the first doors on either side. The door on the left led to the lavatory while the door on the right was to the showers, some of which were already claimed with their curtains drawn closed and water running.

Pip let that door fall closed, then gathered herself to knock on the next door in the row.

A door three down to the left opened, and a female elf with long brown hair and brown eyes stuck her head out. She glanced around, then gestured to Pip as a smile lit her face. "Pippak, right? You are in here with me."

A roommate. Not the worst thing ever, as long as she wasn't the snooty sort.

Pip made her way down the corridor, then stepped

into the room. It was sparse with two stone-posted beds—little better than cots, really—with ropes strung between the stone frame to hold up the thin mattress. A narrow wooden cupboard was set against the wall at the foot of each bed.

The brown-haired elf plopped onto the bed on the left. "I am Aylia Daemaer." Instead of a more traditional elven greeting involving fingertips touched to forehead and lips, the elf stuck out her hand for an Escarlish handshake.

Pip shook her hand. "Pippak Detmuk-Inawenys. But you can call me Pip." If they were going to be roommates for as long as they were both stationed at Dar Goranth, the nickname was probably the easiest, even if she didn't know Aylia well yet.

"Ooh, a nickname!" Aylia's grin widened further. "I find the human concept of nicknames so fascinating. Do dwarves usually have nicknames too?"

"It isn't as common as among humans, but not unheard of either." Pip set her pack on the bed, then opened the cupboard.

There were a few hooks for her things, then some shelves at both the top and the bottom. She wouldn't be able to reach the top shelves, unless she stood on the bottom shelves or reached from the bed, so she wouldn't put much there if she could help it.

She hung up her spare set of coveralls, then glanced over her shoulder at Aylia. The elf seemed fairly straightforward, so Pip was just going to ask rather than beat around the bush in a more elven manner. "You don't mind sharing a room with a half-dwarf?"

Aylia's grin didn't falter. "Not at all. I volunteered to share with you. I figured you would be more fun than sharing with some of the others." She glanced at the closed door, leaned forward, and lowered her voice. "A few of the others come from noble families. The ones in room eight are especially snooty. I would avoid them if I were you."

"Thanks for the warning." Pip stashed the rest of her clothes onto the bottom shelves.

It wasn't too surprising that a few of the elven pilots had the typical snooty elf attitude, especially when it came to elven nobility. There was a small but vocal minority who was still pushing King Weylind to ensure that his children married pure elves, given that all of King Weylind's siblings had not married elves.

Not that such a prejudicial attitude was confined to the elves. There was an element among the trolls who wanted Prince Rhohen to marry a pure troll to strengthen his bloodline after it had been "tainted" by Queen Melantha's elven blood.

The humans of Escarland were less concerned about that and more worried about what would happen to their monarchy if the heir to the throne married a longer-lived race and suddenly a monarch would live unexpectedly longer than was the norm for a human. They were already dealing with the ramifications of King Averett's extra-long reign due to him being an elf friend.

But while the other races certainly held discriminatory attitudes, the elven nobility—with their need to be superior in everything—had seemingly gone out of their way to perfect their prejudices to the point it wasn't just an attitude but a foundational character trait.

"No problem." Aylia waved airily.

Pip climbed onto the bottom shelf, stretched as high as she could reach, and delicately placed the carved wooden train her brother Mak had made for her on the top shelf where she would see it every time she opened the locker.

The little train had, thankfully, survived the attack on Fort Linder unscathed.

She added her bag and closed the locker, her throat unexpectedly tight. She never thought she'd miss Chelsea and the other flirtatious nurses, secretaries, and telephone operators at Fort Linder. But they had shown unexpected depths during the attack, rushing to their stations and doing their jobs with just as much bravery as anyone else on base.

Here, she had a corridor filled with prissy elves for companions. Command over Flight B's mechanics. Not even any aeroplanes for her to maintain just yet.

This stint at Dar Goranth would be more of a challenge than she'd expected.

## CHAPTER
# FOUR

Fieran stepped into the cavernous space that served as the officers' mess hall. Just like on the airship, the two mess halls were set on either side of the kitchens so that one industrial kitchen complex could serve both.

The officer's mess was on the outside of the mountain so that a bank of small, slitted windows let in light and glimpses of the airships hovering over the harbor. The poor enlisted men simply got a cavern with no windows.

Fieran joined the line for food behind Tiny and Stickyfingers, with Merrik and Lije behind him. Pretty Face had wandered off to who knew where. He'd wander back once he got hungry enough.

The food the brawny troll men and women working in the kitchens slapped on Fieran's tray seemed edible enough. Far more edible than the food often served at Fort Linder, at any rate. Some kind of fish, a side of veggies, and a potato. Simple but hearty.

As the island's location meant that all food except fish

had to be imported, they would probably be eating a lot of fish while stationed here.

Fieran faced the room to find a seat. Many of the elven pilots already clumped together at one of the long tables while trolls in naval uniforms were scattered along various other tables.

Pip's dark curls glinted in the light of the sunset streaming through the tiny windows where she sat with her back to the food line. Among all the brawny trolls and tall elves, she appeared a tiny child. One of the female elf pilots sat next to her, and the two of them chatted as if they were old friends.

Fieran slid onto the seat on the bench on the other side of Pip, setting his plate in front of him. "How was the rest of your day?"

"Fieran!" Pip jumped at his voice but grinned. "Meet my new roommate, Aylia Daemaer."

"Nice to meet you." Fieran stuck out his hand, nearly jumping himself when the female elf lieutenant leaned around Pip to actually shake it instead of ignoring the gesture as he'd expected. "I'm Fieran Laesornysh."

Aylia paused mid-shake. "Son of *the* Laesornysh?"

"Yes." Fieran braced himself as he withdrew his hand.

Merrik quietly slipped onto the seat on the other side of Fieran, a stiff presence at Fieran's side as he waited to back him up.

"Then I am especially pleased to meet you." Aylia's grin widened, the expression lighting her brown eyes. "I was too young to fight in the last wars, but my dacha and macha both did, and they told me stories of the great Prince Farrendel Laesornysh. I am honored to fight at his son's side."

Now that was more like it. At least not all the pilots in the elven half of the squadron were stuck-up prigs.

"I will be honored to take to the skies with you. Once Escarland sends my aeroplane, that is." Fieran shrugged as Lije and Stickyfingers joined them at the table, Tiny not far behind.

They went through a round of introductions before they all dug into their fish, the white meat flaking onto their forks.

As Fieran brought another bite to his mouth, he was grabbed from behind and hoisted off the bench. He would have lashed out with his magic at such an attack, but he recognized the voice booming by his ear.

"Cousin Fieran!"

Fieran weakly patted the chest—or perhaps arm—of the exceptionally large and brawny troll warrior pinning him in a hug. "Rokyd. I searched the harbor, but I couldn't tell if the KS *Vanguard* was in port."

"You just caught us. We're finishing up a re-supply before going out on patrol again." Another hand slapped Fieran's back, accompanied by the deep voice of his other cousin.

Fieran was finally set back on his feet, and he tugged on his uniform to straighten it.

Before him, his two cousins grinned broadly. One was a tall troll warrior dressed in a white naval uniform with a lieutenant commander's insignia on his brawny shoulders. He had the typical gray skin and white hair of most trolls, and he kept his hair shorn as short as Escarlish military standards.

The other was a tall human with brown skin and curly black hair. He, too, wore a white naval uniform but with lieutenant stripes instead.

"Good job giving the Mongavarians what-for at Bridgetown." Lucien, the human, gave Fieran yet another backslap, which had Fieran stumbling forward. Lucien might be fully human, but he had been raised among trolls and could whack with troll-like force.

"We'll give them the same beating if they show their faces around here." Rokyd, the troll, gave Fieran's arm a light punch.

Well, light for a troll. Fieran had to resist the urge to rub his shoulder.

"Join us. I'd like to introduce you to everyone." Fieran gestured to the table, where his friends were sitting in what seemed to be stunned silence. Well, not Merrik. He had returned to eating. He was rather used to the cousins' antics.

Rokyd and Lucien obligingly circled the table and took the open seats next to Tiny.

Tiny stiffened, his eyes widening slightly with something of the apprehension Pip showed when Fieran mentioned introducing her to his dacha. For the troll population living in Aldon—like Tiny's family—Uncle Julien and Aunt Vriska were revered.

Fieran's grin stretched so wide it hurt as he returned to his own seat across from his cousins. "Rokyd, Lucien, these are my friends. You know Merrik, of course. This here is Lije, and he's Stickyfingers. The half-troll there is Donkyn Sairdror, but he goes by Tiny."

Rokyd swiveled to better face Tiny. "Related to Erdrol Sairdror?"

"He's my da." Tiny's already high-pitched tenor voice squeaked.

"He's worked with my dasheni on a few projects. Skilled and a hard worker, so my dasheni said." Rokyd nodded with an extra depth of respect that had Tiny sitting straighter. Rokyd's dasheni—grandfather in the troll dialect—was Aunt Vriska's father and one of the founding members of the troll community in Aldon.

Fieran dug his fork into his fish, flaking off a bite. He would have to hurry up and eat before his food grew too cold. "Everyone, these are my cousins Rokyd and Lucien. Uncle Julien and Aunt Vriska's sons."

"Your…cousins?" Stickyfingers swung his gaze from Rokyd to Lucien to Fieran, a furrow between his brows.

"We're brothers." Rokyd threw an arm over Lucien's shoulders. "Can't you tell?"

The two of them couldn't look more unlike brothers. Besides a general similarity in height and burly build, they had no resemblance to each other or to Uncle Julien and Aunt Vriska.

"But…" Stickyfingers gestured vaguely. He might have grown up on the streets of Aldon in a family of crooks, but even he had enough sense not to point out the obvious.

Rokyd and Lucien shared a look before Rokyd laughed.

Fieran worked to suppress his grin. The two of them took far too much pleasure in people's confusion.

Lucien leaned his elbows on the table. "We're adopted."

"Ah." Stickyfingers gave a nod, as if that explained everything for him. "So you aren't brothers by blood."

Maybe not so much sense. But at least Fieran's cousins weren't easily offended. Not these particular cousins, anyway.

"Well, we are. Kind of." Lucien held up his left hand, showing a faint scar across his palm.

Rokyd held up his own left hand, which had a similar scar. "Troll adoptions involve blood. Most troll ceremonies do. We're considered their children by blood just as much as if we were born of their blood."

"Huh. Sounds…messy." Stickyfingers wiggled his

hand on his fork, as if imagining what a troll ceremony might entail.

"Tell them the whole story." Fieran spoke around a bite of fish. No matter how many times he heard it, he always got a kick out of listening to Rokyd spin the tale.

Rokyd's grin widened as he, too, leaned his elbows on the table. "Well, you see, my ma is not exactly the maternal sort. She was not about to put up with pregnancy and squalling babies."

"I do not blame her." Aylia gave a little shudder of her own. "Babies are rather terrifying."

"Exactly." Rokyd nodded to her. "After my da and ma married, they were given Akarak Stronghold and the nearby village as their home in Kostaria. When Mongavaria poisoned grain and killed thousands of trolls, Akarak was hit particularly hard."

Fieran quickly shoveled in the last of his food while he listened to the familiar story.

Stickyfingers, Lije, and Tiny leaned forward, their food forgotten and growing cold. Pip chewed more slowly while Merrik took a moment to finish the last of his fish.

"Kostaria is a bit different than Escarland. Orphans aren't sent to an orphanage. Instead, it's the responsibility of the village to take in those they can." Rokyd's voice kept a steady rhythm. "The rest are raised as wards of the warrior family of the nearest stronghold, usually trained to be low-level guards in the household when they grow up."

"So you were a ward of Prince Julien and Lady Vriska?" Lije blinked, his face twisting as he tried to put it all together.

"I was supposed to be, yes." For the first time, Rokyd's voice went a hint rough. "My entire family except for me died in the poisonings. I went a bit feral after that, living on the streets of Akarak and not allowing anyone to get near me. When Da and Ma finally cornered me to get me off the streets and into the stronghold, I bit Ma's finger so hard I drew blood. In that moment, she decided that I belonged with her and Da. Not just as a ward but as a son."

"Because you bit her finger?" Lije's forehead scrunched. The fish on his plate had to be stone-cold by now.

"Yep. She still has the scar." Rokyd grinned, his eyes going soft.

"What did your da think of that?" Stickyfingers seemed to remember he had food and scooped up another bite.

"Oh, he was thrilled. He loves children, and he was more than happy to turn his parental instincts toward giving love to those who wouldn't have a family otherwise." Rokyd shrugged and gestured to Lucien. "It worked out well. Da got children; Ma got to skip over the baby stage. Not the solution for every couple in their position, but it worked for them. That's where *he* came in."

"I have Aunt Essie to thank for my joining the family." Lucien tipped his head in Fieran's direction. His face and tone had less of Rokyd's lighthearted tone, a hint of the memories he wasn't revealing simmering just below the surface. "I was in an orphanage in Escarland that Aunt Essie supports with her charity work. I had become something of a bully, and those at the orphanage were at their wits' end when it came to me. Aunt Essie asked Da and Ma to meet me, and that was that."

"And then there's Sathrah." Rokyd's gaze flicked to something past Fieran, his smile widening.

Lucien's gaze, too, focused on something—or

someone—behind Fieran, his grin returning. "Oh, we definitely can't forget about Sathrah."

Fieran swiveled on the bench as a female troll warrior stalked to their table, her skin an exceptionally dark gray and her hair tinted a very light shade of brown that was unusual in trolls.

She gripped the back of Pretty Face's shirt as if he were a kitten she had by the scruff of his neck. Pretty Face's nose dribbled blood as he alternately tried to stem the bleeding and tug on his collar to keep from choking. His toes barely touched the ground as he was frog-marched to their table.

Sathrah faced Fieran and gave Pretty Face a light shake. "Does *this* belong to you?"

"Sadly, yes." Fieran sighed and shook his head. "Let me guess. He said something inappropriate."

"Yes, he did." Sathrah plunked Pretty Face onto the bench none too gently, eliciting a whimper. "You really need to teach him a few manners."

"We've been trying. It hasn't stuck yet." Fieran picked up a napkin and passed it to Pretty Face.

Pretty Face took it and pressed it to his nose, leaning his head back. "I'm fine, by the way. Thanks for asking."

"Of course you are. If I'd wanted to hurt you, I would have." Sathrah strolled around the table and plopped onto the bench next to Lucien. "You're lucky all I did was give you a bloody nose. Since you're a fragile human, I held back and didn't even break the bone."

"I appreciate that. I rather like my nose." Pretty Face spoke into the napkin.

"If you want to keep your face intact, then don't go around insulting troll warriors and making inappropriate comments." Sathrah rested a hand on the dagger belted to the waist of her lieutenant commander's uniform.

"We're on a Kostarian base now. Trolls punch first and ask questions later." Fieran leaned over and retrieved another napkin, handing it to Pretty Face.

"You're right, we do." Sathrah planted her hands on the table.

"Their rules about punching fellow officers are far more lax than the Escarlish military's." Fieran glanced between his assembled flyboys. He might need to make a speech about this to everyone tomorrow morning. "As long as no bones are broken—and even then, it depends on the bone—a few punches and bruises aren't against regulations. There won't be any disciplinary action unless a severe beating is given or the fight happened in a dishonorable manner. So keep that in mind, all of you. Especially you, Pretty Face."

"Understood." Pretty Face finally lowered the napkins, giving a few experimental sniffs and exploring his nose with his fingers. "Does it look bad? Is it crooked? Please tell me it isn't crooked."

Pip rolled her eyes. "Your nose is fine."

"Though…" Lije squinted. "I think you might have a black eye starting already."

Pretty Face groaned. "How am I"—he shot a glance at Sathrah—"uh…going to see to shave if my eyes swell shut?"

"At least we don't have to fly anytime soon." Stickyfingers grimaced. "When I broke my nose, it hurt just bending over. I can't imagine flying would feel too good, even if your nose isn't broken."

Flying. How Fieran already missed it. Escarland had better ship their aeroplanes soon. If he thought placing a phone call to his Uncle Averett, or perhaps Uncle Lance, would speed up the shipping, he'd almost be tempted to use his family connections.

"So how did you join the family?" Pip gestured at Rokyd and Lucien. "They were just telling us."

Sathrah smirked, grabbed Sticky's plate, and plucked a bite of the roast potato from it. "Like Rokyd, my family died in the poisonings. Unlike Rokyd, I was from a tiny village in the far western reaches of Kostaria. I was taken in by a family who just wanted an extra hand for mining, and no matter how many times I appealed to the local warrior family to be trained as a warrior at the stronghold, I was refused. Eventually, I ran away."

Sticky's mouth pressed into a tight line. "So the exploitation of orphans and those on the streets isn't only a problem for Escarland."

"No." Sathrah clenched and unclenched her fists. "I spent years living on the streets before I heard rumors that Akarak Stronghold was the place for common trolls to go if they wanted to be trained, not just as guards but as warriors in a shield band. I hitched a ride to Akarak, marched up to the stronghold, and demanded to be trained as a warrior. As you might imagine, Ma took one look at me and saw something of herself. It wasn't long before I was not just in training to be a warrior but also adopted into the family."

"And our little band wouldn't have been complete without you." Lucien threw an arm around the shoulders of each of his siblings sitting on either side of him. "Though you just had to choose the airborne navy instead of seaborne."

"Much to Ma's fond annoyance." Sathrah grinned and gave Lucien a backslap that was part punch. She glanced at the rest of them. "Da and Ma are both army. If we picked either the Escarlish or Kostarian Army, we'd have either our da or our ma as our commanding officer. All three of us jumped ship as it were and picked navy instead."

"I understand that." Fieran gestured at his green army uniform. "I joined the Escarlish Flying Corps for similar reasons."

For a moment, he shared a look with Rokyd, Lucien, and Sathrah. Only his cousins—in their sprawling, interconnected, rather royal family—could understand what it was like growing up as they had, related to the kings of the Alliance Kingdoms and so many highly placed people.

"Speaking of commanding officers..." Fieran leaned a bit closer. "Is—"

A whistle piped from the doorway. "King on deck."

Everyone in the room shot to their feet, spinning toward the doorway. Kings were the exception to the no saluting or standing at attention rule in the mess hall.

Well, that answered the question Fieran had been about to ask. He climbed to his feet and faced the door as a regal troll with an antler crown tucked in his white hair strolled through the doorway. He wore crisp white trousers and a white shirt in a semblance of a naval uniform, but his was cut in an older style that worked with the sword strapped to his waist. The sense of power surrounding him came not just from his muscular arms and sword at his side but also his confident stride and set to his head and shoulders.

Uncle Rharreth, King of Kostaria.

Everyone in the room snapped to salute, and Fieran's hand was nearly to his forehead when a second person trudged into the room behind Uncle Rharreth. His shoulders were slightly hunched, his whole posture slouchy. His long black hair flowed down his back, blending with his gray skin to give him an overall dark and brooding look, emphasized by the pouty expression curling his lips. Like Fieran, his shoulders were broader than the slim build of the elves, but compared to the stocky trolls, he appeared scrawny.

Cousin Rhohen.

Fieran fumbled his salute.

Merrik swayed slightly closer and whispered, "Remember. Be the more mature cousin."

All well and good, but Fieran could only be as mature as Rhohen let him be.

Uncle Rharreth, trailed by Rhohen, worked his way around the room. Despite the rocky start to his reign, the trolls in this room revered him to the point of near hero-worship. He had brought Kostaria out of the poverty of the previous wars into a thriving kingdom as forward-thinking as any of the other kingdoms in the Alliance.

As Uncle Rharreth reached their table, his smile broadened as he stepped in for a hug. "Fieran. Good to see you."

"Uncle Rharreth." Fieran returned his uncle's hug and backslap. Unlike with Uncle Julien and the Escarlish Army where any recognition would be seen as favoritism and make basic training worse, Uncle Rharreth publicly claiming Fieran as family would only help his status here among the trolls.

Then Fieran's smile dropped from his face as his voice came out flat. "Rhohen."

"Fieran." Rhohen didn't even bother to unslouch as he glared back.

Uncle Rharreth didn't do anything as obvious as sigh, but something of disappointment colored his blue eyes. He and Dacha had always hoped Fieran and Rhohen would get along.

There were times Fieran almost wished it too.

Almost. Maybe if Rhohen wasn't so pouty about everything. Right now, he looked like he'd had a whole lemon shoved in his mouth.

All it would take would be a little poke—or a zap of Fieran's magic—and he could turn that pout into a blaze of anger.

But Fieran didn't. He was the more mature cousin, after all.

# CHAPTER FIVE

Fieran forced himself out of bed before dawn. Or what he guessed was the dawn, since his interior room didn't have any windows.

At least the hard military cot was easy to leave. The mattress could hardly be termed such, formed as it was by a packed layer of scrap fabric stuffed inside a thick canvas that was similar to that used for tarpaulins and the sides of dirigibles. It made the bed in the barracks at Fort Linder feel like luxury.

Across the small room, Merrik rolled to a sitting position on his cot, grimacing. "Do you think anyone will notice if I grow a patch of straw to restuff my mattress?"

"As long as you grow enough for my mattress too, I'll cover for you by officially authorizing it." Fieran rubbed his lower back. "I'm going for a morning practice."

He needed to get back in the habit of practicing his magic every morning like he used to do with his dacha and sisters. The rigid structure of Escarlish basic training hadn't allowed wiggle room for a recruit to go off by himself for magic practice. But here, Fieran was a first lieutenant with the freedom to set his own schedule. Somewhat.

"Good. With Rhohen at Dar Goranth, you need to work out your jitters as much as possible." Merrik stretched his arms over his head. "Rhohen is volatile enough for the two of you."

"Very true." Fieran rolled his head, trying to work the stiffness out of his neck. "Maybe you can practice your magic with the elven flyboys and fix our mattress situation."

Merrik snorted and rubbed his own back. "Given the looks Lt. Rothilion and his cohorts were giving us, I do not believe I would be welcomed."

"Aylia might not be as snooty. She doesn't seem to get along with the others." Fieran gripped one foot, then the other, stretching his leg muscles. He would need to get in a good practice to work out all the kinks.

"There might be a few others." Merrik grimaced again and reached for his uniform shirt. "They likely do not dare to speak up and disagree with Lt. Rothilion. Not only is he their commanding officer, but he is from a well-connected, noble family. One with something to prove to regain their status in the king's eyes."

"Insulting the half-elven nephew of that king is a strange way to go about it." Fieran just shook his head and strode for the door. He left his uniform shirt behind, opting to remain in his undershirt and fatigues. It would be chilly this morning, but he wouldn't be cold for long.

Merrik followed as Fieran exited their room. Together, they strode down the short corridor filled with rooms on either side.

Several flyboys were already up. Some were jogging up and down the corridor or performing a basic PT routine in their rooms while joking with their bunkmates.

Others had towels over their shoulders and hygiene kits in their hands as they headed for the showers at the end of the passageway.

The door to the shower room stood open as a pair of the flyboys loitered in the doorway, talking. Inside, one of the flyboys threw open one of the shower curtains. He dragged out a protesting elf, who was scrambling to wrap a towel around his middle. Suds still coated the elf's hair.

"My hair needs more time than this!" The elf clutched at the towel.

"Tough. We're all allotted the same three-minute showers." The flyboy pushed past the elf and yanked the shower curtain closed.

Another flyboy snapped a towel, flicking it so that the end lashed the elf's bare chest. "Go back to your own section and stop hogging our showers."

The elf gave a yip and jumped back, nearly dropping his towel. With a sniff, he spun on his heel and marched from the room, suds dripping from his hair and his wet feet slapping against the stone floor.

Fieran hesitated. Was this something he should deal with as the commanding officer for his Flight? Or was this something minor that would sort itself out if he left it alone?

On the one hand, the elven half of the squadron must have gotten used to taking over the showers not just on their level, but this level as well in the time they'd been at Dar Goranth. That couldn't continue now that Fieran's men occupied these rooms. They didn't deserve to have their showers hogged by elves needing extra time to wash their long hair.

But on the other hand, such animosity between the two halves of the squadron wouldn't be good for morale. They needed to be a united front to fight Mongavaria.

After another moment, Fieran shrugged and decided to let it go, for now. It was only the first morning. Everyone would settle in eventually, especially once the aeroplanes arrived and Fieran's men could take to the skies once again.

Merrik glanced from the retreating elf to Fieran. "I will stay and keep the others out of trouble. Go practice."

"Thanks." If anyone could keep the others in line, it would be Merrik. His repeated failures at keeping Fieran out of trouble weren't a true indication of his ability to watch over others.

After clapping Merrik on the back, Fieran followed the trail of suds and wet footprints from the passageway and up the winding stairs until he stepped into the aeroplane hangar. He didn't see Pip yet, though several of the elf mechanics bustled about, getting a few of the elven aeroplanes ready for a morning patrol.

Fieran strode across the cavern, then out into the gray of the early morning. The frigid breeze cut through his clothes, and he resisted the urge to give in to shivers. Instead, he set out at a brisk pace across the airfield, over the nearest ridge, then through a gully.

Only once a bend in the gully hid him entirely from view did Fieran finally stop. This would be a good spot for morning practice, not just this morning but for every morning he was here. The rock walls surrounding him would keep his magic nicely contained, should he let a little slip.

Fieran held his hands out like he gripped his swords. He let bolts of his magic form, letting it swirl around him while also maintaining two blade-like shapes crackling from his hands.

He threw himself into the first basic sword stance. Without someone to fight, this practice wouldn't be as satisfying as one with his dacha and sister. But he could at least take the edge off the magic crackling inside his chest.

He blasted his magic outward as he threw himself into a whirling sword strike, raising his other hand as if parrying a blow.

As he spun again, a blast of a different, icier magic slammed into his from the side. Fieran nearly stumbled under the blast, his own magic rising in him to blast outward into a shield. He whirled to face the threat.

Not a threat. His cousin Rhohen, which was kind of the same thing.

His long black hair tossing on the slight breeze, Rhohen sauntered down the gully, a sword in each hand as bolts of his white-blue magic—the color of deep lake ice—crackled around him. The magic held some similarities to Fieran's, from the crackle to the power of it coating the air. But it also had an icy edge, a shimmer more in line with the magic Fieran had seen Uncle Rharreth wield.

Fieran crossed his arms, his magic still blasting around him. "Shouldn't you be in your own morning practice with your dacha?"

Rhohen halted a few yards away, that pouty smirk creasing his face. "My da got called away this morning. He is busy, being king."

A subtle dig. Not a very good one, since neither Fieran nor his dacha cared that they weren't going to inherit a throne someday. Thrones were an awful lot of bother.

Fieran gestured, not bothering to tamp down the edge of his sarcasm. "I'd offer you a morning practice, but it seems I'm a bit under-armed, considering you have two swords and I have none."

"That sounds like a problem for you." Rhohen snorted and stalked a few steps closer. "A proper warrior would never let his sword out of his sight."

"Yes, well, I'm hardly a proper warrior." Fieran forced himself to remain relaxed instead of dropping into a fighting crouch. "Besides, I don't need a weapon."

Rhohen gave another derisive snort. He really should get his nasal passages checked out. He seemed to have a condition. "Arrogant as always, I see. Fine. Take this one."

Rhohen tossed one of his two swords, and it landed on the grass at Fieran's feet.

"And you claim to be a proper warrior. That's hardly the proper way to treat a sword." Fieran picked it up anyway.

This sword was all wrong in his hand. Not the familiar leather grip. Not the right length. Not the right weight.

And yet as he clasped his hand around the leather-wrapped hilt, a pang of something almost like homesickness rose in his chest.

He'd never thought he'd miss the feel of a sword in his hand.

Not as much as he missed flying, but perhaps he had something of the elven warrior in him after all.

Fieran had barely straightened when Rhohen struck, stepping into the blow even as he blasted with his magic.

Scrambling to get the sword up, Fieran strengthened the magic crackling around him. His magic clashed with Rhohen's in a popping sizzle.

Fieran blocked Rhohen's blow, the force of it driving all the way up Fieran's arm. Rhohen might be slim for a troll, but he hit hard—harder than Adry or Fieran's dacha.

Fieran danced back to gain space, then unleashed a blast of his magic, burning through the first few layers of Rhohen's magic.

Rhohen growled and rushed forward, hammering with his sword. As Fieran expected, his cousin wasn't too happy to find out Fieran was still magically stronger than him.

Rather than take the blow, Fieran jumped back again. He strengthened the magic both around himself and crackling down the sword before he darted in close, whirling his sword and slicing through Rhohen's magic.

Rhohen parried, his jaw hard, the dark brown eyes he'd inherited from his macha flashing.

Fieran had him riled now, and Rhohen always got more sloppy when angry.

Rhohen pushed forward with a series of strikes and slashes, hammering again and again like he wanted to pound Fieran into the dirt.

It was all Fieran could do to parry the strikes, dancing backward until his back struck the stone cliffs behind him.

Rhohen growled again and gripped his sword with both hands to swing it at Fieran. "You never could stand up to a troll in a sword fight."

Fieran drew deep into his chest and unleashed a crashing wave of his magic. In Rhohen's focus on the sword fight, he'd neglected his magical shield. Fieran's magic exploded through Rhohen's magic, consuming it in a mere moment, and tossed Rhohen backwards.

He landed on his back with an *oomph,* the sword flying from his grip.

Fieran couldn't help his smirk as he stepped forward. "I might be a lackluster sword fighting student, but I still have more magic."

Rhohen snarled, rolled, and snatched his sword from the ground. He launched himself from the ground, lifting the sword high as he ran at Fieran.

"Rhohen!" Uncle Rharreth's stern command boomed off the walls of the gully.

His sword still raised, Rhohen halted, his face twisted in a snarl. "Da…he…"

"It does not matter what Fieran did. You are responsible for controlling yourself and acting in an honorable manner. That means *losing* with honor." Uncle Rharreth strode closer, glimmers of ice magic glinting around his fingers. "I don't care who started this fight, I'm ending it. Rhohen, go back to your room and finish packing."

Fieran schooled his features and held out Rhohen's sword. He was *not* going to smirk at Rhohen getting lectured.

Something of his humor—okay, gloating—must have shown on his face for Rhohen glared as if he wanted to strangle Fieran. After a moment, Rhohen's jaw flexed, and he snatched his sword. He stalked away, murmuring not-so-under-his-breath, "I could have protected Dar Goranth by myself. *He* didn't need to come."

Uncle Rharreth sighed, though he did not speak until Rhohen had disappeared from view. "It is probably just as well Rhohen and I are leaving tomorrow. I'm not sure the island is big enough for the two of you."

"I shouldn't have antagonized him." While both of them knew better, Fieran had the first lieutenant's bar on his shoulder that said he was supposed to be levelheaded enough to lead Flight B. He should have been mature enough to keep a few of those comments behind his teeth.

Though considering the mere sight of Fieran's face tended to antagonize Rhohen, it wasn't like Fieran could have avoided *all* of that confrontation.

"No." Uncle Rharreth wasn't one to tiptoe. He was right. Fieran was due some of the blame. "But the fact that you could antagonize him proves he is not as ready to shoulder the protection of Dar Goranth as he believes."

In a show of his superior maturity, Fieran wasn't going to comment about that, not even to agree.

Rhohen was about the same age that Fieran's dacha had been when he'd married Fieran's mama, was captured, and tortured. Young and not fully in control of his magic, but still considered an adult. Adult enough to marry.

Scary thought, that. Fieran's dacha must have been far more mature back then than Rhohen was now.

Uncle Rharreth shook himself, then clapped Fieran on the shoulder, the gesture firm enough that Fieran nearly stumbled under the force of it. "Well done at Bridgetown. I trust that you will protect Dar Goranth just as competently. I do not need to remind you of how leery the trolls are to trust the protection of their base to a squadron of humans and elves, including the son of Farrendel Laesornysh."

Fieran shifted, clenching his fists to keep his magic contained. "I've gathered as much. I doubt most of the trolls here put much stock in the protection of the Flying Corps."

"No, they don't. They believe the seaborne and airborne navies will be enough." Uncle Rharreth rested a hand on his sword's hilt as he strolled down the gully toward the base.

"They won't be." Fieran fell into step with Uncle Rharreth. "Bridgetown was a warning. The next attack will have much more force behind it."

As bad as the attack at Bridgetown and Calafaren had been, Mongavaria had sent a mere six airships. More than enough to take on an unprepared army base and unprotected town if Fieran hadn't been there.

But six airships were a drop in the bucket compared to Mongavaria's military might.

"Will the Alliance stick with the original plan?" Fieran was tall, but he still had to lengthen his stride to keep up with Uncle Rharreth.

Last Fieran had heard, the Alliance planned to hold a strong front at the Wall. As long as they countered whatever airborne units Mongavaria sent over, the Alliance could simply weather the war behind the Wall, forcing Mongavaria to exhaust their resources until they were eventually forced to ask for peace. If needed, the Alliance would invade, but only once Mongavaria was weakened from trying to fight a war over the Wall.

"I believe so, though there is some talk about what we can do as a retaliatory strike." Uncle Rharreth clenched his fists. "But if Mongavaria keeps targeting civilians, your Escarlish generals and politicians will experience great pressure to end the attacks. The trolls and elves are much more used to war, and they are far more pragmatic about how many civilians will get killed than the Escarlish are."

"Except for those older than seventy, the Escarlish people have never experienced a war." Fieran didn't add that, up until the little taste of it he'd gotten less than a week ago, he hadn't either.

He and Uncle Rharreth hiked up the ridge out of the gully, headed for the edge of the airfield. Fieran worked to keep his breathing even, not wanting to sound out of breath in front of his troll warrior-king uncle.

"The current Escarlish population might not have faced a war before, but after Bridgetown, they are out for blood." Uncle Rharreth's smile was that of a wolf on the hunt. "Something we trolls understand quite well. We've been eager for this war for nearly seventy years. We are not about to be denied now."

"The poisonings." Fieran resisted a shudder. He'd rather face a bullet than poison. He could incinerate a bullet, but he had no defense against poison.

"Yes, but not only that. We fight this war not just for revenge but also to prove our true honor." Uncle Rharreth halted at the edge of the airfield. "Kostaria might be a part of the Alliance, but we trolls have never forgotten that we became a part of the Alliance because we lost a war to the humans and elves. Worse, we were the ones in the wrong in that war. We have more to prove in this war —to Mongavaria, to the other Alliance Kingdoms, and to ourselves—than any of the other kingdoms."

Fieran felt that deep in his chest. Perhaps a need to prove oneself was more universal than one might think.

# CHAPTER SIX

Tapping her pencil on her notepad, Pip swung her legs as she sat at the end of a table in the first row of tables in a small room off the large underground aeroplane hangar. As the chairs had been designed for adult trolls, her feet didn't touch the floor, even when she sat slightly forward.

A common problem. Elven chairs catered toward height as well, and even in Escarland where the chairs were shorter, her feet still didn't touch flat when she sat in a normal chair.

The other mechanics had taken seats near the back of the room. As their commander, Pip probably should have sat with them. But she'd never be able to see if she were in the back. Instead, she sat here, more fully highlighting the divide between her and the others.

Some of the flyboys began to file in, and Pretty Face plopped into the seat at the other end of the table. A dark purple ring surrounded one of his eyes, and his nose was an interesting shade of yellow-green. At least it was still straight.

Pretty Face gave her a smile, then winced. "Ugh. My face is broken."

"Doesn't Dar Goranth have an elven healer?" Pip winced on his behalf. Though knowing Pretty Face as she did, he deserved the punch Fieran's cousin Sathrah had given him. "I thought all important military bases had at least one."

"It does." Pretty Face grimaced and touched his nose. "It turns out this is considered a minor injury and not worthy of direct healing. After confirming that my nose isn't broken, the healer gave me a flask of juice with stored healing magic and sent me on my way."

Stored healing magic like that wasn't as powerful or fast as a direct healing. But Pretty Face's bruise would still heal quicker than it would have otherwise.

Stickyfingers and Tiny took the seats next to Pretty Face. Stickyfingers smirked at Pretty Face and gave him a nudge with an elbow while Tiny nodded a greeting at Pip. Lije slipped into the seat beside Stickyfingers, leaving only one seat between Pip and Lije free at their table.

When Merrik quietly took that seat with a murmured greeting, Pip's heart sank. As much as she liked Merrik as one of the guys, he wasn't the one she'd wanted to sit there.

But as Fieran strolled past the tables to stand at the front of the room, her disappointment vanished. Right. Fieran was leading this meeting. He wouldn't be sitting at all.

Instead, he leaned against a small desk positioned at the front of the room, his hands braced on either side of him with his legs outstretched and crossed at the ankles. Utterly nonchalant, even in his olive-green uniform that contrasted sharply with the bright red of his hair.

And utterly handsome, standing there so casual and confident.

Not that Pip was going to admit that out loud. Or dwell on it. Much. She had a job to do.

As the rest of the flyboys filed into the room and took seats, Baragh leaned against the stone wall next to her and her flyboys' table. Pip shared a nod with him before she faced forward again.

Fieran glanced over the gathering, his gaze not lingering on any of them. "Lady and gentlemen, I know you are all disappointed that we're spending the first weeks of this war grounded."

A murmur of agreement swept the room. Pip resisted the urge to shake her head. Flyboys and their crazy need to take to the skies. Her half-dwarf side preferred to keep her feet firmly on the ground, thank you very much.

"But what we are doing is important." Fieran's bright blue eyes swept the room again. "You more than anyone else know what it's like to go up against an enemy unarmed and unprepared."

Another murmur, then a shout from the back row, "But we had Laesornysh!"

"Laesornysh!" A few echoes rang throughout the room.

Fieran held up a hand, something in his face grimmer at the praise. "Exactly. You had me. But the squadrons stationed at the other aerodromes from here to southern Escarland don't have a Laesornysh."

Now the entire room had that same grim pall over it.

During training at Fort Linder, Pip had only rarely seen this side of Fieran come through. There hadn't been an opportunity.

Now that he was in command, the years he'd spent as a prince of Escarland and Tarenhiel in the public eye were showing. He knew how to make a speech and work a crowd when needed. He might have his father's magic, but now he was very much his mother's son.

"The plan for war has always been that we would stay safe within our borders and let Mongavaria weaken and break against the Wall." Fieran's jaw worked, something flashing in his eyes. "But Mongavaria has made it clear that their plan is to weaken us by attacking not just military targets, but also civilians."

Down the table from Pip, Tiny's knuckles cracked as he clenched his fists.

"It's the duty of the Flying Corps to be the Wall in the sky." Fieran straightened from his casual position leaning against the table. "All across Tarenhiel and Escarland, our fellow pilots will be going up—probably even as we speak—to defend the Alliance Kingdoms from further attacks, and they need to be properly armed. So while we might be sitting out these first few weeks, we aren't wasting our time. What we do here could be crucial to the war effort."

As a cheer rang through the room, Pip couldn't help but join in, a deep sense of duty welling inside her, even if she knew exactly what Fieran was doing.

He'd taken a room full of flyboys despondent at being grounded and given them a sense of purpose and patriotism.

Her stomach was fluttering, witnessing this extra confidence in him. He'd always been cocky. Confident. But he'd never had the command to show it off before now.

She shook herself. Focus on duty, not on the half-elf lieutenant leading the meeting.

Fieran held up a hand for silence again. When the

pilots quieted, Fieran glanced over them again. "So what did we learn in the fight over Bridgetown?"

"That rifles and pistols aren't enough against an airship," someone from the middle row spoke up. "Too small of caliber."

"My machine gun did some damage." Stickyfingers smiled with an unfocused, fond look on his face.

"Yeah, to our wings. And almost to me." Lije scowled at Sticky, giving him a none-too-gentle nudge. "You shot one of our wings nearly to shreds. We're lucky we didn't crash."

"The side mount was less-than-ideal." One of the other flyboys turned to Pip. "No offense, Pip. We don't blame you."

"No offense taken." Pip kept the words light, but her heart still sank. She should have done better that night. Somehow thought of a better way to mount the guns to the aeroplanes.

Could she have come up with a better solution in the less than five minutes she'd had that night?

"Things were less than ideal that night. No time for a proper engineering analysis." Fieran's mouth tipped with a slight smile.

That reminder made her feel marginally better, even if the niggling that she should have done better didn't entirely go away.

If she couldn't have done better back then, she had the time now to do so.

"Even beyond the problem of shooting our own wings, we had only a limited line of fire between the wing and the propeller." The voice came from somewhere behind her to the right.

"Nor could we aim. Aiming didn't matter for shooting

at the balloon but hampered trying to take out the machine guns on the airships."

Pip half-listened to the various critiques and suggestions as the flyboys made them. What would be the best way to mount a gun on an aeroplane?

It would need to be a fairly large machine gun, which would be heavy and bulky. Weight and aerodynamics would need to be taken into account, even beyond all the problems with aim and shooting parts of the flyers.

While Pip had a degree in magical engineering, she'd been mostly focused on the mechanical side of things. Not to mention, her experience was mostly with trains. She wasn't sure she was the most qualified to figure out the complicated engineering that far smarter and experienced engineers in Aldon hadn't solved yet.

Yet as she'd learned with trains, sometimes it wasn't always the most elegant or engineered solution that worked. Sometimes it was the ugly-but-functional methods jury-rigged in the field or trainyard that did what no engineer with schematics and theories could do.

"I have heard of other aerodromes mounting machine guns on the upper wing." Baragh spoke for the first time, though he didn't move from his position against the wall.

"That would be the place to start. Pip, any thoughts?" Fieran turned to her.

For a moment, she sat there, utterly frozen in his gaze. And in the gazes of everyone in the room swinging toward her, though their weight was different than the warmth in Fieran's blue eyes.

Pip swallowed and forced out a few squeaky words. "We'll need to reinforce the upper wing to handle the extra weight and recoil."

Baragh nodded, as did Fieran. Fieran still held her gaze. "Any other suggestions?"

He wanted her to come up with more? Pip cleared her throat, wracking her brain. A tidbit from some of the various journals, papers, and newspaper articles on the early pioneers of flight rose to her mind. "There was cursory experimentation into mounting a larger gun on a flyer a few months ago. The biggest complaint with mounting on the upper wing was that it was very difficult to clear jams or reload or even reach the trigger, especially for shorter pilots."

A difficulty that she could sympathize with, which was why that particular article stood out to her.

She swung her legs beneath the chair yet again. "I could possibly rig some kind of track so the gun could swing up and down from firing position to a more reachable position for the pilot."

A track like that would be best made out of stamped steel to be an interchangeable part, but she should be able to make a workable version with her magic.

Fieran gave a decisive nod. "All right. You and the mechanics can work on that. Use one aeroplane to test a fixed machine gun and the other on a track."

Pip nodded in return. "We'll have a workable model for testing shortly."

"Anyone else have any observations on the fight over Bridgetown?" Fieran's gaze finally swung away from her to scan the gathered flyboys again.

One of the others pointed toward Tiny. "Tiny's ice did more damage than anything the rest of us did, except for your magic, Laesornysh."

Tiny hunched a little lower in his seat, as if embarrassed by being singled out. Pip could sympathize with the feeling.

Fieran nodded. "You nearly had an airship down by

yourself, Tiny. But carrying all that water with you was probably a bit unwieldy."

"It was." Tiny shrugged, his voice squeaking slightly higher than his normal tenor at being the center of attention. "I could barely move the rudder with so much water stacked around my feet."

Not a good long-term solution.

"Pip, would it be possible to add a water reservoir to an aeroplane?" Fieran's gaze was back on her again.

Pip made a note on her paper, sticking to that cool professionalism. "Possibly, but I'd have to run the calculations to see how big of a water tank we could install before the added weight would affect the maneuverability and stability of the aeroplane. The Mongavarians obviously have gasoline tanks in their flyers, so there has to be a way to do it."

Granted, water weighed more than gasoline, so that would have to be factored in.

"Maybe…maybe I could help?"

Pip swiveled in her seat to see Murray, a stocky man with dark skin and curly black hair, with a hand in the air. She hadn't interacted with him much back at Fort Linder as he was so quiet, but the entire training squadron had made a fuss over him when he'd returned to training after surviving his crash.

He was, also, the squadron's one human with magic. Humans with magic were rare, and often their magic wasn't nearly as strong as that of the elves, trolls, or dwarves.

Murray ducked slightly. "I'm only a 2.2 on the Marion Scale and water magic isn't a specialty of mine, but I have some training."

That made sense. Pip had interacted some with the magicians taking various magic-focused classes at

Hanford University, and most magicians were required to take a base set of courses. Likely, if Murray had been skilled with water-related magic, he would have been highly encouraged to join the navy, where most magicians who wanted to join the Escarlish military ended up.

"Thanks for the offer, Murray. That would be helpful." Fieran gestured from Murray to Tiny. "The two of you are exempt from gun testing so that you can work together to figure out the best way to maximize both of your magics."

Tiny and Murray both nodded, sharing a glance with each other as if they were already plotting to disappear into a quiet corner to work on magic in peace.

"The rest of you flyboys, Lt. Rothilion should have a scouting rotation for us shortly." Fieran's mouth only slightly pursed, as if on something sour, while saying Lt. Rothilion's name. "In the meantime, we can study maps and previous aerial photographs, brush up on recognizing ships from the air, and on our air navigation. Flying practice runs over Escarland is one thing. Flying patrols over the open ocean will be another thing altogether. One wrong calculation, and we could find ourselves flying straight out to sea, utterly lost with no landmarks to find our way back."

Great. Another thing for Pip to worry about once Fieran and her other flyboys started actively flying.

A collective groan filled the room. Apparently sea nav calculations weren't something the flyboys enjoyed.

She'd rather do a bit of calculus than fly an aeroplane.

Guess that was why she was the mechanic and not a reckless flygirl.

# CHAPTER SEVEN

"Test Eleven," Fieran called out before he switched on the old, rattling Garrumon Model 2 aeroplane.

Pip jotted a note on the paper on the metal clipboard she held. Merrik stood beside her, a pair of field glasses in his hand so that he could better observe the practice run. The other mechanics clustered a few feet away, also holding clipboards for their own notes.

This was strangely familiar to the routine Fieran had back at his dacha's company—the Alliance Magical Power Company—when testing new engines or other inventions. It had been one of his favorite parts of the job…when stuff blew up. When stuff didn't blow up, it had gotten tedious. He'd chafed under all the restrictions and proper protocol.

Now he was doing everything all over again, just for the army.

Strange how it didn't chafe as much, as long as he was working with Pip.

The aeroplane rolled forward, its nose pointed toward

the end of the airfield facing the interior of the island. Stacked haybales with paper targets pinned to them sat at the end of the airfield.

He bumped and bounced toward it, not moving fast enough to lift the aeroplane off the ground. As old and brittle as this outdated aeroplane was, it might just disintegrate if he tried to fly. He wasn't so sure it wouldn't shake to pieces the first time he fired the machine gun that had been mounted to its nose.

Once he drew close enough, he released the control stick with his right hand—still keeping it steady with his left—and reached for the machine gun's trigger.

The deafening chatter of the machine gun cut through the morning. Hay puffed while large rents appeared in the paper target. Hot gunpowder residue blew back into his face, peppering his skin everywhere that wasn't protected by his goggles.

Another crack sounded, this one louder and closer.

Fieran released the trigger, then grasped the stick with both hands again to swing the aeroplane in a long, arcing turn before rumbling back the way he'd come. When he neared the hangar, he cut the engine and let the aeroplane roll the last few feet.

As the ground crew hurried to chock the wheels, Fieran pushed up his goggles and levered himself out of the cockpit. He jumped to the ground just as Pip and Merrik approached.

The three of them stood before the propeller as it slowly spun to a halt.

Pip reached up, and Fieran sensed her magic building before she cast a small shield of her magic. One of the propeller blades clunked into the magic, forcing it to stop. Pip released her magic, then gestured. "Looks like you hit your propeller several times. This one here is pretty banged up. A few more hits like that, and this blade would sheer off."

"Not unexpected." Fieran sighed and took in the bullet-riddled propeller blade. It was the problem everyone had been running into while trying to mount guns onto aeroplanes, and the reason Fieran had been piloting this particular test aeroplane. If the propeller broke apart and came back toward him, he could incinerate it with his magic rather than be hit in the head with shrapnel like anyone else would have been. "But I suspect we'll find a gun mounted like this is more accurate to fire than one on the wing."

He gestured toward their other test aeroplane, another Garrumon Model 2. This one had a gun mounted to the upper wing with the lowering track Pip had devised curving from the upper wing down to the fuselage so that the pilot could reload and clear jams. Lije currently sat in the cockpit, letting the engine spin up.

"Accuracy does not matter if we shoot ourselves out of the sky," Merrik oh-so-helpfully pointed out as he reached up and rested a hand on the propeller. A hint of his green magic flowed into it, and Fieran suspected that he was examining the integrity of the wood after the hits it had taken.

"True. And it isn't like a lot of accuracy is needed to punch holes in an airship's balloon." Fieran crossed his arms. "But the whole point is to figure out a way for aeroplanes to do more than take random potshots. We need to be accurate enough to take out the machine gunners or disable the airship significantly in some way. Otherwise there is no point in even arming the aeroplanes, and we should just leave fighting airships to our airships."

Not something Fieran wanted to contemplate. The flyers were faster and more maneuverable than the large, drifting airships. He firmly believed aeroplanes would play a bigger role than mere scouts, as many in the military still believed.

"Beyond that, the wing-mounted guns have a few problems." Pip tapped her pencil on her clipboard, her eyes also fixed on the end of the airfield. "The Yshendar aeroplanes favored by the Tarenhieli Flying Corps have a more forward upper wing, allowing for an upper gun mount. But the Soarwings currently used by the Escarlish Flying Corps have their upper wings too far back for a sliding gun mount to work. Not to mention, the upper wing gun mount still isn't short person friendly, even with the lowering track."

Fieran glanced at her. "How so?"

"While you were spinning up, we had the other pilots all sit in the other test aeroplane." Pip gestured to where Lije lined up his aeroplane at the end of the airfield. "The shorter pilots struggled to reach the trigger, and Stickyfingers couldn't reach it at all. Once some kind of firing mechanism can be attached to the control column, that won't matter, except that it would still be difficult for shorter pilots to reach the lowering mechanism in case the gun jams or needs reloading."

"Not much of a problem for the generally tall elven pilots, but not something recommended for Escarlish flyboys." Fieran waved to Lije, giving him the signal to start his run.

Lije waved back and shouted, "Test Twelve!"

Pip made another note on the paper on her clipboard.

Fieran stopped talking as Lije's aeroplane lumbered down the airfield. Next to him, Merrik lifted the field glasses.

As Lije neared the end of the airfield, he opened up. He'd be aiming for the higher of the targets on the haybales, the ones that were set up to be in line with the trajectory of the wing-mounted gun vs. the one on the flyer nose.

Without field glasses, Fieran was too far away to see any of the puffs from the haybales, but spurts of dirt kicked up on the hillside beyond the target.

"It is hard to tell, but I believe he may have hit the haybales once or twice out of that volley." Merrik had the field glasses pressed to his eyes. "The rest went high."

"Still shooting high, then." Pip scratched a few more notes. "Though I'm not sure we can lower the gun's muzzle without risking it also hitting the propeller."

Merrik lowered the field glasses as Lije ended his run and turned back toward them. "It also seems to have a wider spray pattern. The upper wing does not appear to create as steady a gun mount as the nose does."

Another strike against trying to mount a gun on the upper wing. Yet that still didn't solve the main problem keeping them from mounting a gun on the nose.

"Any thoughts on how to fix the propeller problem for the nose-mounted guns?" Fieran waved to his test aeroplane.

"Ideally, there should be an engineering solution to the problem. Perhaps tied into the firing mechanism that will need to be reworked into a trigger on the control stick." Pip sighed and tucked her clipboard under her arm. "But that will take time. For now, I'm thinking something a bit inelegant but simple. If we reinforce the blades with iron plates, the bullets should just bounce off."

Fieran nodded, running the calculations through his head. "The angle of the blades should cause the bullets to ricochet to the side, but we'll want to test to be sure."

Another test he would have to conduct himself. He could incinerate any bullets that strayed toward him.

"I could further reinforce the wooden propellers with my magic to help them take the strain of repeated hits." Merrik gestured at the aeroplane before them. "I know the elven pilots already reinforce their aeroplanes with their magic as a point of practice."

"Perhaps we can talk a few pilots from Flight A into helping so the burden doesn't rest solely on you." Fieran already internally gritted his teeth at having to approach Lt. Rothilion.

Or, perhaps, Fieran wouldn't beg permission. He'd just casually ask a few of the pilots on the side and hope they didn't get in trouble.

Once their aeroplanes finally arrived, that was. The Escarlish military seemed to be taking their sweet time about it.

"Aylia will help." Pip kept her voice low, as if she, too, wasn't so sure Lt. Rothilion would authorize such a thing. "She seems to be a bit on the outs with the other elves in her Flight."

"I noticed." Fieran straightened his shoulders as Lije's aeroplane rolled to a halt at the end of the airfield near them. "Let's try the metal plates and see if that is at least a functional solution until the engineers in Aldon can figure out a more permanent option."

Perhaps he'd give Louise a nudge in that direction in his next letter. Between her, Uncle Lance, and the others at AMPC, surely one of them could figure out a mechanism.

It would take time. Time they didn't currently have. All Fieran could hope was that Mongavaria wouldn't attack before the Escarlish aeroplanes arrived.

FIERAN STRODE out of the hangar and into the chilly mist clinging like a blanket over the whole island. Wearing a fur-lined leather coat that went to his knees and long boots that went above his knees, he was covered from head to toe to stay warm enough while on patrol. A leather hat buckled under his chin while his goggles perched on his forehead, waiting to be pulled over his eyes. The silk scarf—early aviators had discovered that silk chafed less than wool—wrapped around his neck.

Here on the ground, he was just about roasting, but he would be thankful for the layers once in the air.

If only he was flying himself. But today, he was merely a passenger, with a bulky camera in hand instead of the control column.

As he approached the two-seater aeroplane waiting at the end of the airfield, Lt. Rothilion turned toward him, a curl twisting his mouth. "Finally deign to show up, Laesornysh?"

"It wasn't like we could have taken off if I'd arrived any earlier. There wouldn't have been enough light for scouting." Fieran plastered a smile on his face, but he couldn't work up any genuine pleasantness to it.

Lt. Rothilion's face twisted into an even more sour expression as he spun on his heel and stalked toward the aeroplane. "Then let us not waste any more daylight."

As Fieran would like to get this over with as quickly as possible, he had no arguments there. He waited while Lt. Rothilion slid into the front seat before climbing into the rear seat where the wings wouldn't block his view. He rested the camera in his lap and pulled his goggles over his eyes.

Lt. Rothilion flipped the switch to turn the aeroplane on and let the engine spin up before he motioned for the ground crew to remove the chocks.

Fieran's heart beat harder in his chest in that familiar, rising anticipation of taking to the skies once again. He hadn't flown in an aeroplane since the Battle over Bridgetown. He'd missed it. And yet there was a little bit of something extra raw there too. This wasn't just about the skies or the excitement anymore.

Lt. Rothilion pointed the nose of the aeroplane into the wind rising off Dar Goranth's harbor.

Fieran gripped the camera in his lap tighter, his legs braced in the tiny compartment afforded the passenger of this two-seater. Unlike the airfield at Fort Linder, which was huge and flat and bordered by more flat fields, this airfield ended rather abruptly in a cliff. Any mistakes in takeoff would lead to the aeroplane tumbling off and crashing amongst the buildings of the port.

It didn't seem like a great design, but there weren't many open, flat places to build an airfield near the Dar Goranth base.

Lt. Rothilion pushed the aeroplane to full power as it shook and rattled its way down the airfield, bumping along over the grassy hillocks. The craft grew light around them, lifting off the ground, then falling back.

Fieran braced himself, flexing his fingers with the need for that control stick in his hands, the rudder bar at his feet. It took everything in him to grit his teeth and avoid yelling instructions on how to fly to Lt. Rothilion.

The elf lieutenant didn't need a backseat pilot. He gauged the moment and pulled back, pointing the nose toward the sky just as the aeroplane lifted off the ground.

They roared into the air, rising into the sky well before the cliff's edge. The wind buffeted Fieran's face, frigid and biting, yet so freeing. Riding as he was with Lt. Rothilion, he suffocated his urge to whoop.

Lt. Rothilion kept the aeroplane's nose pointed

skyward as they climbed higher with agonizing slowness. As they climbed, Fieran peered over the side.

Brenzuk and Urixidor Islands were dark smudges on the horizon. Long white wakes marked the passages of the various ships—both warship and merchant ship—making their way through the various channels.

Fieran leaned over, gripping the square camera tightly as he used the dial to adjust the large lens. He snapped a few images of some of the ships. Once the pictures were developed, they would be good for training.

Once they finally reached a high enough altitude, Lt. Rothilion leveled the aeroplane off. As they cruised over the two islands, winds shook the flyer, tossing it about. Once the aeroplane steadied, Fieran took a few pictures of the islands and the layout of the icebergs scattered through the channels.

They turned to fly along the sea lane that stretched from the ports of Kostaria and Tarenhiel to the kingdoms on the far continent. A handful of cargo ships steamed together in a cluster, clouds of dark smoke billowing from their funnels as they hurried at full steam ahead to reach a safe port.

In the past few days, word had reached Dar Goranth that Mongavarian warships had already begun harassing shipping headed for the Alliance Kingdoms, especially around the elven port of Sylmare that shared the same bay at the mouth of the Hydalla River as one of the major Mongavarian ports.

A few Alliance warships had been dispatched to deal with the threat, and some minor ship-to-ship skirmishes had occurred. But no major battles yet, and it seemed that Mongavaria was still holding back the bulk of their navy.

Likely for an attack on Dar Goranth, along with a full-scale battle with the Alliance Navies. A showdown was coming where Mongavaria and the Alliance would determine who would rule the seas. Or the Danorbic Ocean, at the very least.

Fieran tried to settle more comfortably on the hard seat, snapping the occasional photograph. They passed over a warship, the lack of funnels and billows of smoke showing that it was a magically powered vessel. A Kostarian battle cruiser, based on the silhouette, though he couldn't tell from this distance if it was the KS *Vanguard*.

Perhaps flying high over the ocean wasn't the time to hash this out, but Fieran wasn't one to just sit there in silence when he could be talking. Or shouting to be heard, as the case might be.

He leaned forward and shouted, "Look. We're going to have to work together as the leaders of our squadron. What happened between my aunt and your uncle was a long time ago. Let's leave it in the past and move forward."

For a moment, Lt. Rothilion remained staring forward. Had he even heard Fieran over the roaring wind with his leather cap pulled tight over his ears?

Then he turned his head and shouted back, "It is not *my* family who has continued the rift. It is your uncle who refuses to return favor to my family before the court."

Perhaps Uncle Weylind was not the most forgiving when it came to those who had hurt one of his siblings. But it wasn't like Lt. Rothilion's family had eased their stuffiness or stopped ostracizing Fieran's dacha because of his illegitimacy.

"Besides," Lt. Rothilion continued, his voice somehow laced with contempt even while yelling, "it is not your family to which I object. I find it disgraceful that the magic wielded by the storied kings of old should be sullied in the hands of a half-breed."

Fieran sighed. That always was the sticking point with the most prejudicial of the elven court. It just stuck in their craw that the most revered magic in all elvendom would find itself first in the hands of an illegitimate prince, and now in the hands of his half-human children.

As much as Fieran wanted to give Lt. Rothilion a little taste of his magic—here in Kostaria, he probably wouldn't even get in trouble for such a minor attack on a fellow officer—Fieran forced himself to smile, even though Lt. Rothilion couldn't see it. But the smile could carry through in his voice.

When Fieran spoke, his tone was cheery with only a trace of the sarcasm he couldn't fully hide. "Glad we could clear that up. It's comforting to know that this is, indeed, quite personal. Good to know where I stand and all that."

Lt. Rothilion didn't bother to reply, and they spent the rest of the scouting flight in silence.

# CHAPTER EIGHT

Pip stared as crate after crate was lowered from the hovering Escarlish airship. Troll workers used wheeled carts to maneuver the crates into the underground hangar.

"Those are our aeroplanes?" Pretty Face gaped in undisguised horror, made even worse by the sparse prickles of the mustache and tiny beard he was re-growing now that the regulations against facial hair were lifted.

"Apparently everyone neglected to mention that some assembly would be required." Fieran sighed as he used a crowbar to lever open one of the crates and peered inside. "I'm not sure what else I expected. Shipping over thirty completed aeroplanes would have been difficult."

"But a lot more convenient." Pip took in the stacks upon stacks of crates. How were her and her four mechanics going to assemble this many aeroplanes? Perhaps Baragh could shift some mechanics from elsewhere in Dar Goranth to help, though doing so would put those mechanics behind in their other duties.

Fieran fished out a roll of paper and held it out to her. "I think these are instructions."

She unrolled it, discovering a schematic of the aeroplane with the parts somewhat spaced out and arrows showing where they belonged. But everything was so layered over each other that it was hard to tell what she was looking at for a moment, even though she was an experienced mechanic. "These schematics leave something to be desired."

Fieran left the crate and peered over her shoulder. "No kidding."

"It's going to take us weeks to build all of these." Pip grimaced, not wanting to see the look on Fieran's face. "Sorry."

"Put us to work." Fieran gestured to the cluster of gawking flyboys. "You have thirty out-of-work flyboys itching to get into the sky."

Right. Why hadn't she thought of that? Most of the flyboys wouldn't be skilled labor. Some, like Pretty Face, probably didn't even know the difference between a wrench and a screwdriver. But they would be extra hands to hold things in place for those who did know what they were doing.

"That's a good idea." Pip rolled the schematics up and turned to better face him. "You and Merrik have just as much experience as some of the mechanics."

"I think Tiny has some experience in mechanics and stuff like that as well." Fieran pointed to where Tiny was helping the troll workers unload the cargo. "His da works on engineering and infrastructure projects in Aldon."

Pip nodded. "Good call. Divide up your men into eight teams. We can all start unloading and organizing things, then set up stations like one of your Escarlish assembly lines. We can put Tiny and the less experienced mechanics on the first few stations, then work up to my team as the final one."

Perhaps building these aeroplanes was doable after all.

FIERAN QUICKLY HAD his men divided up. He assigned Stickyfingers and Lije to Tiny's team but kept Pretty Face for his own team. Pretty Face was apt to whine over extra work, and his background as a wastrel noble's son meant he was about as unhandy as it was possible to get.

As the men set to work opening the crates, moving the elven aeroplanes to make room for stations in the hangar, and gathering tools, an airman approached Fieran and Pip. He glanced between them, then faced Fieran. "Lt. Laesornysh?"

"That would be me." Fieran stepped forward.

The airman held out a clipboard. "Could you please sign for the shipment of the aeroplanes?"

Fieran took the clipboard, glanced at the shipment list, and counted the crates. He counted a second time. "There are twenty crates, but this list has only eighteen."

"Those two over there are from this shipment." The airman reached over and flipped to a second page. "I'll need you to sign for those as well."

Fieran caught a glimpse of the AMPC header on the second paper, and the contents made him grin. He quickly signed both sheets and handed the clipboard back. "There you go."

"Thank you, sir." The airman saluted before spinning on his heel and marching toward the rope ladder stretching from the hovering airship.

Fieran grinned at Pip, motioning to her. "Come on. You'll want to see these last two crates."

Pip trotted next to him as he hurried across the hangar. He tried to remember to temper his stride so he didn't make her run, but it was hard when all he wanted to do was dig into those crates.

When he reached them, he found an envelope taped to the top of one of the lids. He peeled it off and ripped it open.

*Fieran,*

*Uncle Lance talked the war office into letting your squadron test the air-to-air radio prototypes, given that you have two certified magical engineers as pilots and a certified engineer mechanic as well. A few squadron captains at some of the other aerodromes are squawking at favoritism to the king's nephew and blah, blah, blah, but Uncle Lance and Uncle Julien got their way. Your squadron is the only one that can properly test the prototypes and give accurate feedback.*

*I've also thrown in the new shielded, gyroscopic compasses. You're welcome.*

*Stay safe. Don't crash.*

*Louise*

"WHAT IS IT?" Pip had a crowbar in her hand, but she hadn't yet started prying the lids off the crates.

Fieran's grin was so wide it nearly hurt. "A gift from Weezer."

"Weezer?" Pip's eyebrows rose at that.

"My sister Louise." Fieran laughed at the look on Pip's face. "When she was born, Adry and I couldn't pronounce her name. Louise ended up Wo-weez, then just Weez. And from there everyone started to call her Weezer, and the nickname stuck."

"What a nickname." Pip shook her head. "That makes Pipsqueak—my brother's nickname for me—seem normal."

"Pipsqueak, huh?" Fieran nudged her, still grinning.

"Yeah, don't get any ideas. I've been purposely not telling any of you flyboys that tidbit." Pip scowled at him, then gestured at the crate. "What did your sister send?"

"Well, technically it's from my Uncle Lance." Fieran patted the crate. "Radios for our aeroplanes to test out, along with compasses that have been shielded so they won't be thrown off by the magi-magnetism of the engines."

"That will be handy for navigation." Pip attacked the first crate with the crowbar. "I've been worried about you flying off and getting lost somewhere out there in the wild blue yonder."

As she pried out the nails, Fieran levered the boards the rest of the way off. "No worries about me or Merrik. But Stickyfingers still can't seem to get his calculations right. I won't be sending him off on any patrols by himself."

Pip gave a shudder before she pried at the next nail. The crowbar glinted with her magic, and Fieran guessed she was sending her iron magic down the crowbar into the nail as she pried it off. While her magic flowed directly like an elf's, using it in conjunction with a tool like that was a very dwarven way of going about it.

Once he and Pip had the lid off, the two of them peered inside the crate. A row of what looked like metal boxes with a few switches on the front and wires curling from the back rested inside, padded with sawdust to keep them from shifting.

A paper lay on top, and Pip picked it up and opened it. "A diagram of the radio and a brief explanation of how it works. A few suggestions on how and where to install it, but it seems some of that still needs to be figured out."

"Perhaps once the teams have put together a few aeroplanes, you can shift to figuring out how to hook up the radios and install the compasses." Fieran tilted a radio to inspect first the face, then the wiring at the back. It appeared to need power from the magical power cell to operate.

A part of him wanted to put everything aside to fiddle with it and figure out exactly how it worked.

But no. He was the flyboy here. He'd leave this to Pip's capable hands.

Pip glanced first from the schematics to the radio before finally lifting her dark brown eyes to meet his almost shyly. "Perhaps we could do it together? Apparently the radios work using both radio waves and a magical resonance, and that's more your area of expertise, given it's your family's magic powering it. If we could find a magical power cell fueled by your magic, that would be even better for our initial testing."

"I'd be happy to help." Fieran met her gaze, something like excitement filling him, though it was warmer and deeper than merely that.

He hadn't wanted to step on her toes. She was the chief mechanic for his Flight, and she had a great deal of experience. She could install this herself easily enough.

But if she asked for his help, then he'd gladly give it.

WITH EIGHT TEAMS of flyboys and mechanics working on them, the aeroplanes took shape far more quickly than Pip had expected, even if more than a few of the flyboys grumbled about having to build their own aeroplanes.

At least they'd been sent the very latest T-05 Soarwings. Those were worth the wait.

Pip had her head down in the engine compartment, her toes barely touching the top of the ladder, as she positioned the radio box behind the engine. "How's this? Do your knees hit it?"

Fieran, sitting in the cockpit of one of the nearly finished Soarwings, shifted as he worked the rudder bar. "No, I think that's good now. Neither my knees nor my shins knock into it."

"Good. It will be easy to wire the power in this way." Pip used her magic to secure the box into place. She'd have to work out some kind of bolting system later so that the other mechanics could get the radios in and out as needed, but this would do for now. "I can wire the channel and talk toggles onto our new front panel."

"Would it be possible to put the talk toggle onto the control stick instead?" Fieran folded himself in half so that he could peer at her. "Until someone figures out how to rig the gun firing mechanism on the control stick, we'll already have to let go to fire the guns."

"Good idea. Yes, I can do that easily enough. Perhaps a button that you can press and hold to talk instead of a toggle?" Pip worked her way out of the engine compartment and more firmly onto the ladder. "I was thinking we would wire the receiver and earpieces into your flying caps. If I add a connector built into the aeroplane about here"—she tapped the side of the aeroplane's frame near Fieran's elbow—"you could just plug in the wire there. Perhaps it could even run under your coat down your back. That would keep the wire from getting in the way of your hands."

"Another good idea." Fieran grinned at her, wide and open.

The expression had her grinning back, an effervescent kind of bubbling in her chest. There was just something *more* about working with Fieran like this. He saw her skills, appreciated them, and didn't just dismiss them because she was a female.

She didn't feel like she had to prove anything with Fieran. He let her carry the heavy stuff, do the mechanics, and expected her to know what she was doing. And that was awfully nice.

After sticking her head and upper torso back into the engine compartment, Pip uncoiled the heavy gauge wire that had come with the radio. The connection to the magical power cell's terminal was, at least, easy and already thought-out for her. Fieran's sister or the inventor Lance Marion must have designed that connection while they were building and testing the radios.

"Which aeroplanes do you want the two-channel radios in?" Pip took out her wrench to loosen the bolt holding the wiring harness in place on the power terminal.

Most of the sixty-some radios had only a single frequency channel. But five of the radios were an even more complicated design, featuring two separate frequencies so that those five radios could talk to each other without the others overhearing.

"Lt. Rothilion and I should each have one, then Merrik and whoever Lt. Rothilion has as his second-in-command for his Flight." To Fieran's credit, he only grimaced slightly on Lt. Rothilion's name.

"Then this aeroplane is either yours or Merrik's, since I already have this two-frequency radio half-installed." With her wrench, Pip removed the bolt holding the ending of the wiring harness that ran from the power cell to the engine.

The thump that reverberated through the aeroplane's wooden frame around her was likely Fieran patting the wooden side. His voice drifted down through the open space by his feet to the engine compartment. "I'm already growing fond of this one. Merrik will have to get the next one."

"We'll let him pick his favorite." Pip removed a few more bolts, taking off the single output end from the magical power cell connection housing. She dug the new double end out of her pocket, then bolted it on instead, appreciating the design and workmanship of whoever had designed these to be easily switched out. It was the work of a moment to bolt both the engine wiring and the radio wiring into place. "Who should get the fifth radio?"

"I was thinking that one should go here for the ground support." Fieran shifted his feet slightly, accidentally knocking her shoulder with his toe. He scrunched his legs up higher with an apology before he continued, "We'll want one of the radios here on the ground anyway so that we can radio in alerts once we are in range."

"I'll have to see if I can rig an antenna so we can install the radio in a corner of the hangar somewhere." Pip inspected her connection one last time. If she'd done everything right, then the radio should have power. "Perhaps I can boost the ground radio's range with as big an antenna as the trolls will let me build. These radios will be nice, but they have an incredibly short range."

"A long range isn't necessary for communicating during battle, and that's what we need them for, mostly." Fieran tapped his fingers on the control column, like he was itching to take to the sky now that he had an aeroplane built. "But, yes, a longer range for the ground radio would be very handy if we spot something while out at sea. The extra few minutes' warning that we could give Dar Goranth might make all the difference."

Pip patted the radio and withdrew her head. "Turn the power on."

A click sounded as Fieran flipped the switch that let the magic flow from the power cell into the engine, and now the radio. A hum filled the space as the engine wound up. A slightly less noticeable buzz came from the radio.

She couldn't test if the radio was functioning as a radio yet, but at least it had power and there weren't sparks of magic or the smell of overheating metal indicating it was about to explode. "All right. It's getting power. You can turn it off now."

Fieran flipped the switch off, and the engine's humming slowed. "Do you still need me here?" He braced his hands on either side of the cockpit, preparing to lever himself out.

"No. Actually, could you grab a roll of wire? I have a wire cutter and pliers." Pip climbed down her ladder. "I'll start working my way inside the aeroplane, but I need your legs out of the way."

"Got it." Fieran pushed out of the cockpit, then hopped out of the aeroplane easily.

As he strolled away with that ground-eating, long-legged stride of his, Pip pushed the ladder closer to the wing. She stepped from the ladder to the step built into the side of the plane, using one of the wing supports to pull herself up and onto the wing. She was careful to place her foot on one of the wooden braces that formed the wing instead of the stretched canvas.

While Fieran could step over the side of the cockpit with ease, it was thigh-high for her. She rather awkwardly lifted her knee to her nose to get her foot high enough to clear the side. Straddling the wooden side, the slight leather padding around the edge making it not too uncomfortable to sit on, she reached her toe for the seat. Once she found it, she swiveled her weight onto that foot, then hopped as she angled her other leg up and over.

After settling in the cockpit, sitting down wasn't too much trouble. She wasn't sure why Fieran always found it so tight. There was plenty of room for her to not only sit but also kneel and crawl into the space where his legs were normally jammed.

When she was comfortably lying in the space with the radio just above her head, she set to work getting the terminals ready to attach the various wires.

The ladder squeaked again before Fieran's head appeared by the engine compartment hatch. "Glad I'm not the one wedging myself in there."

"You know, everyone expects mechanics to be large and brawny men, like Baragh or my brother Mak. But there's something to be said for being conveniently tight-space-sized." Pip reached out a hand. "Give me the end of the wire."

"Very true. A highly overlooked qualification." Fieran gave her the end of the wire, then held the spool so that it easily unrolled while she tugged. The tone of his voice changed. Still light, but also a touch more serious. "I have a question I've been meaning to ask you."

"Go ahead." Pip tugged out several feet of wire, gauging how much she'd need and giving herself a little extra just in case, before she cut it with her wire cutter.

"You don't have to answer if it's too personal." Fieran set down the spool of wire and leaned an elbow against the side of the aeroplane beside the open hatch. "But I'm curious. You went to Hanford University for a magical engineering degree because you were inspired by my dacha. So why didn't you get a job at the AMPC? With your skills and magic, you could have had one easily if you'd wanted one."

Pip stilled partway through stripping the end of the wire. She had to take a breath before she could force her hands to continue moving to hook up the correct wires to the right spots in the radio. "I thought about it. I thought about it a lot, actually. But when the time came, I just…I just couldn't do it. After four years away, I missed home. Sure, I'd visited during breaks, but it wasn't the same."

Fieran waited as she paused, as if he sensed there was more to it. How could he possibly know her so well already to sense such a thing?

She fiddled with the wire, not looking at him. "I hate to admit it, but I was scared. I couldn't shake the terror of applying and having my childhood hero turn me away. It would have crushed me. Silly, I know. With my magic, I would have been hired. And your dacha probably has nothing to do with the actual hiring. Yet no matter how much I told myself that, I just couldn't bring myself to apply. I had an application. I had it filled out and everything. I carried it around with me for weeks during my last semester. I guess…I guess I just wasn't ready, you know?"

"Yeah, I know." Fieran's voice was soft.

Pip scooted back toward the cockpit, stringing the wire as she went. She'd either need some kind of tacking nails or an elf to secure the wire to the wooden frame so it wasn't dangling loose.

Perhaps she'd ask for Merrik's help. She'd need him to encase the wire in the wooden control stick anyway.

But not quite yet. She was enjoying her time with Fieran too much at the moment.

"What about you?" She sat up on the cockpit seat,

smoothing the wild tendrils of hair that had frizzed out of her messy bun. "Why didn't you start flying before now? You could have bought or built your own aeroplane, gone to one of those flying schools, and become a pilot well before now if you'd wanted to. I know how badly you wanted to fly. So why didn't you just do it?"

Fieran stilled, even his hands freezing for a moment before they took up fidgeting again by sliding over the side of the aeroplane as if he was petting his favorite horse. "I just wasn't ready, I guess."

He flicked a small, lopsided smile her way at the echo of her words before he dropped his gaze back to the aeroplane. "I thought about it. Lots of times, in fact. But while I don't mind being involved with the inventing side of things, I don't love it. So flying for the sake of invention didn't hold as much appeal to me. And as much as I love the thrill of flying, I just couldn't risk myself without a purpose. I couldn't do that to my family. But the Flying Corps—defending the Alliance Kingdoms—that was the purpose in flying I needed."

"You wanted to be a warrior like your dacha." It was Pip's turn for her voice to go soft with a shared understanding. "Following in his footsteps without actually following in his exact footsteps."

"That too." Fieran shrugged. "It was both the military and the flying that drew me. I needed both, together, to finally be ready."

"I get that." Pip pretended to be inspecting the control stick and the end of the wire she'd strung. "Were we ready, you think?"

"Probably not as much as we thought we were." Fieran's lopsided grin flashed again before he bent down and retrieved another roll of wire. "I brought the wire for the receiver and earpiece as well."

"Good. We can string that, then I'll need Merrik's help to finish up." Pip pushed off the seat, preparing to wiggle back into the footwell.

"With what do you need my help?" Merrik strolled over to them, a set of work goggles pushed up into the strands of his growing hair. Thanks to the fast-growing property of elven hair, it was now long enough past Escarlish regulation length to appear slightly shaggy.

"Securing the wires." Pip ducked her head and crawled into the aeroplane's body before Merrik could catch a glimpse of any kind of disappointment on her face.

# CHAPTER NINE

Fieran ran a hand over the canvas stretched over his aeroplane's frame as he waited for his turn to take to the sky. With the entire squadron—both Flights—flying today, he had a long wait as a constant roar of aeroplanes taking off sounded from the airfield outside the hangar.

They'd barely finished assembling the final flyer and installing all the radios and compasses. Pip had even added a small elven light to the dashboard next to the new compass. The light included a sliding wooden cover that could be pushed down to cover the light as needed. Should they have to fly at night again, they could open the cover to illuminate their compass and switches but close it again to prevent being as much of a target.

Most of the aeroplanes had guns mounted. While Lt. Rothilion's elven half of the squadron had the guns mounted on the upper wing with a track to lower it for clearing jams and reloading, the Soarwings flown by Fieran's Flight had the guns mounted on the nose, shooting through the propellers. All the propellers had been reinforced with iron plates to help prevent the wooden propellers from shattering.

They hadn't had a chance to paint the aeroplanes yet, and the tan resin-coated canvas appeared about as boring as it was possible to get.

But the aeroplanes were assembled, and right now that was enough.

A few yards away, Pip inspected one of the newly assembled aeroplanes one last time before she shut the engine compartment hatch, climbed down the ladder, and gave the ground crew a nod to let them know the aeroplane was cleared to take off.

So competent. So good at her job. Watching her did something inside him that he wasn't ready to name.

Pip pushed her ladder across the hangar, halting beside Fieran and his aeroplane.

Fieran grinned at her, pushing away those thoughts. "Come to make sure my aeroplane won't crash?"

"Making sure it won't crash because of any mechanical issues." Pip climbed the ladder and opened the engine hatch. "It will be up to you to get my aeroplane back in one piece."

"Of course." Fieran leaned against the fuselage as Pip inspected his aeroplane's engine.

She finished quickly and closed the hatch. "You're cleared for takeoff."

Fieran grinned and stepped aside as the ground crew converged on his aeroplane to push it from the hangar. "I'll see you when I land."

"You'd better." Pip propped a hand on her hip, giving him a stern look that made him want to do something stupid. Like wink at her. Or brush a strand of her hair behind her ear. Or lean in closer and…

Where had that thought come from? Was it hot in

here? He tugged on his silk scarf. It must be all the layers of leather and wool he was wearing. Of course he was roasting while here on the ground.

Giving himself a good mental shake, he tugged his goggles over his eyes and strode after his aeroplane.

Once he stepped onto the mossy green of the airfield, Fieran drew in a deep breath of the crisp air, trying to clear his head from whatever that had been a moment ago. The crystal blue sky arched overhead, perfect for a day of flying.

Flying. Everything in him soared yet again, this time with the anticipation of the sky above and sea far below and the wind rushing past his face.

Another aeroplane soared into the sky, joining the cluster of aeroplanes circling overhead.

Fieran climbed into his aeroplane, settling into his seat and plugging the new wire running from his cap into the port Pip and Merrik had created just to the right of the seat.

He flipped the switch to turn the engine on, power flowing from the magical power cell into both the engine and the radio.

The elven moss speakers secured in the flaps over his ears crackled to life with voices.

"…new radios."

"I can hear you."

"What do you think about…"

The voices garbled over each other as various members of his Flight talked at the same time in their excitement to be able to communicate.

Fieran tuned out the chatter as best he could as he let his aeroplane's engine spool up and waited for several more aeroplanes to take off ahead of him. Merrik commanded the aeroplane taking off just ahead of him, leaving Fieran's biplane as the last one.

Once it was finally his turn, the ground crew raced in, grabbed the wheel chocks, and dashed out of the way.

Fieran's heart leapt as his aeroplane rolled forward, gaining momentum. He pointed the nose toward the end of the field, not letting himself dwell too much on the edge of the cliff looming closer.

His Soarwing biplane bumped and jostled over the grassy stretch as it gained momentum. He waited, sensing the moment the air caught his wings before he tilted the control stick and sent his aeroplane hurtling into the sky. It clawed its way upward as he headed for where Flight B circled.

Amid the chatter, another more supercilious voice cut through the garble. "Lt. Laesornysh, channel 2."

Fieran gritted his teeth at Lt. Rothilion's tone as he reached forward and flipped the switch mounted next to the switch for his engine, changing his radio from channel 1 to channel 2. As soon as he did, the chatter disappeared, leaving only a vague static. He pushed the talk button on his control stick. "Changed to channel 2."

Without the chatter, Lt. Rothilion's voice cut sharp and clear. "Tell your motley Flight of humans and half-breed mutts to cut the chatter. The radios are to be used for military matters, not idle chit-chat."

Fieran swallowed back his sarcastic retort at Lt. Rothilion's insult to him and his men. "Will do. Anything else?"

"Take your Flight and circle north and west along the coast. I will take Flight A east and then circle south." Lt. Rothilion's tone was stuffy as he gave the order that put his Flight on patrol over the crucial eastern and southern sea lanes while Fieran patrolled the northern route and the channel between the outlying islands and Kostaria's coast. While it was possible a Mongavarian fleet could circle around to come from the north, they would most likely come from the south or harass the Alliance's sea trade to the east.

But all Fieran could say was, "Understood. Switching back to channel 1."

Little as Fieran liked it, Lt. Rothilion was his commanding officer. At least he didn't have to call Lt. Rothilion *sir*.

"Flight B, listen up." Fieran finally reached his circling Flight, waiting a beat for their chatter to quiet. "We've been assigned the northern and eastern patrol. Cut the chatter. These radios are for military matters."

A chorus of "yes, sir" echoed through the radio before it fell silent except for the static.

Fieran swung his aeroplane into the position at the fore as the others assembled behind him, with Merrik taking his spot to the side and just behind Fieran.

They flew in silence for several minutes as they crossed the length of Drogenvroh Island. Besides the heavily industrialized southern tip around the Dar Goranth base, the rest of the island was heather-covered hills, rocky crests, stands of trees, and tiny inlets with quaint fishing villages comprised of stone huts and a few docks, places where life for the rural trolls hadn't changed all that much in the last thousands of years.

A few of the trolls working around the docks or tending gardens looked up, shading their eyes as they peered at the very modern aeroplanes flying over their peaceful little villages.

Finally, Fieran's Flight reached the far northern end of Drogenvroh Island and headed north over the ocean. Below, a maze of icebergs clogged the sea, making it difficult for anyone unfamiliar with the waters to navigate close to the island. A few fishing trawlers puttered between the icebergs, a glow of troll ice magic showing how they were finding their way without issues.

Fieran waited another half an hour before he broke the radio silence. "All right. Location check."

He pulled out the notebook, chart, pencil, and tools for taking readings for the sun's location. Keeping the aeroplane steady with one hand, he spread the chart over his legs, took a few measurements, and ran through the calculations both by using the chart and the sun's location and using his biplane's airspeed and the length of time they had been traveling. The new compass also provided a heading.

After giving his Flight time enough, he pressed the talk button on his control stick. "All right, everyone. Sound off what numbers you got."

The radio burst with the various members of the Flight reporting the numbers they got in their calculations all at once.

"One at a time. In order." Fieran had to just about shout over the others.

Everyone paused again. Then Merrik's voice came over the radio, reporting numbers that matched Fieran's. Not a surprise, but also a reassurance that Fieran's numbers were the correct ones. Not that he was doubting himself, but he'd rather check with Merrik.

Pretty Face and Tiny both had the correct numbers. Several more members of the Flight had the correct numbers, but a few didn't. Lije was only a few numbers off.

When it was Sticky's turn, a long pause filled the radio before Stickyfingers spoke, his tone coming across sheepish even over the crackling radio. "Um…"

Not a surprise either. With his lack of formal education, Stickyfingers had barely passed the tests during training and only managed it thanks to Fieran and the others helping him along. Doing quick calculations while flying was still beyond him.

He wasn't the only one. About a quarter of the Flight got the wrong number or hadn't been able to finish their calculations in the time he'd given them.

Fieran made a mental note of those who struggled. After this first patrol, the Flight would be divided up into a rotation of constant patrols around Dar Goranth. Fieran would assign the patrols to make sure those struggling were always placed with more capable navigators.

Packing away the rest of the items, Fieran pulled out the logbook and made a note of his Flight's position and the time. Once that was done, he slid the logbook into the wooden pocket formed in the side of the fuselage beside him.

A few fishing trawlers bobbed on the waves far below among the icebergs, the large white bergs more scattered the farther they flew from Drogenvroh Island. A smudge to their west was the mainland's coastline. Besides that, there was nothing but dark empty ocean.

Lt. Rothilion had sent Fieran's Flight on the useless patrol, but Fieran would make the most of it. His men had been shortchanged two weeks of vital training. They were seriously behind on the number of flight hours they should have, and the near disaster of the Battle over Bridgetown proved how badly his flyboys needed more training. Most of his fellow pilots who had died during that battle had crashed because of their own inexperience rather than the enemy guns.

His men needed practice, and it was up to him to figure out some kind of drills.

Fieran couldn't help a lopsided grin. He was starting

to sound like his dacha.

He pressed the talk button. "All right, men. We're going to run a few drills before we continue our patrol."

Now he just had to come up with the drills. He didn't have the personal experience to even know what orders to give.

Keep it simple to start. He could work up from there.

Fieran led the Flight in a series of loops, dives, and climbs. Thankfully, no one stalled, though a few got close and had to tumble before they regained control.

After about an hour of drills, Fieran divvied up the squadron into pairs and sent them off in various directions to extend the amount of ocean his Flight could cover on this patrol. They'd already flown far out to sea in the north as they'd gone through their drills, and he checked that everyone had the right heading before he sent them off.

Fieran and Merrik swung into their route, flying over the rippling waves. Fieran peered over the side, noting the various boats they spotted.

Fishing trawler. Fishing trawler. Oh, an older style, outrigger canoe. Fishing trawler.

After another hour of boring flying, Fieran turned back to the south and paralleled the coast. The rest of the squadron checked in and fell in behind him until all thirty-some aeroplanes returned.

That was a relief. Given the calculation mistakes of earlier, he'd been a little worried a few of them wouldn't be able to find their way back.

As they flew down the coast, the breeze picked up, tossing and buffeting their aeroplanes.

A turbulent gust shoved Fieran's aeroplane into a sudden drop before another smack sent him bouncing sideways.

He braced himself in the cockpit as his shoulders knocked against the leather padding around the edge. He pressed the talk button. "Everyone, give each other plenty of space. We don't want to be knocked into each other with this turbulence."

Fieran fought against the rudder bar and the control column to keep his aeroplane as steady as possible. The closer they got to Dar Goranth, the more intent the wind seemed to be on sending them through the blender. In the calm skies over Fort Linder, they'd never faced winds like these sea breezes.

As they veered toward the airfield at Dar Goranth, a few flyers from Flight A remained circling in the sky, waiting for their turn to land after their patrol.

Fieran started a new circle farther away. "We'll wait for Flight A to finish landing before we start our runs." He set an order for landing, then finished with, "I'll land last."

More acknowledgments came through, along with a little chatter.

One of Flight A's aeroplanes came down for a landing. The wind must have hit it because it skidded sideways and nearly landed on the underground hangar instead of the airfield proper before the elven pilot regained control and managed to salvage the landing.

"Whoo-whee, what a landing. Looks like he nearly ate it," Stickyfingers observed over the radio.

Before Fieran could reply, Lt. Rothilion's voice cut over the radio. "Do not forget that Flight A can hear you."

"Oh, right. Sorry about that, sir." Stickyfingers still sounded far too cheerful.

Fieran would have smacked himself in the forehead if he hadn't needed both hands on the stick to keep his aeroplane under control in the freshening wind.

"I agree with you, Sticky." Aylia's voice rang through the headset, speaking in Escarlish, likely for the benefit of Fieran's half of the squadron. "That was not Thalanil's most graceful landing."

"Just wait until your turn. The winds down here are quite strong." Another elven-accented voice came over the radio, also speaking Escarlish. Thalanil, presumably.

Fieran could imagine the elven first lieutenant grumbling about how Fieran's mutts were rubbing off on his elven pilots.

But Fieran wasn't about to quell the banter. It would be good for more banter to spring up between his Flight and Lt. Rothilion's. Thanks to Lt. Rothilion's stuffiness, the two halves of the squadron hadn't interacted much, and most of those interactions had been stiff and official.

Once the ground crew wheeled Thalanil's biplane out of the way, another elven pilot lined up for a landing. The aeroplane also crabbed sideways before it touched down.

Aylia's voice crackled over the radio again. "Thalanil was not joking. The winds are fierce. Take care with the landings, Flight B."

"Thanks for the warning." Fieran paused, debating. He didn't want to admit his squadron's weakness over the airwaves where Lt. Rothilion and Flight A would hear.

But his men's safety came first over any kind of pride.

Fieran pressed the talk button again. "Ground radio, switch to channel 2." After the person on the ground radio acknowledged, Fieran switched to channel 2.

A moment later, the voice came again. "Ground radio on channel 2. What is it, Lt. Laesornysh?"

"Could you alert Mechanic Pippak Detmuk-Inawenys to be standing by outside the hangar to use her magic to assist with the landings?" Fieran wasn't sure how badly these landings would go, but Pip's shield might be able to stop an aeroplane from crashing into the cliff or one of the surrounding hills if necessary.

"Will do. Anything else?"

"No, that's all. Returning to channel 1." Fieran swapped back to channel 1 just as the last of Flight A's aeroplanes touched down safely. "All right, Murray, you're up."

Fieran's chest squeezed as Murray lined up for his landing. Now just to hope that all his flyboys survived their first truly difficult landing here at Dar Goranth.

Pip raced outside, her stomach already in her toes. As soon as she stepped from the hangar, a gust of breeze slammed into her so hard that she stumbled.

No wonder Fieran had asked for help in making sure the flyboys landed safely. The wind gusts had picked up even in the past few minutes since the elven half of the squadron had landed.

With the radio tucked in a corner of the hangar, hooked up to the temporary antenna that she planned to rework to extend the range, Pip couldn't talk to the flyboys as they came in for their landings.

She stepped aside as the ground crew wheeled the last of the elven aeroplanes into the hangar.

High above the inland cliffs of the island, the first of the Soarwings lined up into the wind for the landing. A gust came from the side, crabbing him sideways in the air.

Pip called up her magic, keeping it at her fingertips, readying herself for anything.

The aeroplane dropped lower and lower until it

skimmed right above the grass at the far end of the airfield.

A gust slammed the aeroplane into the ground hard enough that one of the wheel struts cracked, the wheel spinning away. The broken shaft dug into the ground as the aeroplane toppled over, skidding on the grass. Thankfully it remained upright, coming to a halt after digging a furrow in the grass.

Pip released a breath, even as the ground crew rushed to remove the biplane from the airfield to clear it for the next flyer.

Once the airfield was clear, two more aeroplanes landed badly but safely without her assistance.

Then the fourth aeroplane came in for a landing. Right as it neared the ground, a particularly strong side gust of wind caught one wing and just about turned the flyer onto its side.

Pip threw out her magic, trying to press on the aeroplane without smacking into it with enough force that *she* caused something to break.

For a moment, the aeroplane hung there, pinned between the competing forces of wind and magic. Then it flipped back onto its wheels, slamming into the ground.

Pip saved several more aeroplanes from crashing before Merrik, then Fieran landed without incident. She finally took a breath, her hands shaking.

FIERAN STRODE THROUGH THE HANGAR, slapping each of his pilots on the back and letting them know they'd done well, despite their rough landings. After the mostly smooth landings of the elven half of the squadron, Flight B had looked like a fumbling mess.

But it wasn't their fault. The wind had picked up, and they'd never landed in rough conditions like that before. Frankly, he was just thankful they were alive and all the aeroplanes were in more or less one piece. Or, at the very least, in few enough pieces that it wouldn't take Pip and the mechanics that long to repair them.

"Lt. Laesornysh." Lt. Rothilion's strident tone forced Fieran to halt, even though all he wanted to do was keep walking.

Lt. Rothilion stepped in front of Fieran, a few of the elves from Flight A trailing him as they always did. Lt. Rothilion's gaze swept first over Fieran, then past him to the pilots and slightly damaged flyers of Flight B. "Disgraceful performance this morning. Though one could not expect much better from such a rabble."

As much as Fieran wanted to retort, he gritted his teeth and forced his words back. He could point out that the elves of Flight A had had their full training—two weeks more of training than Fieran's men—plus an additional two weeks of flying experience here at Dar Goranth.

But saying such a thing would only invite Lt. Rothilion to remark on how sloppy the Escarlish Flying Corps must be, if they sent such inexperienced, undertrained pilots to an important base like Dar Goranth.

Worse, it was generally known that elves, as a whole, made the best pilots. They *did* have slightly superior reflexes and a better head for heights than the average human.

But that didn't make humans inferior. There was a heart—a fire—in many humans that Fieran had rarely seen in the elves. That was not to be underestimated.

Having delivered his set down, Lt. Rothilion sniffed, turned on his heel, and marched away.

As he walked away, Merrik joined Fieran, crossing his arms and speaking in a low tone that wouldn't carry even to the elves with more sensitive hearing. "The insults were unnecessary, but it is difficult to refute him when our showing today was poor."

"Our lack of training definitely showed." Fieran grimaced, also keeping his voice barely above a whisper.

"What are you going to do about it?" Merrik raised an eyebrow.

Fieran sighed, already wishing he didn't have to say it out loud. "Put together better practice routines and figure out how to add them to our schedule on top of the patrol rotation."

"Now you sound like your dacha." Merrik's mouth curved with just a hint of a smile.

"I know. Don't remind me." Fieran heaved another sigh. Growing up, he'd chafed under such rigid practice all the time, both with his swords and with his magic.

He could better understand the necessity of them now. Perhaps his dacha, who had spent his formative years living in an army camp, didn't know any way to go about teaching his children except to fall back on his military-style training.

Then again, Dacha had known for the past seventy years that war was coming. Maybe he didn't know any other way to teach than by military discipline. But he also knew that Fieran and his siblings would need that military discipline once war broke out.

Dacha had spent years preparing Fieran for this. It was time Fieran stepped up and fully took on the mantle of Laesornysh.

But did that mean he had to become as hard and dour as his dacha? Or could he still retain some of his more carefree, easygoing personality?

# CHAPTER TEN

After climbing down the flights upon flights of stairs—no one took the lifts for going down—Pip strode out of the mountain into the bustling port of the Dar Goranth base. She hadn't had the chance to search out the dwarves working on the base in the first few weeks she'd been there, thanks to the long hours of testing the aeroplane guns, then the scramble to build the Escarlish aeroplanes.

Now that Fieran and the flyboys were out on another patrol—thankfully with good, calm weather—she had a few moments to explore the base.

She dodged around the various human and troll seamen—as well as a few seawomen—and naval base workers as they hauled freight and bustled between various buildings.

Most of the trolls, standing a foot or more taller than her, didn't even seem to see her. Several almost ran into her, and one nearly clocked her in the face with an elbow as he swung to say something to the person next to him as she was wiggling her way by.

But she was used to dodging elbows, so she rocked back on her heels, the elbow missing her nose by a mere inch, before she ducked around the troll and squirmed through a tiny gap in the crowd.

Surrounded by tall trolls and even taller buildings, she might have gotten lost in the sprawling base if the pounding beat of hammers and the earthy, metallic taste of dwarf magic hadn't provided an unerring guide through the streets.

Finally, she popped out of the general bustle before the giant dry docks—large concrete structures built stretching out into the bay. Most of the dry docks were, well, dry with their large doors at the end sealed shut against the water. The ships in these were resting on large bracings, keeping them upright and steady as dwarf, troll, and human workers swarmed over them.

In the nearby harbor, the nearly complete ships floated on the water while work crews of mostly humans with only a few trolls and dwarves labored over the finishing touches.

Beyond the dry docks, more ships' hulls were in progress, resting on more bracings as they were built on solid ground before they would be sent down slipways to plunge into the bay at their launch.

Teams upon teams of dwarves worked on each ship. Other teams of trolls and humans were interspersed among the dwarves, but the dwarves were the ones in charge here.

On the nearest hull under construction, a team of dwarves pounded in the rivets that held the hull plates together. One dwarf heated the rivet in a small, portable forge. Once the rivet was red-hot, the dwarf used a pair of tongs to toss it up to another dwarf, who caught it in a bucket. This dwarf then plucked the still hot rivet from the bucket with another set of tongs and placed it in the hole pre-drilled in the two sheets of iron being clamped together.

While Pip couldn't see the inside of the ship, she could imagine a dwarf on the inside holding the bucking bar against the back of the rivet. A dwarf on the outside then pounded the rivet with his large ball-peen hammer, flattening the outside head and smushing the base of the rivet against the bucking bar on the inside. When the rivet cooled, it would shrink, holding the two sheets of iron together.

All the while, the dwarves kept up a steady rhythm with their heating, tossing, and pounding, at one with the metal. Magic curled around them as they worked it into the rivets, the metal plates, the very bones of this ship in progress.

Pip couldn't work her magic the way a dwarf did, but she tapped her hand against her thigh in time with the rhythm as she approached the working dwarves.

The noise of all the drilling and hammering reverberated in her ears, and she dug into her pocket and pulled out a set of elven moss earplugs. While full dwarves like her mother or a half-dwarf like her brother had an extra flap inside their ears that they could use to plug their own ears when working, Pip had inherited her dacha's elven, sensitive hearing.

Pip waited to one side of the massive hull, simply soaking up the presence of so many dwarves.

A pang shot through her. Would she still be gone fighting this war next winter when her family made their yearly trek to the dwarven mountains to visit her grandparents?

With Dar Goranth so remote, letters came sporadically every few weeks. Unlike at Fort Linder, they no longer could call home, unless it was a dire emergency, and even then they had to go up the chain of command to request such a thing. There were only two telephone lines sunk in the channel running from Drogenvroh Island and Kostaria's mainland, and those had to be reserved for military purposes.

Between the phone calls and frequent letters, she hadn't felt so cut off from her family at Fort Linder. Plus she was surrounded by the familiar Escarlish culture.

Here, everything was foreign, and her family felt so very far away. She'd finally received a packet of letters from home, making her miss her parents and Mak all the more.

After several more minutes, a female dwarf who had been shouting out orders to the others wandered in Pip's direction. The dwarf's beard was braided in an intricate pattern, the colors of the bands and beads telling Pip the dwarf came from Clan Herfaed, a dwarf clan from one of the more northern dwarven clans.

The dwarf glanced over Pip, taking in her height to the hand Pip still tapped against her thigh. The dwarf pounded her fists together in front of her in the dwarven greeting. "Kiddakak of Clan Herfaed."

Pip made the gesture as well. "Pippak of Clan Detmuk."

"A good meeting." The dwarf nodded, then pointed toward one of the hulls only starting construction. "Dwarves of Clan Grustraen are down that way."

Clan Grustraen was part of the same dwarven kingdom as Clan Detmuk, their mountain only a few mountains over from Mount Detmuk.

"*Nomdet*." After so long of speaking Escarlish and elvish in the last few months, the dwarvish thank-you felt rough on Pip's tongue and deep in her throat. She pounded her fists against each other again in farewell, then turned to head in that direction.

The interaction likely would have felt abrupt to a human or an elf. But dwarves didn't linger over conversation during a workday. Socializing was for when the work was done.

But when they did socialize, well, dwarves knew how to party.

Pip strode along the shipyard until she reached the hull the female dwarf had indicated.

Here, a male dwarf with a thick, black beard down to his waist shouted orders in between tapping out a rhythm of his own against the hull with a small hammer.

Pip halted next to him and knocked her fists. "*Durid mouna*. Pippak of Clan Detmuk."

"Clan Detmuk! *Durid mouna.*" The other dwarf didn't pause in his rhythm as he wished her good morning, though a large grin spread beneath his thick beard. "I'm Yamrarlig of Clan Grustraen. I've been to Mount Detmuk many times."

"Perhaps you know my *grandak,* Jordrouth?" Pip spoke in dwarvish as she mentioned her grandfather.

"Jordrouth! Yes, I know him well! Didn't he have a daughter who married an elf?" Yamrarlig eyed her, as if taking in all the elven features that made her slimmer and slightly tall for a full dwarf.

"My muka." Pip kept her shoulders straight, facing the other dwarf without flinching. This was the part where most dwarves said something disparaging about her dacha.

"Ah, quite the story there. Made its way all the way to Mount Grustraen." Yamrarlig nodded, still pounding out a rhythm with his hammer. A swirl of his magic spread through the ship's hull every time the hammer clanged against the metal, merging with the dwarven magic from all the other dwarves matching this lead dwarf's rhythm. "Not judging, mind you. I'm here with my crew, after all."

"I was surprised to see so many crews of dwarves working here." Pip waved toward the long line of dreadnoughts and battle cruisers under construction.

"The Alliance pays quite well." Yamrarlig grinned, showing off his large teeth. "Ships built by dwarves are far superior. We infuse our magic into the iron as we build the ships, and that makes the hulls all but impervious to the newfangled guns and torpedoes."

"Of course they are." Pip dared to reach out and pat the hull in rhythm with the dwarf's pounding. She hesitated, then added, "Do you know if there are any crews of dwarves working for the Mongavarians?"

"Not that I know of." Yamrarlig shrugged, still not breaking his rhythm. "The dwarven kingdoms might not have any closer alliance with the Alliance Kingdoms than a few trade treaties, but we have no such trade with Mongavaria. We all know how Mongavaria treats those they deem inferior. Perhaps a few crews will be taken in, but it will not be many. We dwarves might not be willing to get involved in fighting the actual war, but we will send our iron and work crews to build the weapons so that the Alliance Kingdoms can fight your war."

That was a relief, at least. Mongavaria already had the benefit of a large coastline and many seaports. At least the Alliance would have the advantage of better, dwarven-made ships.

Would it be enough, once the Alliance navies and the Mongavarian navy came to blows?

Pip shook herself and gestured toward the ship. "Care for a little help for a while?"

Yamrarlig grinned and pointed toward a nearby tool cart with several extra hammers. "Always room for another hand on a crew."

"Did you have a good time with the dwarves today?"

Pip glanced up at Fieran's question, craning her neck since they were walking side-by-side through the tunnels of the Dar Goranth cliffs. "I did. There aren't any dwarves from Mount Detmuk here, but there's a crew from a mountain not far from there. It was good to spend some time with dwarves again. And neat to see how they are building the dreadnoughts and other warships with their magic."

She'd enjoyed helping Yamrarlig and his crew. Even though she couldn't work her magic in conjunction with a team the way the other dwarves did, she wrapped her magic through theirs, using her magical sense to guide her. The dwarves had been rather fascinated by her dwarven iron magic that was wielded so directly in the manner of the elves.

"Really? I know dwarves have iron magic, but how are they using it in building warships?" Behind Pip and Fieran, Lije trotted a few steps closer to join their conversation.

Pip half-turned, walking at an awkward sideways hop-skip to talk to Lije and the others while also including Fieran. "Full dwarves use rhythm to craft their magic. It's hard to describe, but it's a union of skills, tools, and magic. While the dwarves are riveting and constructing the battleships, they are also infusing the very iron with their magic. According to Yamrarlig, the crew leader of the dwarves from Clan Grustraen, the hulls will be nearly impenetrable."

"A good thing for the navy boys." Stickyfingers gestured around them, as if to indicate the whole of Dar Goranth base.

"And navy girls. Don't forget about them." Pretty Face smoothed the still thin beginning of his new mustache. "You're always ragging on me about giving women their proper due courtesy."

Lije rolled his eyes and slugged Pretty Face's shoulder. "I'd say you're improving, but I know you're only thinking about the women in the navy because you're still plotting ways to flirt with them without getting punched."

"Getting punched by my cousin wasn't enough?" Fieran walked backward for a few steps.

Pretty Face gave a small cough. "Um, well…"

"Word got around that Pretty Face is to be avoided or punched." Stickyfingers sounded almost too happy about that.

"It has really cramped my style." Pretty Face heaved a sigh as he waved at the passageway ahead of them. "This is the first time in my life I have gone to the cinema without at least one girl on my arm. It's a dismal blot on my record."

"It's good for you." Stickyfingers rolled his eyes before he turned back to Pip. "I'd like to meet the dwarves, if you go again when we're not on patrol."

"If you don't mind us tagging along," Lije added, his gap-toothed smile on display.

"I wouldn't mind." Though it boggled her mind to think of introducing her flyboys to the dwarves.

While the dwarves here didn't seem all that opposed to elves or humans—not like some dwarves she'd met back in the dwarven mountains—she was glad she'd gone by herself this first time. She'd been able to establish herself as a dwarf before showing up with a gaggle of humans and half-humans trailing her.

"We can make it our group excursion, the next time we are all off duty." Fieran glanced at the others before his gaze rested on her.

Was she imagining the warm and lingering look in his eyes? Something in her chest jolted at the thought of introducing Fieran to the dwarves.

Though it wasn't the dwarves in the harbor she was thinking of. For some reason, her mind jumped to an image of Fieran in the dwarven mountains, feasting at her grandparents' table with her parents and brother there.

Pip had to look away as she worked to keep her voice casual. "I'd like that."

What *was* that? She'd thought she'd set aside her attraction to Fieran, but lately it seemed to be getting worse again.

When Fieran continued speaking, he didn't seem at all affected by whatever had come over Pip. "Do you think any of the dwarves will come tonight? I think everyone on the base is invited."

Right. Just friends. Casual conversation. Pip plastered a smile on her face. "They might. Dwarves are always up for a good time."

"Are there any dwarven women in the crews?" Pretty Face slicked his hand over his hair.

Both Stickyfingers and Lije punched Pretty Face's shoulders. Pretty Face winced, trying to rub both shoulders at once. "What?"

Pip rolled her eyes. Pretty Face sure was in a mood tonight. "Yes, there are. But don't bother with your smarmy flirting. You won't get any farther than you would with the female troll warriors. Not with that beard."

"What's wrong with my beard? It's considered quite stylish in Escarland." Pretty Face rubbed a hand over the meticulously trimmed and sculpted beard on his chin.

"Stylish in Escarland, maybe. But for dwarves, a small beard is worse than no beard at all." Pip grinned, perhaps a little too gleeful about that. She could just imagine her muka and brother Mak hassling Pretty Face for his little sissy beard.

"Huh." Pretty Face rubbed a hand over his chin, as if contemplating what he should do with his beard. Keep it to appeal to Escarlish women or shave it to flirt with dwarven women.

Pip shook her head and trotted to catch up with Fieran's long strides. She reached his side just as Merrik pulled open the door at the end of this corridor.

As soon as the door swung open, the reverberation of voices thundered from inside the large space on the far side.

This was one of many doors that led into the large arena built deep underground. The stone had been carved into a large, domed ceiling above tiers upon tiers of benches. Sand covered the floor of the arena in the middle where the monthly fighting bouts were held. Many of the troll warriors stationed at Dar Goranth scheduled various training sessions here, so it was rare that the arena wasn't in use by someone.

Tonight, though, a large white sheet had been stretched across a stand on one end of the arena. Ropes marked the places to sit to see the screen.

Many trolls and humans already packed into the tiers of seats. A few dwarves had even managed to get there early enough to claim the first few rows on the left-hand side.

"There." Fieran pointed slightly to the left.

Tiny stood up, waving. In the rows above and below him, most of the other flyboys in Flight B clustered on the benches, but the row beside Tiny remained empty.

Merrik was already halfway down the row in that direction, and Pip followed, edging down the narrow aisle. Many of the troll warriors were so bulky that their shoulders and elbows filled the aisle as they sat at the very end of their rows to pack in as many people as possible.

"It's a good thing Tiny saved us seats." Fieran's voice came from directly behind Pip.

"Yes." Pip reached the row Tiny had saved and followed Merrik into it. Who knew a showing of an Escarlish moving picture starring an elf would be so popular?

When she sat down, she found herself wedged between Merrik and Fieran. Even though Tiny had saved seats, the benches were crowded enough that they all had to cram so close together that she tucked her elbows to her sides to avoid bumping arms with Fieran and Merrik. Lije, Pretty Face, and Stickyfingers crowded in on the other side of Fieran.

As they settled in, Lije glanced around, then leaned closer to Fieran. "I don't see any elves besides the three of you." He gestured at Fieran, Pip, and Merrik. "You'd think the elves would like a moving picture starring an elf."

"Well, the Star Forest movies aren't exactly historically or culturally accurate, so some elves can be bothered by that." Fieran shrugged, his movement knocking his arm into Pip's. "The elven nobility especially."

"Not all of us are so stuffy." Aylia's voice came from the aisle. Pip's elven roommate halted next to the end of their row, her long brown hair flowing around her shoulders. "Is there room for me?"

"Sure." Pretty Face scooched over so fast that Stickyfingers was squashed against Lije.

As everyone shifted down, Pip lost the little room she had. She was all too aware of the way her side pressed against Fieran.

Fieran, of course, seemed utterly oblivious.

Just as well. It was bad enough fighting her slight attraction to him without him acting like anything more than a friend toward her.

Aylia gave Pretty Face a stern glare before she sank onto the bench. She leaned forward to speak past him. "The amount of stone does not help either. Many of my squadron mates are not willing to brave the possible headache to watch a moving picture."

"This would not be a comfortable room for most full elves." Next to Pip, Merrik's quiet addition to the conversation was nearly drowned out by the general hubbub of the room.

Still, Aylia must have heard, for she nodded, pulling out the stone she wore on a cord around her neck. "Exactly. We all have our healing stones to keep the headaches and other physical symptoms at bay, but even the healing stones do not erase all the weight of so much surrounding stone."

Merrik nodded, all too grave.

Did he, too, feel the pressure of the stone around them? While she was half-elf, Pip had never felt the weight of stone the way her dacha described it.

The lights in the large training arena dimmed as the bright light of the projector flared. As the murmuring voices faded, the clicking, whirling sound of the reel spinning in the projector echoed through the room. The first strains of the music blared scratchy from the phonograph.

The title page of the moving picture came to life on the white sheet, announcing they were watching *Star Forest and the Princess of Estirinfel,* the very first Star Forest book and moving picture.

After a few moments, the title page switched to a page with words. *In the time of the elven empire, when the elves ruled the continent from the sea to the great dwarven mountains, the young elf warrior Star Forest travels through the forests far from his home.*

The page of words blinked into the black-and-white images of the actor Tenian Daefiel bounding lightly through a sun-dappled forest, his bright blond hair flowing in a breeze the audience couldn't feel.

The musical score changed to the recognizable Star Forest theme, a jaunty tune of elven flutes and stringed instruments. For all the inaccuracies of the plot, the characters, and, well, everything, the score at least made an effort to use elven music to denote the elves.

Pip settled as comfortably as she could on the hard stone bench. Too bad it didn't have a back.

She'd seen this moving picture several times, but it was her favorite. There was just something about the original, the first introduction to Star Forest and his lady love, that couldn't be surpassed by the sequels. Not to mention, the leading lady wasn't quite as helpless in this one as she became in the later ones, where the repeated kidnappings and Star Forest rescues grew increasingly ridiculous.

Here at Dar Goranth, so far from home, there was something extra cozy about re-watching a favorite.

All that cozy warmth vanished when Fieran reached

around her to brace a hand against the bench behind her. Not touching her, but still invading her space in a way that made her all too aware of him.

He leaned closer, his breath warm and tickling her ear. "Star Forest is so obviously modeled after my dacha. Blond hair, a renowned warrior, powerful magic, falls in love with a human princess."

"Your dacha and macha inspired a generation," Pip whispered back as quietly as she could.

On the screen, words flashed again. *Suddenly, a scream pierces the forest.*

The words flipped back to the scene of Star Forest. He halted, cocking his head and going rigid, as if hearing a scream that the audience couldn't hear.

*Deeper in the forest, he spots a fair maiden being carried off by bandits.*

The scene showed a dark-haired young woman in an elaborate dress struggling in the arms of four rough-clad dirty men, which, of course, signified that they were evil minions. The music changed from the lilting elven notes to a more bombastic score, showing the transition to the action scene.

Fieran leaned closer to Pip once again. "The only reason she doesn't have red hair like my mama is that the dark brown shows up much better in a moving picture. She has auburn hair in the book."

*"Unhand that maiden, you foul villains!"*

A moment later, the picture showed Star Forest mouthing those same words, though the audience couldn't hear him say them, of course.

The villains halted what they were doing, gaping at Star Forest. Then two of them continued dragging the maiden away while the other two drew their swords.

*Star Forest rushes to confront the dastardly fiends.*

Drawing his two swords, Star Forest gracefully launched himself forward.

This time, Pip tilted her head to whisper to Fieran. "Two swords, of course."

"Of course." In the darkness of the arena, the light of the screen before them highlighted Fieran's smile and glimmered in his eyes.

In the moving picture, a furious, choreographed sword fight ensued. Star Forest easily took on the bandits.

"And skilled with those swords." Pip let her back rest against Fieran's arm braced behind her. Just getting comfortable. Nothing more.

"Though he somehow manages to get his shirt ripped off." Fieran had his head bent so close to hers that his mouth nearly brushed her ear. "A Star Forest Moment, as my family calls it."

On the screen, a triumphant Star Forest, indeed, had his shirt in tatters. Only one sleeve remained partially on his arm while the other was entirely ripped off, baring his shoulder and muscular pectorals. The remaining strips of his shirt fluttered rather artfully as the maiden he'd rescued swooned in his arms—because apparently maidens were supposed to be overcome after such things.

Though who could say if she was overcome by nearly being kidnapped or by the sight of the handsome, all-but-shirtless elf rescuing her.

Pip snorted, then pressed a hand to her mouth to stifle her laugh.

Stickyfingers leaned around Lije. "Would the two of you stop talking? Some of us are trying to watch."

Fieran grinned back in a way that was far too unrepentant. "Merrik isn't complaining."

Merrik rolled his eyes and heaved a sigh. "You always

talk during moving pictures. You and Adry. I am used to it by now."

The flyboys on the rows above and below shushed them so loudly that those sitting farther up and farther down also started shushing.

Pip poked Fieran in the ribs. "See how disruptive you're being?"

"Me? You've been talking just as much as I have." Fieran's smirk sent far more flutters through her than the too-handsome Star Forest currently sharing a romantic first meeting with the maiden he'd rescued, a maiden he doesn't yet know is a princess.

"Shush!"

Pip wasn't sure who said it this time, but she shared one last amused look with Fieran before she turned to better face the screen.

As the moving picture continued, Pip dared to lean her head against Fieran's shoulder. Just a little bit. Not too snuggly. Just getting as comfortable as she could on a stone bench not designed for comfort. Since Fieran didn't seem to mind, she wasn't going to pull away.

Because this moving picture was a two-reeler, there was an intermission when the first reel finished and the crew had to swap it out for the second reel.

A spread of donuts and ice cream had been laid out on tables in the mess hall, and Pip hung back rather than join the shoving for the food. Two of the trolls got into a punching match over the chocolate sprinkles they both wanted to put on their ice cream, and a few of the others were about to come to blows over the donuts. Not a safe environment for someone vertically challenged.

"What would you like? I'll fetch it for you." Fieran gestured to the troll warriors, dwarves, and flyboys descending on the food like a pack of scavengers.

"A maple donut, if they have any. Or any donut, really." Pip placed her back to the wall where she wouldn't be trampled in the continued stampede for the refreshments. "Thanks."

"All right." Fieran glanced around the rest of their group. "Well, men, there's our target. Form up."

On cue, Tiny took station to Fieran's left with Merrik to his right. Lije and Pretty Face took the spots to either side of Tiny and Merrik so that they now formed a wedge with Stickyfingers, the shortest and smallest of the flyboys in their group, filling in the wedge as a rearguard.

Fieran led the way, and their wedge sliced into the tumult. They didn't get into wrestling matches or engage in too much shoving. There was just something about the confident way that Fieran strode into the melee that had those around him moving out of his way.

Aylia leaned against the wall next to Pip. "Good thinking, finding a spot by the wall."

"I didn't want to be trampled." Pip searched the seething mass, but Fieran and his flyboys had disappeared into the fray. "Fieran is getting me a donut."

"Pretty Face is getting mine." Aylia grinned, shrugging. "He offered, and I was not about to brave *that*. Not even for food."

Pip opened her mouth, but Fieran stepped from the crowd a moment later, followed by the others.

With a triumphant grin, Fieran held out a plate containing a cake donut with the brown, maple-syrup-flavored icing. "Your donut."

"Linshi." The elvish thank you rolled off her tongue as Pip took the plate and picked up the donut. It was still warm, so the base's cooks must have made the batch fresh, perhaps even missing the moving picture to make them.

Fieran held a bowl of chocolate ice cream topped with chocolate fudge and chocolate sprinkles.

Tiny gripped a bowl with two massive scoops of vanilla ice cream sporting just about every topping available, from the chocolate sprinkles to nuts to strawberries. Stickyfingers had both a donut and a bowl of ice cream while Lije's chocolate ice cream sported as much additional chocolate toppings as Fieran's.

Pretty Face bowed and flourished a plate with a powdered-sugar-coated donut. "And here is your donut, milady."

"Linshi." Aylia took the donut with a smile that was kind but not flirtatious.

"Let's move back to our seats and get away from this crowd." Fieran once again led the way.

Pip fell into step behind him so that he could part the way for her. Having tall men around was so convenient when they were providing a shield for her in a crowd.

The strains of the Star Forest theme still blared from the phonograph as they returned to their seats while the screen simply said "Intermission."

After they all polished off their food, Merrik gathered all their plates and bowls to return them to the mess.

Just as Merrik returned and shuffled past them to reach his seat on the other side of Pip, Captain Gradrah strode down the center aisle and halted in front of the screen.

The music abruptly cut out, and the conversations all around the arena staggered into silence.

Pip tensed. If only Fieran would brace his arm behind her again. Whatever Captain Gradrah was about to say, she was likely going to need the comfort of his strength.

Captain Gradrah swept her gaze around the arena before she spoke in a carrying voice. "We received word from Tarenhiel that a few hours ago Mongavaria bombed the eastern forests with incendiary bombs using human magic."

Pip stilled, a sick weight sinking into her stomach. Fire that was powered by human magic would be much more difficult to put out than a normal fire. How much of the forest had burned? Was it, perhaps, still burning as the elves struggled to put it out?

On either side of her, Merrik hunched as if sick to his stomach while Fieran had gone unusually still. Farther down, Aylia's jaw worked as she blinked far too rapidly.

To an elf, the destruction of the trees was a profound loss. Perhaps not as mourned as the loss of lives, but a close second.

Pip's donut churned in her stomach. It felt so wrong, sitting there enjoying a donut and watching a favorite moving picture while far away to the south the forest was burning.

"We enjoy a moment of rest today, but our time will come to fight back." Captain Gradrah's gaze scoured those gathered in the arena again. "The Escarlish Intelligence Office has picked up rumors of a planned attack on our navy. Nothing concrete yet, but our day is coming."

All around the room, the troll warriors shouted in a howling, growling kind of cheer that was the traditional war cry of the trolls.

Pip wasn't sure if she wanted to cheer or quail. When the attack came, would she be strong enough?

## CHAPTER ELEVEN

Fieran circled his aeroplane high over the middle of Drogenvroh Island. Below him, four other aeroplanes circled.

Tethered by a several hundred foot rope, an old weather balloon hovered above a rocky ledge. Farther down, targets had been set up, one pinned to a stack of haybales, another on a steep hillside.

Fieran pressed the talk button for the radio. "Lije, you're cleared to start your run."

"Got it." Lije's voice came crackling through the headset in Fieran's cap.

One of the aeroplanes broke off from the pattern. Lije flew his aeroplane at the balloon, unleashing short bursts of machine gun fire at the hovering balloon once he was in range. After a few bursts at the balloon, Lije dove toward the first target, strafing it, before sweeping up to the final target.

Fieran tipped his aeroplane on its side to better observe. He still couldn't see well but based on the puffs of dirt and the way the balloon had danced, Lije had hit the targets or gotten close enough.

"Well done, Lije." Fieran kept circling with his aeroplane on its side. "Murray, your turn."

After Murray, then Tiny, and finally a flyboy by the name of Grady each went through their practice runs, Fieran had them all go through it again, this time in pairs. Once Fieran was satisfied with their practice, he ran through the course himself, aiming for the targets as he swept past and squeezing off short bursts of gunfire from the machine gun mounted on his aeroplane's nose. One bullet ricocheted off the metal plate on the back of his propeller, but the rest hit around or on the target.

To the south, building storm clouds filled the horizon, dark and looming. Weather reports from Tarenhiel reported that a large storm was sweeping slowly up the coastline, bringing days of high winds and rain. This would be the last chance the squadron had to fly before it would be grounded for at least a few days.

In the sky over Dar Goranth, a crowd of airships hovered, waiting to be directed to a berth to ride out the storm. Winding their way through the field of icebergs guarding the islands, Alliance warships converged on Dar Goranth, seeking shelter before the storm.

Fieran led the way back to the airfield, waiting for the other four pilots to land before he brought his aeroplane in for a landing, bumping along until he rolled to a halt before the hangar.

As he climbed out of his aeroplane, Commander Druindar strode down the last few steps leading to the observation tower, where he could watch the target practice with a pair of field glasses.

Fieran saluted as the commander approached, standing at attention.

Commander Druindar returned his salute. "That practice seemed to go well."

"It did, sir." Fieran remained staring straight ahead.

"It was a good suggestion on the part of Lt. Rothilion." Commander Druindar gave another nod, then strolled off.

Fieran gritted his teeth. The practices hadn't been Lt. Rothilion's idea but Fieran's. Following military protocol, Fieran had to run the idea past Lt. Rothilion, and of course the elf lieutenant had made it sound like it was all *his* idea when he asked permission from the troll commander to set up the targets and designate an area for practice strafing.

No matter. Fieran didn't need to go to such lengths to kiss up to Commander Druindar. Once the Mongavarians attacked, Fieran and the rest of Flight B would show their worth.

Surely the attack was coming soon. The Mongavarians had been relentlessly bombing the eastern forests of Tarenhiel and the military bases along the eastern edge of Escarland for the past week.

Much of the Alliance fleet of both seagoing warships and airships had retreated to the safe harbor of Dar Goranth to weather the coming storm, the largest gathering of the navy so far. Rumor around Dar Goranth was that Mongavaria would attack on the heels of the storm while the Alliance fleet was still bottled up in the harbor.

Lt. Rothilion was currently leading Flight A on a scouting mission to the south, getting one last look of the area before everyone was grounded.

Of course he had given himself the more important task, along with a snide jab about Flight B not being ready to face the turbulent flying and landing just before the storm.

Probably true, but Lt. Rothilion didn't need to be so snooty about it, making Fieran's idea of target practice sound like a punishment instead of a good idea.

As Fieran strode into the hangar, he found the rest of Flight B hard at work at the task he'd set them while he'd been out running practice runs with four at a time.

All across the hangar, the aeroplanes of Flight B were in various stages of painting, from some which still had the first layer of gray-blue paint to those that were fully dry.

At the nearest aeroplane, Merrik stood on a ladder as he painted the upper wing. Pip stood below the aeroplane, painting the bottom of the fuselage. Gray paint liberally spattered her dark brown curls, her face, and her coveralls.

Fieran strolled up to them, then lifted a particularly paint-smeared section of Pip's hair, which had frizzed out of her messy bun. "What happened to you? You look like you lost a paint fight."

"No." Pip sighed, though it held a trace of a laugh. "I volunteered to paint all the lower parts of the aeroplanes since I didn't have to duck as much, but some of your flyboys aren't so neat when it comes to painting."

Fieran glanced over the hangar. Paint coated the floor all around each of the aeroplanes. "I can see that. At this point, it might be easier just to paint the floor gray rather than try to clean it up. Merrik, you were supposed to be supervising."

"I tried." Merrik's tone was almost grim as he slathered paint on the upper wing. "Messy paint was the least of our worries."

Fieran glanced from Merrik to Pip. That sounded rather ominous.

This time, Pip rolled her eyes, laid her paintbrush

across the top of her can, and stepped out from under the aeroplane. "Come on. You need to see Pretty Face's aeroplane."

Fieran sighed and trailed after Pip. Any trouble involving Pretty Face was bound to be inappropriate in nature. So far, Pretty Face hadn't crossed too many lines too egregiously, and Fieran had hoped that Sathrah's punch in the nose had knocked some sense into him.

Apparently not.

As they meandered between the aeroplanes, Fieran nodded at a few of the other flyboys, who were hard at work on their aeroplanes' paint jobs.

When they reached the back corner, Pretty Face stood on a ladder, putting the finishing touches on an additional painting on the side of his aeroplane.

The not-regulation artwork depicted Pretty Face with a rose clamped between his teeth and lounging in nothing but what appeared to be a towel—or perhaps a loincloth—draped around his middle, his shirtless chest especially well-defined.

He had a talent for painting. Fieran would give him that much.

Fieran resisted the urge to drop his head into his hands. "Pretty Face, extra artwork is not in the regulations."

"Exactly! There's nothing in the regulations that forbid it." Pretty Face put a last flourish to his self-portrait's hair, his tone all too cheerful. "I checked."

Probably because no one had thought to forbid it just yet. The Flying Corps was still too new as a branch of military service.

"It's not exactly appropriate." Fieran nearly pinched the bridge of his nose the way his Uncle Weylind did whenever the elven nobility was being especially aggravating.

From the next aeroplane over, Stickyfingers leaned farther out on his ladder to peer under the upper wing at them. "Just be glad Merrik put his foot down on Pretty Face's original design before he got too far with it. That was truly inappropriate."

"Dare I ask?" Fieran gave in and rubbed at his temples. Between Lt. Rothilion's harassment and trying to wrangle the flyboys of Flight B into shape, he was getting nostalgic for the carefree days of basic training and yelling drill sergeants.

"The first version was a girl with very little clothes on." Stickyfingers sent a glare in Pretty Face's direction. "Totally disrespectful."

"What? I changed it." Pretty Face pressed a hand to his chest. "Besides, this is better. If my aeroplane had a girl on it, the ladies might think I'm taken. This way, I display my own magnificent attributes."

"You're just asking for another punch in the nose. Apparently my cousin didn't knock enough sense into you last time." Fieran sighed. What should he do about it? He could order Pretty Face to paint over it. He could forbid all extra art entirely.

And become exactly the kind of stuffy lieutenant he didn't want to be.

Or he could let it go. At least the art would make Pretty Face's aeroplane easy to identify while they were flying. And of the two artwork options, this was the better—less inappropriate?—of the two.

"Fine, you may keep it." Fieran raised his voice slightly so that more of the surrounding flyboys would be able to hear. "Since you possess such painting skills, Pretty Face, I'd like you to help everyone else with painting art on their aeroplanes so that each flyer is more identifiable in the air."

"Yes!" A few of the others nearby pumped their fists.

Pretty Face's grin dropped, likely as he realized that Fieran was giving him additional work. A more subtle punishment, perhaps, than having him just paint over the art, but a punishment nonetheless.

When he'd enlisted, Fieran had wanted to be in charge. But now…Fieran hated having to discipline his friends. Basic training had been so much easier, when they were all equals and he could just be one of them.

Despite that, he kept his tone firm. "However, there will be no art of scantily clad women, understand? We are not that kind of unit, and here in Kostaria, we have the honor of Escarland to uphold."

A louder cheer this time, though there were a few groans.

Some of the other flyboys shouted over at Pretty Face.

"I want a portrait of my mama, can you do that?"

"How about a heart with my girl's name in it?"

"I'd like an eagle!"

Fieran released a slow breath, trying to relax the tension in his shoulders.

Pip nudged him with her elbow, her voice low. "That was handled well."

"Linshi." Her quiet words banished the last of his tension.

Her mouth curved into a smile, the expression tugging at some of the dried paint on her face. "What are you going to have Pretty Face paint on your aeroplane?"

"I don't know." Fieran shrugged, his mind going blank. What would he want painted on his aeroplane? Something heroic? Something sentimental? "I'll let Pretty Face work on everyone else's first."

That would keep him busy for a while, considering the shouted requests kept getting more and more elaborate.

By the time he got up to Fieran's aeroplane, hopefully Fieran would have come up with something good.

A LOUD CLANGING rang through the passageway, yanking Fieran from sleep. He was sitting up and reaching for his uniform shirt before he'd fully registered what was going on.

Across the tiny room, barely visible in the darkness, Merrik sat up as well.

Footsteps ran down the corridor before someone pounded on Fieran's door. "An airship has been sighted above Dar Goranth."

"In this weather?" Fieran was on his feet and crossing the room without taking the time to finish buttoning his shirt. He yanked the door open to find Lije standing there. He must have been one of the flyboys on watch, for he was fully dressed and turned out already. Fieran gripped the door. "I'm assuming the storm hit?"

"Just the edge of it, so far. Lots of rain and some gusting wind." Lije shifted from foot to foot.

Along the corridor, Stickyfingers was going from door to door, pounding on each one and shouting to be heard over the ringing warning bell. He must have been the other one on watch.

Merrik appeared beside Fieran, a wince creasing his face every time the alarm clanged. While the Escarlish forts still used the older bugles, Dar Goranth must have installed a newer bell-style alarm to send alerts throughout the base.

Fieran scrambled to button his shirt the rest of the way. "Wake the others and head for the hangar. I don't know if Commander Druindar will order us up in this weather but be prepared."

Lije nodded and hurried off to spread the word.

Fieran returned inside the room, sat on his bed, and quickly stuffed his feet into his thickest wool socks. He tugged on his boots but didn't lace them, though the laces had been tucked inside and were now pressing against his feet. He'd switch to the warmer flight boots up in the hangar if they were ordered into the air.

Merrik threw his boots on as well, then the two of them raced from the room toward the stairs leading to the hangar. The lift would be too slow.

They took the stairs two at a time, reaching the landing for Level 24 just as Lt. Rothilion skidded into the stairwell. Lt. Rothilion merely acknowledged them with a glance before all three of them raced up the final set of stairs.

The hangar was lit with low red lights, a black curtain blocking the light from showing into the night.

Commander Druindar met them at the top of the stairs, somehow already fully put together in his white uniform. "Lt. Rothilion, Lt. Laesornysh, the observation post on Urixidor spotted the shape of an airship flying low and running dark, headed this way. We've checked, and it isn't one of ours."

There was a slight chance it was a private airship blown seriously off-course. But if that were the case, it would be frantically signaling and trying to get help, not running dark.

A Mongavarian scout, then, trying to use the storm for cover, dangerous as the high winds were to an airship.

Commander Druindar glanced between the two of

them. "I'd like you to pick thirty of your best pilots from both Flights and take them up to confront the airship. The others will be kept here in reserve."

In case there were high casualties due to the airship or the weather. No sense risking the entire squadron.

"And Lt. Laesornysh, I'd like you to avoid using your magic." Commander Druindar's gaze landed squarely on him.

"Sir?" Fieran flexed his fingers, not wanting to protest, but also itching at the restriction. His magic was his best weapon against airships. Without his magic, he was just another pilot with a gun.

"Right now, we don't know if the Mongavarians know you're currently stationed here." Commander Druindar's tone remained unwaveringly final. "Once you use your magic against one of their airships, they will know, and I'd rather save that surprise for the main battle, rather than waste it on what is likely a scout."

That made far too much sense, even if Fieran didn't like it. "I understand, sir."

"Good." Commander Druindar waved them off as the rest of the squadron, both elves and humans, poured into the hangar. "Now get up there and either chase off or take down this intruder before they get too good of a look at our defenses."

Not to mention the fleet of docked airships and warships currently sheltering in the harbor. A fleet that comprised the bulk of the Alliance's air and sea navies.

As Fieran and Lt. Rothilion headed for where their men and women had assembled in rows, gathered into Flights A and B, Fieran lowered his voice so only Lt. Rothilion could hear. "Don't just pick your pilots from Flight A. Commander Druindar said to pick the best of both Flights."

Lt. Rothilion sucked in a breath, as if he were about to retort that, naturally, Flight A had all of the best pilots since they were all full elves. Instead, his nose lifted slightly. "It would be unwise to risk all of my Flight for a paltry scout. Your Flight is more disposable than mine. Pick fifteen of your men, and I will pick fifteen of mine."

And there it was. Even while complying with the order, Lt. Rothilion still managed to be insulting.

There was no time to dwell on it. Every moment, the airship was getting blown closer to Dar Goranth, and it would take time to get the flyers in the air.

Fieran faced his flyboys, Merrik halting next to him. "Only fifteen of us will be going up. The rest will stay back in reserve in case this turns out to be a larger battle than a single airship. When I call your name, grab your gear and head for your aeroplane."

Now to decide who would go up and who would stay.

"Lije, Pretty Face, Tiny, Murray." Fieran rattled off ten more names, leaving Stickyfingers behind. While he was a decent pilot, he wasn't yet up for a flight like this, and his navigational skills were still abysmal. If he got blown out over the ocean in the storm, he'd never find his way back. "And Merrik."

Because of course he wouldn't go up without Merrik.

"The rest of you, help the ground crews get the aeroplanes onto the airfield." Fieran gestured at the rest of the hangar, where Pip, the mechanics, and the ground crews were scrambling to push the various aeroplanes toward the hangar door.

With his orders given, Fieran raced for the lockers in the back, joining the others in throwing on his leather coat, the leather boots, his cap, and his goggles. It was going to be a wet one tonight, and even these warm layers were likely going to be soaked before the night was out.

Within a few minutes, Fieran reached his aeroplane as the first of Lt. Rothilion's pilots turned on their aeroplanes. Some of the ground crew drew back the black curtain as the lights near the front of the hangar were switched off. Instead of having the ground crew push the aeroplanes all the way outside, the pilots maneuvered them out under power, disappearing into the driving rain.

Pip met him by the wings of his aeroplane, her hands clasped in front of her, then tucked in the pockets of her overalls, then pulling out a wrench and fiddling with it.

"I know. Bring your aeroplane back in one piece." Fieran kept a grin on his face rather than match her grim look.

"Not even a scratch. We just got them painted." Pip's light words didn't match her tone, and her smile didn't reach her dark eyes.

"Got it." Fieran gave her one last grin before he grabbed the wing support, stuck his toes into the footstep on the side, and bounded into his aeroplane.

As he plugged the end of his headset cord into the side of the aeroplane, voices bombarded his ears.

"...turbulent..."

"...cannot see..."

"...reported sighted to the southwest." That last was Lt. Rothilion's voice, muffled by the resounding roar of many aeroplane engines winding up inside of the hangar.

Most of the elven pilots of Flight A were spooled up and already leaving the hangar one by one. Several must be climbing into the sky already.

"Flight B, listen up." Fieran tried to tune out the chatter that didn't apply to him as he switched his aeroplane's engine on to start it spinning up. "Stick in your pairs. You are each other's right hand man."

"Don't you mean right *wing* man?" Pretty Face somehow managed to get a laugh to carry over the radio.

Pretty Face had a measure of wit, when he wasn't using it for inappropriate comments.

"Yes, wingman. Stay with your wingman, wingelf, wingtroll, or whatever the case might be." Fieran liked the term. He'd have to keep using it. "As Commander Druindar believes this airship is a scout, he has asked that I refrain from using my magic so that I don't give away that I'm stationed here just yet."

A chorus of disbelief and dismay filled the airwaves, nearly drowning out Lt. Rothilion attempting to give orders to his pilots already in the air.

"Since I won't be able to shield us as I did in the Battle over Bridgetown, Tiny, Murray, I'd like the two of you to take the lead." Fieran settled his goggles into place over his eyes. "Troll and human magic won't be out of place here at Dar Goranth."

A man from the ground crew standing by the door of the hangar motioned for the next aeroplane to leave. As others of the ground crew removed the wheel chocks, Lt. Rothilion let his aeroplane roll forward into the lashing rain.

The fifteen pilots chosen from Flight A had taken far too long to take off. Fieran pressed the talk button, hoping his pilots would be up for this next order. "We'll be taking off in pairs."

They had practiced this, but that had been in fair weather in the daylight. Not in darkness and driving rain.

Another motion from the ground crew, and both Tiny and Murray waved to the ground crew to take away the wheel chocks. Once freed, they maneuvered their aeroplanes one after the other outside.

Lije and Pretty Face went next, then the other pairs before it was Fieran and Merrik's turn.

As Fieran's aeroplane rolled from the hangar, the rain was a slap, stealing his breath with the wash of cold dousing every inch of exposed skin. Rain ran down his goggles in such a torrent that the world was reduced to a watery, dark blur.

Fieran scrubbed at his goggles as he turned the aeroplane to position it near the end of the airfield, slightly forward and to the left so that Merrik had room for his aeroplane behind and to the right.

At the far end of the airfield, the previous two aeroplanes rose into the sky, banking into the wind as they clawed their way into the tumultuous storm.

High above, a shimmer of white icy magic traced across the sky, briefly highlighting the flyers already climbing into the sky. Tiny's voice came over the radio. "I think I sense something to the south."

"Headed to intercept." Lt. Rothilion's reply came sharp and quick.

"On our way." Fieran pushed his aeroplane to full power as it rumbled forward over the ground, jouncing and bouncing over the tiny hillocks of grass even as crosswinds buffeted the wings, threatening to tumble his aeroplane onto its side before he even had the chance to get into the air.

He fought both the control stick and rudder to keep control even as the aeroplane rushed forward.

Almost before he was ready, a gust picked his aeroplane up, tossing him into the sky. Before it could slam him back to the ground, potentially damaging the wheel struts, he worked the ailerons. For a moment, his aeroplane hung, caught between sky and land as if unsure which force would win.

Then the solidness returned beneath his wings, and his flyer climbed into the sky, fighting for every inch rather than being the graceful craft it normally was.

When he risked a glance over his shoulder, Merrik's aeroplane was a dark shape in the flashes of lightning, following in Fieran's wake into the sky.

Crackling static filled the radio, punctuated by garbled voices. The storm was interfering with their radios, and the distance wasn't helping.

Fieran pointed the nose of his aeroplane toward the faint sense of Tiny's magic whispering across the sky. The higher he got, the harder the rain pounded against the wings and drove into his face until he felt like he was drowning in the sky every time he choked in a breath.

This was insane. They were all going to get themselves killed trying to intercept this airship.

What did the mystery airship even hope to gain, trying to scout Dar Goranth in this weather? In these winds and with this rain, the airship must be struggling as much as—or more than—their aeroplanes were.

The tiny pinpricks from the elven lights mounted inside the cockpits of their aeroplanes were the only things marking the location of the various squadron members, and even those couldn't be seen more than a hundred yards away.

Fieran tried to count the lights as his aeroplane struggled into the sky, but the water streaming down his goggles and the roiling waves of rain made it impossible to count more than a handful at a time.

With a slash of something almost like pain, bits of sleet and ice sliced through the air along with the rain. From Tiny's magic? Or was the storm turning even worse?

"Tiny, do you still sense the airship?" Fieran shouted into the radio. Was he close enough for Tiny to even hear him?

"…lost…can't see…"

Was that Tiny or someone else? Fieran couldn't make out enough of the voice through the static.

"Lt. Rothilion." Fieran fought the buffeting winds, his aeroplane skidding sideways, then slamming downward before yet another gust nearly rolled him. The canvas on the wings strained at the pummeling forces. "Lt. Rothilion, can you hear me?"

A long, crackling pause. Then, barely discernible above the static, "Yes, Laesornysh."

"We need to go back. We can't fly in this, and we'll lose thirty of our best pilots if we keep trying." If they hadn't lost some already. Besides Merrik valiantly keeping his aeroplane stationed behind Fieran's, Fieran had no idea where the rest of his men were.

A longer pause. More sleet arrowed downward. A hint of ice shimmered on Fieran's wings.

Hang their orders. That airship wasn't getting much information in this storm, and for all they knew, it had been taken down already by the sleet and relentless, now freezing rain.

"Rothilion, we will all die out here. We need to land." The control stick was nearly ripped from Fieran's hands at an even more violent gust.

This might not be something even Fieran could survive, if Lt. Rothilion didn't give the order to land.

# CHAPTER TWELVE

Lt. Rothilion's voice crackled over the radio. "Return to base. Everyone, return to Dar Goranth."

Could the pilots hear the order?

Fieran fought his aeroplane to fly closer to a few of the pinpricks of light, joining Lt. Rothilion in shouting the order into the radio. "Everyone, return to base."

When he let go of the talk button, he might have heard a few acknowledgments. Hard to tell over the pounding of the storm and the crackling radio.

He let his aeroplane continue on its course for another few minutes, shouting into the radio for the others to return to base.

Where was Dar Goranth? The sky? The ground? As the rain tumbled and the wind churned, a chill swept through him, his heart beating harder and sharper in his chest. A fuzzy sense of disorientation muddled his senses as he cast about.

There. Twin dots of light far below. The lighthouses marking the passage between Brenzuk and Urixidor

Islands. That meant he was flying south, and he needed to turn around to return to Dar Goranth himself.

He held down the talk button. "Merrik, I'm going to make a turn to the right and return to Dar Goranth. I don't see anyone else out here."

He didn't see the airship either. Not that he could even see his own aeroplane's nose in this sleet.

"Understood."

Fieran dove into the right-hand turn, gaining extra speed to fight the force of the wind. As he straightened out going north, the wind was now coming out of his rear quarter, driving his aeroplane before it. It was all he could do to fight the control stick to keep the wind from tumbling his craft tail over nose

He glanced over his shoulder long enough to ascertain that Merrik had survived the turn as well.

With the wind propelling them, they crossed over the southern point of Drogenvroh Island and approached Dar Goranth within a few minutes.

The dark shapes of other aeroplanes danced through the sleet, more voices once again crackling through the radio. One after another, the flyers made a run for the ground, not even waiting for the airfield to be fully cleared before they came in for their landing.

Fieran tried to count the aeroplanes, but he didn't know how many had already landed before he'd arrived. The only thing to distinguish the black shapes of the aeroplanes from each other was the dark outline of the gun on the upper wing of the elven aeroplanes.

"Fieran, your wing!" Merrik's voice yanked Fieran's gaze from the other aeroplanes. He peered left, then right.

The tip of his right front upper wing flapped, no longer attached to the support to the lower wing. The wind snatched the loose piece, peeling back a whole section of canvas on the upper wing.

On instinct, Fieran released a slash of his magic, slicing through the canvas before more of it could be yanked away. The piece of his wing soared past his head, then out of sight as the wind whipped it away.

At this point, it didn't matter if he used his magic. That mystery airship wasn't close enough to see, and right now, Fieran just needed to survive.

With most of his upper right wing gone, the lower wing on that side was straining, his aeroplane tilting in that direction with the unbalanced lift.

"We need to land. Now." Merrik's voice cut sharply over the headset.

"We should wait…" Fieran didn't want to cut in front of the others. He should stay up here until the last of his men had landed.

"No. We land. Now." Merrik's tone left no room for argument. "If you lose any more of that wing, you will crash. Now, land."

He couldn't really argue with that. Already, some of the other wing supports were moving in a way that they weren't designed to move. If more cracked, the rest of the right wings would rip off entirely, and he'd go down.

Fieran dropped lower and took the next place lining up for a landing, Merrik far too close behind him, considering the likelihood that this landing wasn't going to be smooth.

Already, the airfield was littered with crashed or stuck aeroplanes that the ground crews hadn't had a chance to move out of the way.

Fieran tried to line up on a spot that was still clear, but the squall made his aeroplane nigh impossible to control. As the gale shoved him over Dar Goranth harbor onto the cliffs above, he was slammed down to earth to the left of the designated airfield.

His wheels skidded on the slick grass a moment before his right wing clipped a boulder and disintegrated the rest of the way. With the greater weight of the intact left wing, his aeroplane tipped sideways, and he came to a grinding halt against the hillside.

For a moment, Fieran just sat there, water streaming down his face, his breath making wet, silvery puffs before his mouth. Water pooled in his lap and sloshed in the cockpit by his feet. His heart still hammering in his chest, he couldn't seem to make himself move, not even to peel his fingers off the control stick.

That might have been the first time he'd ever been truly terrified while flying. He'd never considered he could be killed, not even in the Battle over Bridgetown.

But that just now…that had been worse. So much worse.

Another aeroplane flashed past before jouncing to a stop fifty yards away, also to the left of the airfield.

Merrik, completing a much better landing than Fieran had.

Something about the sight of his friend also safely on the ground finally jolted energy back into his limbs.

Fieran shakily disconnected the lap belt, yanked out the headset wire, and levered himself out of the cockpit. He stumbled to the ground, then jogged toward Merrik's aeroplane.

Merrik scrambled out of his aeroplane, slipping on the waterlogged grass as he ran toward Fieran. Merrik's hair—grown past his ears—was plastered to his neck beneath his cap. But Fieran didn't see any injuries or hesitation in the way Merrik moved.

Merrik must have done a similar assessment of Fieran

for injuries because as one, they turned and sprinted toward the hangar. They had to halt and wait beside a crashed elven aeroplane as another two aeroplanes landed—both from Flight B, though Fieran couldn't make out the nose art—before they could make the final dash for the hangar.

The shock of stumbling from the whipping wind and freezing rain into the dry hangar nearly sent Fieran to his knees. His waterlogged goggles instantly fogged.

Hands were there, peeling off his soaked flight jacket and easing his goggles and cap from his head. He shivered violently, aware of just how sodden and chilled he was now that he was out of the storm.

Then Pip was before him, steering him farther into the hangar as someone else draped a blanket over his shoulders.

"I didn't bring your aeroplane back in one piece." His words came out strange between his numb, wind-chapped lips. "The right wing broke."

"I don't care about that." Pip all but shoved him to a seat next to the wall. "I'm just glad you're back safe."

Stickyfingers approached, his eyes wide, his jaw set in a line Fieran had never seen on him before. He held out a steaming mug. "Coffee to warm you up."

Fieran took it with shaking fingers, wrapping both hands around the mug, the heat searing to the point of nearly painful. "Linshi. I mean, thanks."

Merrik sagged against the wall next to Fieran, and Stickyfingers handed him a mug as well, though the color was far lighter than the dark brew in Fieran's mug. Rather thoughtful of Stickyfingers to remember that Merrik preferred tea over coffee.

Fieran leaned forward, peering down the line of sodden pilots. Aylia was there, her hair straggling over her shoulders. Tiny curled over his stomach, his gray pallor tinged a bit green. The buffeting winds must have made him airsick, something he usually didn't get while flying.

Fieran counted six of his men sitting there, including Merrik, Pretty Face, Tiny, and Murray. Even as he counted, two more raced inside. They must have been piloting the aeroplanes that had landed just after Merrik and Fieran.

The members of Flight B who hadn't gone up converged on them, helping them out of their sodden flight jackets and giving them blankets just as they had Fieran.

Fieran glanced down the line again, his stomach sinking. "Sticky, where's Lije?"

Lije and Pretty Face had been paired together. Unless they had gotten separated in the storm, they should have landed together. But while Pretty Face was slumped next to Tiny, Lije was nowhere in sight.

Stickyfingers halted as he was reaching for another mug on the rolling cart. "He's in sick bay. Just a few broken bones, nothing too serious. He was able to get out of the aeroplane himself after he crashed. Two of the elven pilots are also down there for injuries they received on landing."

Fieran released a breath. Lije was alive. That was the main thing right now.

He gave himself another few moments to soak in the warmth of the coffee in the mug. A puddle grew beneath him and Merrik as they dripped rivulets of rainwater onto the floor.

As another rather sodden pair of elven pilots stumbled inside, Fieran forced himself to his feet. He tottered down the line of pilots, taking the time to check if they were all right regardless of whether they were humans of Flight B or elves from Flight A.

As he reached Tiny, Tiny lifted his head, his cheeks still a little green. "I'm sorry, Fieran. I thought I had the airship. I was so close. But then it began to sleet, and there was just so much ice in the air that I couldn't…I wasn't strong enough…I just…"

"It's all right, Tiny. There was nothing more you could have done." Fieran couldn't hide the weariness in his voice.

There was nothing any of them could have done, even if Fieran had used his magic. There was just no fighting a storm like this.

"Lt. Laesornysh."

At Commander Druindar's voice, Fieran spun and saluted, bracing himself. If Commander Druindar was angry that they'd come back early without so much as engaging the presumed enemy airship, then Lt. Rothilion was sure to place the blame on Fieran for pushing for the return to base.

But Commander Druindar's returning salute had a weary lack of crispness to it, his blue eyes pained. "I am… glad you have returned safely."

"Thank you, Commander." It was likely the closest the commander would ever come to admitting that perhaps they never should have gone up in this weather.

But those were the kinds of decisions a leader had to make. Either keep his pilots safely on the ground and risk an airship spying on the base or send his pilots into a storm that had only gotten more violent by the moment.

One could only know which option was the wrong one when deaths happened and the recriminations came afterwards.

Or, perhaps, there were no right options, only less bad ones.

Pip stood on the ladder, the steel of her wrench cold in her already icy fingers.

Fieran's aeroplane was a sorry sight, dripping rainwater onto the hangar floor. What was left of his right wing dangled in tatters while the left wing had sustained damage during the landing.

All around the hangar, the mangled aeroplanes the ground crew had managed to retrieve from the storm crouched in piles of tangled wires, tattered canvas, and sagging wings.

So many of the beautiful, brand-new aeroplanes reduced to this.

Worse, Lije was in sick bay recovering from broken bones. Several flyboys and elven pilots were still missing. And there was nothing any of them could have done. There was no fighting a storm like this.

Pip blinked back tears as she fumbled to loosen the bolts holding what remained of the lower wing to the fuselage. Her fingers shook so much she couldn't seem to get a good grip on the bolt to work it loose.

"Here. I got the wing."

Pip jumped at the sound of the voice, and she scrambled to wipe her sleeve over her face.

One of the human mechanics stood below, gripping what remained of the wing to hold it steady while she loosened the wing from the aeroplane.

Not Fieran coming to help. She shouldn't be disappointed at that. He paced near the mouth of the hangar, his steps sharp, the slouch to his shoulders almost tortured. He wouldn't be reaching out to comfort her any time soon.

Perhaps she should be over there, comforting him. But her own emotions were too raw. Right now, she just wanted to throw herself into the work.

Clearing her throat, she glanced down at the mechanic bracing the wing for her. "Thanks."

It was the first time one of the other mechanics had reached out to her like this. She wouldn't dismiss that, even if she wished it was Fieran helping her.

With the other mechanic's help, she loosened the rest of the bolts and the ruins of the wing fell from the aeroplane.

She climbed down from the ladder to better assess if there was any other damage to be fixed or if all this aeroplane needed was new wings bolted on.

At least a shipment of replacement aeroplane parts arrived from Escarland before the storm hit.

"What are your orders, Pip?" The other mechanic didn't salute her, but he was looking at her with something almost like respect.

"We need to get these aeroplanes back into shape as soon as possible. With an attack coming, we can't have half the squadron grounded." Pip swept a glance over the wrecked aeroplanes. "Let's prioritize the aeroplanes that only need new parts bolted on. Those can be fixed the quickest. We'll then worry about the ones with more extensive structural damage."

Focusing on the work steadied her. As long as she stayed busy with the mechanical side of things, she wasn't thinking about the missing flyboys.

Fieran paced back and forth, too restless to sit still. Of the pilots of Flight B who had gone up into the storm, only Merrik remained in the hangar. Fieran had sent the others to hot showers, hot food, and warm beds.

A pilot each from Flight A and B, ones who hadn't flown in the storm, kept station by the radio, monitoring it for distress calls from any of the seven missing pilots: three from Flight A and four from Flight B.

Lt. Rothilion, too, was pacing, though he marched several yards away from Fieran.

To one side of the hangar, Pip and the other mechanics were more silent than usual as they worked on the damaged aeroplanes.

Merrik stepped in front of Fieran, halting his pacing. "Go check on those in sick bay. I will stay here to wait for word."

Fieran hesitated for a moment longer before he nodded. Neither he nor Lt. Rothilion had checked on the wounded pilots yet. While there was nothing more he could do for the missing men, he could do this for those who had made it back.

He took the lift this time, wearily leaning against the wall as he used the hand crank to lower the metal cage down the shaft. At Level 3, he halted the lift, opened the cage door, and stepped into the large central space beside the lift and winding stairs. Across the space *Sick Bay* was painted on the gray rock wall next to closed, metal double doors.

Crossing the entry space, Fieran pushed one open and halted just inside, letting the door swing closed behind him as he took in the long hallway, the various doors and rooms.

A male troll looked up from where he sat behind a desk beside the doors. "May I help you?"

"I'm Lt. Laesornysh. I'm here to see the injured pilots."

"They're all in the ward at the very end of the hall." The troll pointed in that direction.

"Linshi." Fieran strode the length of the hallway, then entered through another set of double doors.

Inside this room, a large hospital ward stretched in either direction. Beds lined each wall. A few seemed occupied with various trolls who had received injuries from one thing or another on the base. The two elven healers stationed here moved between their beds, a hint of green magic glowing around their fingers.

To the right, Lije, the two human pilots who had been rescued after they had crashed in the harbor, and the three elves who had been injured upon landing lay in beds next to each other.

Beside the bed of the nearest elf, an elf woman with long, straight black hair that sported various braids woven with leather in the troll style rested her hand on the elf's arm, green magic glowing around her fingers. Behind her, a hulking young male troll shifted from foot to foot, his shoulders hunched as if he was trying to appear smaller. His face, hands, and waist still had the pudgy adolescent look of someone who still had more growing to do.

Fieran hurried down the aisle between the beds. "Aunt Melantha? Sontar? What are you doing here?"

Aunt Melantha glanced up from her work, her dark eyes warming slightly as her mouth curved in a hint of a greeting. "Healing your downed pilots, it would seem."

"Something I greatly appreciate." Fieran halted beside Aunt Melantha, refraining from giving her a hug as she was still finishing her healing. "I hadn't realized you were here. When did you arrive?"

"Only a few hours ago on the last ship to make the harbor as the storm hit." She dropped her gaze to her patient again.

Sontar gave a slight shudder, mumbling something Fieran couldn't make out. Something about a rough ride.

One would never guess that Rhohen and Sontar were brothers. Rhohen was all pouty emotions and icy magic, looking more elf than troll. While Sontar had inherited the troll build, he was shy and gentle in the extreme. Whereas Rhohen's magic was a combination of troll ice magic mixed with the magic of the ancient kings, Sontar had inherited the rare troll trait of having two different types of magic. He was showing signs both of his mother's healing magic and his father's ice magic, something that could make him a great healer if he could develop a strong enough stomach for it.

Aunt Melantha's magic vanished, and she gave a slight smile to the elf on the bed. "Rest your shoulder tonight as it finishes healing. The tear in the ligament will be repaired by the morning."

"Linshi, Maresheni." The elf gave her a respectful nod, using the elven title for queen.

Aunt Melantha turned to Fieran, though she waited to speak until the three of them had walked away from the elf's bedside. "Your pilots will be fine. We have mended a few broken bones and staved off pneumonia and hypothermia for those two who spent more time in the water than they should have." She gestured toward the two pilots who had been fished from the harbor.

"Linshi." Fieran glanced from her to Sontar and back. "I didn't expect to see you here. Not with…" He dropped his voice. "Not with an attack coming."

He couldn't see his Uncle Rharreth being happy about sending his wife and younger son into harm's way. Even though they had staggered their visits to Dar Goranth to ensure that the entire troll royal family wasn't at the place of a likely attack all at once.

"The very reason we are here." Aunt Melantha's tone held a grim note, even as her mouth pressed into a line, highlighting the almost sharp angles of her face. "I needed to ascertain that the healers here at Dar Goranth are prepared for such an attack. The plan was for us to leave well before an attack, but it seems we will be here at least through this storm."

Hopefully the supposition that the Mongavarians would attack once the storm lifted was more rumor than based on actual intelligence. Low on the command structure as Fieran was, he wasn't the person being told what information Escarland's Intelligence Office was sending to the troll military leadership.

As much as Fieran would have liked to continue talking to his aunt and cousin, he edged a step away. "I'd better let you continue your work."

Aunt Melantha nodded. As Fieran walked away, she led Sontar in the opposite direction, heading for the other two elf healers.

Fieran spoke with each of the other pilots until he reached Lije's bed. "How are you feeling?"

Lije was sitting up, his arm in a sling. "Just a broken arm and collarbone. Your aunt said the bones would be all healed by morning. Hard to believe that, but it hurts a whole lot less than when I broke my leg falling out of a tree as a kid. We didn't have any elven healers in Frogg's Hollow."

Fieran nodded. He'd always been rather spoiled, growing up. All his bumps, scrapes, and broken bones were promptly healed by an elf healer. One was never all that far away from wherever Fieran's family happened to be staying. "I'm glad the healing magic is working quickly."

"So they're a few more of your relatives." Lije gestured with his good hand, shaking his head. "And here I thought I had a bunch of cousins. I think you might have me beat."

"I don't have that many." Fieran sighed, though with more fondness than exasperation. "My family just happens to be rather noticeable."

Being related to every king in the Alliance would do that.

Lije's gap-toothed smile vanished. "Did all of the squadron return?"

Fieran hesitated, then shook his head. "No. We're still missing four pilots from Flight B and three from Flight A."

Seven men were missing somewhere out in that squall. No one was quite prepared to give them up for lost just yet, but there was nothing they could do but wait. There would be no search parties until the weather lifted.

If those men were still alive, they would just have to hang on until they could be found.

## CHAPTER
# THIRTEEN

Fieran paced along the passageway of their assigned rooms, trying to pretend he was merely stretching his legs and not so filled with restless energy that it took all his willpower to keep his magic from dancing around his fingertips.

This deep in the cliffs of Dar Goranth, he couldn't hear the wind howling or feel the sleet pounding the earth. But last he'd checked, the storm still raged outside, a full two days after it had begun.

He might have braved the storm anyway, if there was anything he could do to save his men.

Two of the missing elves had come trudging into the hangar during the night, soaked through and near hypothermic from the cold. They had landed farther inland on Drogenvroh Island and hiked back to Dar Goranth when they couldn't seem to get a message through on their radios due to the storm.

At dawn—or what counted as dawn during the storm —a telephone call had come from Brenzuk Island that a pair of the missing human pilots had managed to land on that island and were now sheltering in the lighthouse with the keeper and his family.

That still left one elf and two humans unaccounted for. With each hour that passed, the likelihood that they were dead increased.

Losing men in his unit had been hard enough during basic training and the Battle over Bridgetown. But to lose men under his command? That ached in a way he couldn't describe and just couldn't face at the moment.

Nor could he or their unit truly mourn just yet. Going down to the mess, raising a glass to their fallen comrades, would mean accepting that they *were* fallen. Right now, there was still a chance—a slim, nearly impossible chance—that they were still alive somewhere, riding out the storm.

He might have joined those watching the radio for any attempt to make contact or see if Pip and the mechanics needed any help repairing the damaged aeroplanes, but he'd already spent hours up there, getting underfoot.

His utter inability to *do* anything roiled through him until he might just combust if he didn't do something soon.

The glimpses Fieran got through the various open doorways into the rooms showed that everyone else seemed infected by a similar restless energy. The more dedicated of his men were polishing boots, cleaning sidearms, or remaking their cots to the peak of military perfection.

Stickyfingers had taught Lije how to pick locks, and now the two of them sat across from each other as they locked and relocked the same two padlocks over and over again. Tiny and Murray were absently rolling balls of ice back and forth across their room. Pretty Face had somehow gotten his hands on a bottle of cologne and, after spending an inordinate amount of time in the shower, had duded himself up as if about to go on a date with a pretty girl and then proceeded to re-read the stack of letters he'd received from various girls pining for him in Escarland.

Fieran halted at the end of the corridor, eyeing the stairs that wound twenty-three stories downward.

Merrik planted his feet next to him and crossed his arms. "You have that look in your eye. The one that says you are about to get us all into trouble."

"But we are going to have so much fun doing it." Fieran spun away from the stairs to face Merrik. "Do you want to lodge an official protest to protect yourself in case this goes badly?"

Merrik sighed but promptly shook his head. "No. Whatever trouble you get us in, we will go down together."

"That's the spirit, especially since a quick way down is what I have in mind." Fieran raised his voice. "All right, everyone. Anyone who wants to have a little fun grab your mattress and gather at the stairs."

As Fieran hurried to their room, the noise of boots hitting the floor, voices passing his words along, and the scramble of mattresses being hauled off bunks filled the corridor.

Fieran yanked the sheets and blankets off his mattress, dumping all of it onto the floor. The mattress was comprised of a tough, waxed canvas and the internal padding was barely softer than the stone frame it rested on. Perfect for what Fieran had in mind.

Merrik copied his actions, then the two of them toted their mattresses out of their room and into the passageway. Already, many of the others were also stepping from their rooms, carrying their own mattresses. Even those who had been working so hard on their perfectly taut blankets and sheets had cheerfully ripped off all their hard work.

"What are we doing?" The end of Sticky's mattress trailed on the ground. Short as he was, the mattress was more unwieldy for him.

"Penguin sliding down the stairs." Fieran grinned, clamping down on his magic to keep his restless excitement from breaking free. He'd wanted to try this from the moment he'd seen all those stairs.

"Yes!" Several of the men pumped their fists.

Fieran raised his hand. "Now we need to keep this somewhat quiet. We can't go waking up everyone on the other floors as we go by. So as much as you might want to, you can't whoop or holler on the way down."

The others nodded. Then Fieran led the way to the top of the stairs. Well, it wasn't fully the top, but he wasn't going to lead them up to Level 24 and risk Lt. Rothilion catching them. He'd ban this for sure.

"Okay, who wants to go first?" The words had barely passed Fieran's lips before someone was shoving his way forward.

"I do!" Holleran took a small running leap forward, then bellyflopped onto his mattress on the stairs. His momentum sent the mattress shooting downwards, and he gripped it as he tha-tha-thumped down the flight of stairs. At the landing for Level 22, the stairs made a sharp turn. Going too fast to either stop or turn, Holleran whammed headfirst into the stone wall.

Fieran leaned over the railing at the top. Maybe this hadn't been the best idea after all. "Are you all right?"

Holleran lifted his head. Blood trickled down his face from split skin on his forehead. "I'm fine. I've got a hard head." He swiped at the blood, as if he found it more annoying than painful.

Change of plans. "Everyone, grab your helmets."

"I'll grab yours, Holleran," the man's roommate called down the stairs before he joined the stampede back to the rooms.

Fieran picked his way between the piles of mattresses left at the top of the stairs. "Still not going to lodge a protest?"

"Giving it serious consideration." Yet Merrik joined him with just as much alacrity as they fetched their metal, Escarlish helmets from their kits and buckled them into place.

Once everyone was helmeted, a line quickly formed. Holleran, now also safely helmeted and a bandage from a med kit wrapped around his forehead to staunch the bleeding, adjusted his mattress and whooshed down the next flight of stairs. The faint *tonk* of a metal helmet hitting stone echoed up from below.

"Still fine!" Holleran called back to them.

Fieran found himself shuffled to somewhere in the middle of the line, after Stickyfingers and Pretty Face but before Merrik, Tiny, and Lije. He would have dropped back to let others go first as a proper leader should, but he was just too eager for his turn.

As soon as one person cleared the landing below, the next person took a running start and shoved off. Each time, their helmets clanked into the stone wall at the bottom, but the helmets served their purpose and prevented another injury.

Within minutes, Stickyfingers dove onto his mattress, grinning nearly as broadly as he had when hugging his machine gun. He was still grinning when he clanged into the wall at the bottom.

Once he cleared the landing below, Pretty Face shoved off, the speed and juddering mattress knocking his mustache out of its sleeked style.

Finally. Fieran's turn. He gripped his mattress, ran a few steps forward, and flopped both himself and the mattress onto the stairs. His breath whooshed out of him as the mattress connected with the stone steps. The hard, canvas-covered mattress bumped downward with exhilarating speed, each stair a breath-stealing shudder. It was all Fieran could do to bite back his shout of elation and clamp down on his magic.

He crashed headfirst into the wall at the bottom with a painful jolt. But the helmet did its job. He quickly turned the mattress, checked that Pretty Face had already cleared the landing below, then pushed off the wall with his feet to send him and his mattress sliding downward again with a rapid *thump-thump-thump.*

Now this was exactly what he'd needed. The whoosh, the thrill, the reckless abandon. A moment to forget the weight resting on his shoulders.

At each turn in the stairway, he thunked into the wall, adjusted his mattress, then thump-slid down the next set of stairs.

By the time he was on the last set of stairs headed toward Level 1, he was nearly dizzy with the constant turns and motions, his head drumming from the hits against the stone walls.

How suspicious would Aunt Melantha be if Fieran and his whole Flight trooped into sick bay with headaches?

His mattress shot into the parade ground space on Level 1. He had only a heartbeat to notice those who had gone before, all standing at attention with their backs to him, their mattresses scattered and abandoned, before he and his mattress slid right into the back of Pretty Face's legs.

Pretty Face fell backwards, landing on Fieran with a weight that drove the breath from Fieran's lungs. Pretty Face's elbow dug into Fieran's back, his boots clunked against Fieran's helmet, and Pretty Face's helmet knocked painfully against Fieran's ankle.

Fieran's mattress slammed into Pretty Face's mattress, which shot into the next mattress over. That mattress collided with Stickyfingers, and he went down, landing on the mattress instead of the stone floor. More mattresses pinballed across the parade ground, knocking still more men over.

Fieran's mattress skidded to a stop with the sound of canvas grinding on gravel.

Pretty Face rolled off, scrambling to his feet and facing forward again.

Following his lead, Fieran hopped to his feet. As he did so, his gaze landed on where Commander Druindar was standing at the front of the room, his arms crossed, a scowl twisting his face. Behind him, Captain Gradrah leaned against the wall, her arms folded as if she were taking in the entertainment. What appeared to be a gathering of the ship captains, their white uniforms sporting lots of gold braid, stood in one of the rooms to the one side, peering out and openly smirking.

Fieran's stomach plummeted into his toes. They were in so much trouble.

The thumping sound of another mattress whooshing down rang from the stairway. Standing at attention, Fieran couldn't turn around to look or jump out of the way. All he could do was semi-brace himself as much as he could.

Canvas scraped against stone. Something slammed

into the back of Fieran's legs, taking his feet out from under him. He toppled backwards, landing on Merrik with an *oof*.

Fieran's mattress knocked into the next one over, setting off the chain reaction of sliding mattresses and falling men yet again.

As soon as the mattress stopped sliding, Fieran rolled off, trying to subtly scramble a few feet away from the sliding zone before he stood and came to attention once again.

Beside him, Merrik leapt to his feet and straightened to attention.

Was that the twitch of a smile to Captain Gradrah's mouth? Probably wishful thinking. Perhaps it was a barely suppressed scowl. Commander Druindar, certainly, was making no effort to hide his increasingly wrathful glower.

The whooshing sound came again from the stairs. Fieran mentally braced himself.

Merrik went down, landing on Tiny.

Something—a mattress, presumably—slammed into the back of Fieran's ankles hard enough to knock him over. He fell backwards, landing on an empty mattress this time instead of on Merrik.

Pretty Face, Stickyfingers, and several others toppled like bowling pins as mattresses skittered and ricocheted across the floor. The parade ground was quickly becoming clogged with mattresses.

Fieran had barely gotten back to his feet, facing the cluster of captains and the commander, when scraping came from behind him. He caught a glimpse of Lije's straw-blond hair and lanky form before he slammed into the back of Tiny's legs. Tiny tumbled and landed on Lije with a grunt that was echoed by Lije's muffled groan.

Fieran only had time to spare an internal wince on Lije's behalf before he was once again taken out by a mattress.

How many more men were still coming down? He tried to mentally count those standing around him as he scrambled back to his feet and came to attention yet again. There were at least fifteen men standing around him. Perhaps seventeen or eighteen. That meant they still had nearly half of Flight B to go.

Another flyboy and mattress skidded into the room. More pinballing mattresses and toppling men. The captains gathered in the room behind Captain Gradrah seemed to be taking bets on which flyboy would hurtle the farthest with each new mattress that came zooming down from above.

Fieran would have gritted his teeth, but he'd probably crack a tooth the next time he was bowled over by a mattress.

By the time the last flyboy and mattress skidded to a halt, the mattresses clogged the parade ground so much that Fieran struggled to find a place to stand to come to attention yet again. Beside him, Merrik stood precariously balanced on a mattress that was half-shoved onto another mattress.

Commander Druindar had been forced to retreat to the wall beside Captain Gradrah to avoid being knocked over in the chaos. Now the two of them were talking quietly. Perhaps discussing just how to punish Fieran and his flyboys for this.

At least it would be highly unlikely for them to formally reprimand Fieran and his men. While they had been placed under Commander Druindar while stationed here at Dar Goranth, they were still, technically, part of Escarland's chain of command. Commander Druindar and Captain Gradrah would have to send a formal reprimand up Escarland's chain of command, something they wouldn't do unless they were absolutely certain they could both prove and defend their actions if any of the Escarlish commanders disagreed with them on the severity of the punishment.

Grady, the final flyboy to descend the stairs and not the brightest bulb among Fieran's flyboys, picked up his mattress and began hauling it back toward the stairs rather than standing at attention as he ought in the presence of his commanding officers.

Fieran opened his mouth to call Grady back before he got all of them into even more trouble, but Commander Druindar beat him to it.

"Where do you think you're going, Lieutenant?" Commander Druindar glared at Grady.

Grady, still grinning, kept hauling his mattress toward the stairs. "I'm going to go again, sir. That was fun."

"Fun." Commander Druindar's dark tone would have quailed the most hardened troll warrior. "You think you're here to have fun."

Grady's grin faded with just the hint of dawning comprehension.

Fieran braced himself for whatever Commander Druindar said next. He was getting a gleam in his eye that was probably similar to the look Fieran had worn when getting them into this mess. Commander Druindar might not have been able to formally reprimand them without getting the Escarlish military involved, but there were plenty of other ways he could punish them by making their lives miserable.

"Well, then, gentlemen, let's have a little fun, shall we?" The edge in Commander Druindar's voice held all the glee of their drill sergeants back at basic who had come up with an especially creative punishment. He faced Grady once again. "You like building sand castles, don't you, Lieutenant?"

Grady grinned once again. "Oh, yes, sir."

If Fieran hadn't been Grady's commanding officer where physical violence to those in his command was frowned upon, he would have given Grady a smack upside the back of the head once this was all over.

"Good, good." Commander Druindar pointed toward the double doors leading out into the storm. "Take off your helmets, go outside, and fill your helmets. All the way to the top now. You can't skimp on your sandcastles. Move."

Fieran spun on his heel and raced toward the doors with the others, tugging off his helmet as he went.

As soon as two of the flyboys hefted the stone doors open, a sheet of rain gusted inside, instantly drenching those nearest the door. A flash of lightning gave a brief glimpse of the several inches of water running over the road and sluicing off the cliffside above their heads.

This was going to be cold. And wet. And miserable.

Only right that Fieran lead the way. After all, he was the one who led them into this mess.

He dashed into the storm, and it was like stepping into the cold gush of a ginormous faucet. Rainwater dumped on him from the cliffs above while the icy rain sliced through his clothing to chill his skin.

Beside the main road that ran through the Dar Goranth base, the rain had turned the gravelly sand into a gloopy mess.

Fieran located a spot that was slightly higher and hadn't yet become a puddle. He scooped a helmetful of the sand, using his hand to shove in more sand until his helmet was filled all the way to the top.

The others crowded around him, also frantically shoveling sand and gravel into their helmets.

Despite the downpour, Fieran waited for all of his men to rush outside and fill their helmets before he returned with the last of them, carrying his helmet in front of him.

Once inside, he joined the line of his men assembling on the slightly cleared spot before their mattresses. Each of them held a helmet filled with sand and dripped water into growing puddles on the stone floor.

Commander Druindar strode in front of their line, his hands clasped behind his back. "Now it's time to build your sandcastles. Line up your mattresses, then dump your sandcastle onto your mattress. Don't let it fall apart. It needs to be a good sandcastle."

At that order, Fieran and his men scrambled to disentangle the mattresses and straighten them into neat lines, all while holding their helmets and not letting so much as a single pebble of gravel spill onto the floor.

Once they'd lined up the mattresses, Fieran knelt on a mattress, suppressed a grimace, and turned his helmet over to form a sandcastle, just as he used to do with a bucket when making castles by the shores of the lake at the elven summer palace of Lethorel.

The sand and gravel made a slurping, sucking sound as it glopped onto the mattress. With so much water content, it flattened in a gloopy mess rather than staying in the shape of the helmet, rivulets of sandy water running across his mattress.

Fieran patted the sides of the pile, mud coating his hands, until he corralled the castle back into shape.

Commander Druindar and Captain Gradrah strode between the mattresses, commenting on the sandcastles and making "suggestions" for improvements, such as

*Move that rock there for a gate. Every good castle needs a strong gate.* Or *Use that leaf for a pennant. Every good castle must fly the proper flag.*

When they reached Fieran's castle, Commander Druindar and Captain Gradrah spent an exceptionally long minute inspecting it before Commander Druindar pointed to a collection of pebbles that had rolled off. "Don't neglect the battlements."

Fieran hastily picked up the pebbles, flattened the top of his sandcastle, and delicately placed the pebbles in a ring around the top as if they were the crenelations on the top of a tower.

Seemingly satisfied, the two troll warriors moved on to Merrik, who ended up having to dig a moat and add a low earthen embankment around his castle.

Once they'd gone through all the sandcastles, Commander Druindar and Captain Gradrah brought out the ship captains to vote on the best sandcastle out of the bunch. The collection of ship captains—mostly trolls, but with a few humans from the Escarlish ships in the harbor—walked between the castles and debated the merits of each one with the seriousness of inspecting actual military fortifications.

Fieran's face burned. Commander Druindar was succeeding with the humiliation part. The whole base was going to hear about this by morning.

The ship captains voted Lije's sandcastle as the best. Lije had gotten a scoop with some larger rocks that he'd artfully balanced to form towers on the corners. For the "honor" of winning, Lije was sent back out into the rain to find a flat rock to act as his winner's medal.

Once Lije returned, Commander Druindar turned to Grady once again. "Is this enough fun for you, Lieutenant?"

"I think so, sir." Grady's brown hair was plastered to his forehead while sand smeared his clothes.

Fieran bit back his groan. Not the right answer.

That gleam returned to Commander Druindar's eyes. "You *think* so? Hmm. That means you might still be in need of more fun."

As Fieran expected. Apparently Grady hadn't learned his lesson well enough back in basic training.

"Every castle exists to protect a kingdom from an enemy." Commander Druindar swept a glower over all of them. "You'd better build your enemy sandcastle."

With that, they were all sent back into the storm to fill their helmets yet again. After fetching another helmet's worth of sand, they all built a second sandcastle on their mattresses. At least this time Captain Gradrah and Commander Druindar didn't make such a production out of it, and there was no voting by the ship captains on these castles.

Instead, Commander Druindar's glower deepened as Fieran and his flyboys finished their sandcastles and stood. "In case you have forgotten, we are at war with the Empire of Mongavaria. We might even find ourselves under attack once this storm lifts. As it seems you need a reminder, your castles will come under attack."

With that, Commander Druindar and Captain Gradrah walked between the mattresses. One by one, they had each of the flyboys shake his mattress back and forth so that the castles "attacked" each other, the rocks and gravel breaking apart and sliding all over the place and onto the floor.

At the end of a seemingly random, indeterminate amount of time, the troll warriors called a halt, then assessed the amount of sand left of each castle to declare a "winner" of either the Alliance castle or the Mongavarian castle. How they could possibly tell which sand belonged to which castle, Fieran had no idea. They were probably just making it up at random.

Those who had the Alliance declared the winner were told to rebuild a single, large castle with all the sand on their mattress and the surrounding ground. The unlucky ones had Mongavaria declared the winner. They had to go back outside, fetch two more helmets' worth of sand, and conduct the battle again until Commander Druindar and Captain Gradrah were satisfied that the Alliance was the winner.

When it was Fieran's turn, he had to conduct the sandcastle battle three times—going out into the rain an additional four times for all the extra castles—before the troll officers declared the Alliance the winner. When he piled all the sand and gravel on the end of his mattress, it formed a sandcastle mountain nearly two feet tall and as wide as his mattress. Parts of it kept sliding off onto the floor.

At last, Commander Druindar declared the battles over, and all the sandcastles had been rebuilt into large, victorious Alliance strongholds.

Commander Druindar faced Grady. "Have you had enough fun now, Lieutenant?"

Fieran held his breath, willing harder than he'd ever willed in his life that Grady would come up with the right answer.

There were no grins this time as Grady, even more begrimed and bedraggled, replied, "Yes, sir. I've had enough fun now."

"Good." Commander Druindar's tone had a sharp edge. "Then you'll all sleep here tonight, guarding your sandcastles. I want to see them intact when I inspect them tomorrow morning."

With that, Commander Druindar, Captain Gradrah, and the ship captains went their separate ways, finally leaving Fieran and his flyboys alone on the Level 1 parade ground.

Fieran let his shoulders slump as he faced his men. They were a sorry-looking lot. Smeared with sand. Clothes still dripping. Hair plastered to their heads. Instead of lifting their spirits, all he'd succeeded in doing was getting them into trouble. "I'm sorry. That didn't go according to plan."

"It was fun while it lasted." Grady cheerfully plopped onto his mattress, almost absently fixing the part of his sandcastle that had collapsed with the movement, before he curled onto his side, heedless of the sand smeared over his entire mattress.

Fieran waited for someone to pipe up that it hadn't been worth it. Yet, strangely, no one did.

Instead, the rest of them followed Grady's example and lay on their mattresses in various curled and contorted positions to avoid knocking over their sand-castles.

With a rather pointed *I told you so but I did not try too hard to stop you either* look at Fieran, Merrik crossed the room and switched off the magically powered lights, plunging the room into darkness, lit only by the warm glow of lights in the stairwell, which were never shut off.

As Merrik headed back toward them, Sticky's voice broke the silence. "You know, I think the commander was just as bored as we were."

"You think?" Pretty Face snorted. "What gave that away? The sandcastles? The overblown sandcastle competition? The sandcastle wars? The utter glee they all took at the whole thing?"

"So glad we could provide their entertainment."

Fieran lowered himself onto his mattress with his head just below his sandcastle and his legs below his knees hanging off the end. Tall as he was, there was no way he would fit on the mattress unless he curled into a tight, uncomfortable ball.

Not that he was comfortable as it was. His clothes were still soaked through, sticking cold and clammy against his skin. The canvas of the mattress, while more or less waterproof, had soaked up some of the water from the sand, making its surface both damp and gritty. He didn't have a pillow or any blankets.

This was going to be one long, cold, uncomfortable night.

# CHAPTER FOURTEEN

The next morning, Fieran stood at attention once again, grimy and gritty.

Commander Druindar paced before them, sweeping an eye over their sandcastles. "I see your sandcastles survived the night. But now it's time to stop playing and get back to work."

With a few orders, Commander Druindar had them dump all the sand off their mattresses and sweep it into a pile in the center of the room while all the mattresses were stacked to one side. Once they were finished, they lined up at attention once again with Merrik and Fieran standing in the middle of the row.

"You men..." Commander Druindar swept his hand to indicate Merrik and the half of the Flight to the left. "Return the mattresses and helmets and set your rooms to military standards. You may not use the lifts. Only the stairs."

Fieran internally winced on Merrik's behalf. He and the others would have to traverse twenty-two flights of stairs carrying the mattresses, and they'd have to do it twice since only half the Flight had been assigned to that job.

"The rest of you…" Commander Druindar indicated Fieran and the men standing on the right. "You will return all of the sand outside using only this one spoon."

The commander held out the basic metal spoon used in the mess hall. He set it on the floor at the front of the room.

Fieran gave another mental wince as he surveyed the massive pile of sand without turning his head. That was going to take forever.

"Each group will have one hour to complete your task." Commander Druindar's tone remained hard, no hint whatsoever of the glee he'd shown the night before. "Whichever group finishes first before the hour is up will get breakfast and the other will not. If neither of you finish before the hour, neither group will receive breakfast."

Fieran flicked a glance from the mattresses to the five-foot-tall mound of sand. Sure, they would move as quickly as they could in the hope of getting breakfast, but he might as well face it now. There was no possible way any of them were eating that morning.

With that, Commander Druindar dismissed them to their tasks.

Fieran lunged for the spoon even as Merrik raced toward the mattresses. Ignoring the orders Merrik was giving to his half of the men, Fieran gestured to the men assigned to him. "Form a line. We'll pass the spoon back and forth. Every fifteen minutes we will rotate those stationed inside and those outside."

Perhaps sooner, if the men outside seemed to grow too chilled too quickly. While fifteen minutes might only seem like three or four rotations, it would be many more than that, given that this would take much longer than an hour to clean up.

Tiny and Stickyfingers, who had ended up with Fieran, flung the doors open. While the outdoors appeared a marginally brighter gray than it had the night before, the gusting wind and driving rain hadn't let up.

Fieran handed the spoon to Murray, the first man in line, before he headed outside to take a place at the end of the line in the downpour, standing next to the spot that had become a puddle-filled pit thanks to all the sand and gravel they'd shoveled out of it the night before. He had to rapidly blink to see through the deluge.

Within a few moments, the spoon appeared, oh-so-carefully passed from hand to hand to avoid spilling even a grain of the sand resting on it. As the spoon reached the downpour outside, the flyboys bent over and used one hand to shield the spoonful.

Fieran took the spoon from Tiny next to him, then dumped the spoonful into the puddle beside him. The teaspoon of sand barely made a plop amid all the ripples and splashes of the rain.

He handed the spoon back to Tiny, and it was passed back the way it had come.

Forget breakfast. They'd be lucky if they finished before lunch. His men hadn't mutinied over the humiliation the night before, but if his reckless idea cost them two meals, they just might.

WITH THE UNCANNY knack of officers, Commander Druindar reappeared just as Fieran and his flyboys swept the last of the sand onto the spoon, using their fingers to capture the last few grains.

"Lt. Laesornysh, a word." Commander Druindar spun on his heel and marched toward his office set to one side of the parade ground.

Fieran paused just long enough to tell the others, "Dump that spoonful outside, then go get cleaned up. Well done."

The others nodded, solemnly escorting Stickyfingers—the one with the steadiest hands—outside to dispose of the last of the sand.

Fieran trudged after Commander Druindar, his heart already lodged somewhere in the pit of his stomach.

As he stepped inside the office, Commander Druindar barked, "Close the door behind you."

This really wasn't going to be good if the door needed to be closed.

Fieran closed the door, then took his place at attention before the commander's large desk formed of what appeared to be a single slab of stone molded into a table shape.

For a long moment, Commander Druindar sat in his large, leather-padded chair and regarded Fieran with cold, dark brown eyes set in his hard, gray-skinned face. While he wore a modern military uniform with a sidearm at his hip, a traditional Kostarian sword—heavy-bladed and honed—hung on a rack on the wall next to a broad shield behind Commander Druindar's chair.

Finally, the commander leaned forward. "Given the glowing report I received from your previous commander and who your father is—not to mention your relation to my King Rharreth, my Queen Melantha, and the Generals Julien and Vriska Ardon—I expected better of you, Lt. Laesornysh."

It took every scrap of steel Fieran still possessed not to

openly flinch at that. Commander Druindar certainly knew how to hit Fieran where it hurt.

Whatever tales Lt. Rothilion had been spinning to Commander Druindar, this would just confirm them.

"We are at war, Lt. Laesornysh." Commander Druindar might as well have been flaying Fieran with knives for the sharpness to his tone and gaze. "I trust you will not forget it again, and there will be no more similar shenanigans."

"No, sir, there will not." Fieran was too tired and hungry to squirm.

"I will not be writing up an official report of this incident. Nor will I give you and your men an official reprimand." Commander Druindar's voice held little mercy, despite the reprieve. "But this will be your only warning, Lieutenant. Cross the line again, and I will not hesitate to write a thorough and scathing reprimand, no matter the difficulties I might face for it."

"I understand, sir." Fieran nodded, swallowing.

He waited, but Commander Druindar didn't dismiss him. Instead, the commander's gaze dropped briefly, as if gathering himself for the next thing he wished to discuss with Fieran.

When the commander lifted his gaze again, the hard anger had disappeared into something more like regret.

"I received word this morning from the mainland." Commander Druindar made the slightest motion toward the communications room where the telephones connected to the mainland via the underwater cables were located. "Wreckage has washed up on the Kostarian shoreline. Pieces of an Escarlish aeroplane. Perhaps two aeroplanes."

Another blow, and this time Fieran couldn't help his flinch.

His missing men were dead, then. Their bodies would never be found, unless they, too, happened to wash up on the Kostarian shore.

"The missing elven pilot?" Fieran's voice rasped out far more hoarse than he intended.

"Still no word. But it is assumed that he, too, is dead."

Three dead. And for what? A Mongavarian scout airship that had gotten away.

It brought up the memory of Capt. Arfeld after the Battle over Bridgetown. At the time, Fieran had been too focused on the promotion and the praise to do more than subconsciously note the other paperwork on the desk.

But he remembered it now. The stacks of letters addressed to the families of the pilots who had died.

That was Fieran's job now. Lt. Rothilion and Commander Druindar were the ranking officers and the official telegram informing the families of the loss would go through them to the proper military channels.

But Fieran was the only one who was also Escarlish. Those men had been lost under his command and his watch, even if the orders that had sent them into the sky that night had been Commander Druindar's. A more personal letter of condolence should come from Fieran.

"Thank you for informing me, sir." Fieran wasn't sure what else to say.

"You are dismissed."

Fieran hurried from the room. As none of the lifts were on this floor at the moment, he trudged up the numerous flights of stairs, ignoring the stares—and worse, the whispered words and laughter—of those he passed.

Once he was on his floor, he found the rooms set to rights and most of his men rotating through the showers.

Some had curled up on their newly made beds for a quick nap before lunch.

At last, it was his turn for a shower, and the three minutes of hot water was the most luxurious thing he'd ever experienced. He dressed in a clean uniform and dumped his grimy fatigues into the bag for wash day.

Merrik fell into step with him as he headed for the stairs again, even though Merrik's muscles must have been aching as much or even more than Fieran's after scrambling to right the rooms. Neither of them said anything as they plodded downward.

As they entered the mess hall, Fieran kept his head high, not meeting anyone's gaze.

Lt. Rothilion sat with his cronies at the table nearest the door. One of them leaned away from the table, calling out, "Done building sandcastles?"

The others snickered.

Lt. Rothilion gave a haughty sniff, his voice plenty loud enough, as if he wanted to be sure Fieran heard. "What else could one expect from the half-breed son of a —" He ended that sentence with the crude and derogatory term for Dacha's illegitimate birth.

Fieran halted, something inside him boiling, his gaze filling with blue. He was done. So done.

"Fieran, do not—" Merrik grabbed his arm to prevent him from doing whatever he was going to do. Even Fieran wasn't quite sure what that would be.

Shrugging off Merrik's grip, Fieran stalked toward Lt. Rothilion's table. Letting just a hint of his magic rage inside him, he swept out a hand. His magic flashed out, in an instant consuming every scrap of food on the elves' plates, including the bite of food one was bringing to his mouth and the piece of fruit Lt. Rothilion had pinched between his fingers.

Lt. Rothilion lunged to his feet, swearing in elvish. "What the…are you crazy, Laesornysh? You could have hurt someone."

"But I didn't." Despite his anger, Fieran had kept his power under control. Nothing had been harmed besides the food.

And if the lash of his magic had stung a few fingers, that was all it had done. It hadn't left so much as a mark on the skin.

Fieran planted his palms on the table, glaring at Lt. Rothilion. "Insult me all you want. Right now, I deserve it. Call me a half-breed; I don't care. That's what I am, and I'm proud of it. But don't you dare say that about my dacha again, or I'll do far more than sting your fingers."

Lt. Rothilion glared right back. "I should report you for this."

"Go ahead. Report me." Fieran was too tired, too hungry, and too done to care. "You'll also have to report what you said, and I'll appeal and protest this all the way up the chain of command. Once that report lands on the desks of your commander-in-chief and mine, who do you think King Weylind and King Averett will side with? The lieutenant who insulted the brother of whom they are famously protective or their nephew?"

Lt. Rothilion's jaw worked as he held Fieran's glare for another moment before he finally dropped his gaze. "You will regret this, Laesornysh."

Merrik grabbed Fieran's arm again, and this time he succeeded in yanking Fieran away. As he all but dragged Fieran across the mess hall, he muttered so that only Fieran could hear, "He is not worth any more trouble this morning."

That was probably true. And he had his flyboys to

consider. He couldn't shame them any more than they were already humiliated this morning.

Fieran collected his tray of food without paying much attention, plopping down in a seat at their usual table without taking in who else was there.

Next to him, Pip's eyes were wide, dark circles smudging her face as if she'd had as rough a night as he had. She briefly rested a hand on his arm before dropping her fingers back to her lap, as if she wasn't sure how to go about offering comfort.

Across the way, Aylia leaned forward, her voice lowering even if her eyes danced. "Good job on giving Lt. Rothilion a good smack. He deserves it. But I do have one bone to pick with you."

"What?" Fieran wasn't sure if he could take another scathing dressing down this morning.

"Next time you get up to something recklessly fun, make sure you invite me." Aylia's face twisted into an exaggerated pout. "I cannot believe you did something like penguin sliding down the stairs without me."

Fieran gestured farther down the table at where Tiny, Stickyfingers, Pretty Face, and Lije were wearily scarfing down their food. "Are you sure you want in next time? My shenanigans tend to be a lot of fun right at first, then end in unmitigated disaster and the possibility of a formal reprimand."

"You said it, not me," Merrik murmured under his breath.

"So? I am still missing the reason why I should not join in the fun." Aylia grinned before she took another bite of her pulled beef sandwich.

"Do not encourage him." Merrik picked up his own sandwich.

After the rebuke he'd gotten that morning, Fieran

agreed with Merrik on this one. No more shenanigans. He needed to be a model lieutenant from now on.

Just maybe a different model from whatever model lieutenant Lt. Rothilion was. One that came with less schmoozing and more heroic epicness.

A group of trolls strode in. They glanced toward Tiny, then bent their heads together as they said something in a low tone before chuckling.

Tiny hunched farther on the bench, pushing his food around his plate.

Fieran winced. Apparently, he wasn't the only one getting hassled. He should have realized that Tiny—half-breed troll raised in Escarland that he was—would also find himself a target.

"I heard you had a rough night." The large, muscled figure of Fieran's cousin Rokyd slid onto the bench on the other side of Merrik, followed a moment later by Lucien sitting across the way next to Aylia.

Fieran blinked at them for several seconds, his mind still trying to process. "Rokyd? Lucien?"

"We finally got shore leave. Everyone is getting a little cooped up in the ships after three days of riding out this storm." Rokyd picked up his fork. "The KAS *Dominion* is tied to one of the piers, but I haven't seen Sathrah yet. Hopefully she'll be one of those chosen to attend the fighting bouts tonight. You know how she loves those."

"Fighting bouts?" Fieran glanced from Rokyd to the others at the table. He'd missed something. "Aren't the fighting bouts not for another few days?"

Once a month, the trolls held their traditional fighting bouts here at Dar Goranth. Fieran and his flyboys had missed the last set of fighting bouts since they'd been held the day before they arrived.

Years ago, the fighting bouts were a way for the

warriors to test their mettle and earn honor by defeating others in single combat. In the years since Uncle Rharreth and Aunt Melantha became king and queen, the fighting bouts had been toned down to be less dangerous and more entertainment than a vital peg on the social structure. Yet the trolls hadn't dispensed with them entirely.

"Yes, but between the likelihood of an attack once the storm breaks and how stir-crazy everyone is becoming, it seems the base commanders decided to move it up a few days." Rokyd shrugged, then waved his fork in Fieran's direction. "Yours wasn't the only ruckus last night."

Lucien gave a snort. "Seamen from the KS *Indefatigable* stole their captain's skivvies and flew them from the masthead. And seamen from the ES *Norholdt* jumped ship and swam to the ES *Frielan* to exchange copies of their moving picture reels. They came close to drowning."

"The situation is getting dire." Rokyd spoke around a bite of his beef. "The commanders needed to do something to restore order, otherwise the entire base would be in shambles by the time the storm lifts."

At least Fieran hadn't been the only one causing trouble.

He let the conversation about the fighting bouts drift around him, watching as the talk perked up the rest of his men.

He'd have to tell them about the wreckage, and they'd take a moment to mourn before the storm lifted and the Mongavarians likely attacked.

But not just yet.

# CHAPTER FIFTEEN

Only a few hours before the fighting bouts were set to begin, Fieran sat with his back to the stone wall near the hangar mouth, hiding in the shadows as he stared into the pounding rain. After days of nearly nonstop rain, the airfield was nothing but puddles and squishy hummocks of grass.

Perhaps he should be catching a nap after the rough night. Or stretching out his tight muscles.

But he'd told the men about the aeroplane wreckage after lunch, and they'd raised a glass of troll mead to their fallen comrades, leaving two glasses untouched.

Perhaps it should have been three glasses. They still had no word on the missing elf pilot, but after this long, he was more than likely dead as well. Fieran hadn't had a chance to know him as well as he knew the two pilots from Flight B, but the elf was still a part of his squadron.

With a whisper of boots on stone, Merrik walked around the aeroplane hiding Fieran from view. He slid down to sit next to Fieran, not saying anything. After a month here at Dar Goranth, Merrik's hair was long around his ears, nearly long enough to brush his collar.

Fieran sighed and leaned his head against the stone behind him. "I thought I wanted to be in command. But leading is harder than I thought it would be."

Especially when he took it in his head to do something especially reckless. Sometimes, the need to just let loose without a thought for the consequences was so strong he almost couldn't help himself.

Almost.

Impulsiveness was no excuse for not thinking things through and controlling himself.

"Fieran." Merrik heaved a sigh of his own, shaking his head. "Life has always been so easy for you. I do not know if you have ever been challenged in your life before now. You never missed a meal or had to worry about material things. You are smart enough that our university classes never truly tested you."

Fieran grimaced at that. If he'd actually studied, he might have gotten perfect scores. But as it was, he did well enough without studying to graduate toward the top of the class. Why work for a few meaningless extra points?

Merrik continued, still not looking at Fieran. "Thanks to being the son of one of the owners, you got a job right out of university at the AMPC, a company with a waitlist of applicants. Most of those in our university classes would have begged on hands and knees for a job there, but you just took it for granted that you had one."

"All things true of you as well." Fieran winced as those words came out more defensive than he meant them to be.

"Yes." Merrik didn't flinch. They'd been friends long enough that perhaps he'd expected a bit of edge, pushing

Fieran as he was. "But my parents were not born into wealth as your parents were. Not to say your parents didn't face their own struggles. All our parents had far harder childhoods than we did."

Also true.

Fieran was well aware that he had been rather blessed when it came to looks, intelligence, wealth, and the privilege of being born to royalty. No, he'd never struggled. But he'd never been given an opportunity to struggle. Everyone seemed to expect *more* from him because he'd been given so much, and yet he'd never found something hard enough to actually test his mettle and stretch his mind and skills.

As Merrik had said, everything was too easy.

Except perhaps morning practices with Dacha. Those were hard.

Basic training had come close to testing him. Yet even with how much the drill sergeants pushed him, he'd never reached his true limits. Did he even know his limits of physical and mental endurance?

"What do I do now?" Fieran slumped even more heavily against the stone behind him.

"You either break or you rise to the occasion." Merrik glanced at something in the hangar before he lightly punched Fieran's shoulder and stood. "Looks like someone else wants to talk with you."

What? Who? Fieran wasn't ready to speak with anyone else right now.

But then Fieran saw Pip standing there in the shadows of the aeroplane, shifting from foot to foot as if she hadn't wanted to interrupt.

Never mind. Merrik was the absolute best wingman ever.

Pip lingered in the shadows of the aeroplane, not sure if she should interrupt Fieran and Merrik.

But Fieran had seemed so down after his punishment the night before and the news that his two flyboys were dead. Why she thought he'd want her comfort, she didn't know. But she felt compelled to give it anyway. Pesky more-than-friends attraction.

Merrik glanced up, and he must have spotted her for he stood, said something to Fieran, then strode away. As he passed Pip, he gave her a nod, something gleaming in his eyes.

Pip froze, then gaped at Merrik's retreating back. He *knew*. Merrik totally knew she was attracted to Fieran. Or, at the very least, he wasn't above playing a bit of matchmaking.

She halted in front of Fieran, not quite sure how to stand, as if her body had forgotten what was her normal. She tucked her hands in her pockets, then took them out and clasped them in front of her instead. That didn't feel right either, so she crossed her arms. That still didn't feel natural either, but she forced herself to remain as she was. "You look like you could use some cheering up."

"Yeah." Fieran straightened slightly from his slumped position. "What did you have in mind? I know this is going to sound strange coming from me, but it probably should be something that doesn't get me into trouble. Well, more trouble."

What did she have in mind? She hadn't given too much thought to it besides just spending time with Fieran.

She glanced about, spotting the sleeting rain outside. Ah, that would work. She gestured that way. "What about a little magic practice? That always seems to help. We won't go far in case you're needed, and I can make a shield with my magic to keep us dry."

Well, mostly dry. She couldn't do anything about the puddles and wet grass. Their boots, socks, and trousers would get soaked.

"That...sounds like exactly what I need." Fieran braced himself, preparing to stand.

She held out a hand to Fieran. He took it, and she had to lean back to put her whole weight into pulling him the rest of the way to his feet.

Pip called up her magic, letting it spread out in a small dome above her and Fieran's heads as they stepped outside. While their boots squished on the saturated ground, they stayed otherwise dry as the rain sluiced off her magical shield.

"That's a handy skill." The hint of a smile returned to Fieran's face.

"It is." Pip expanded her shield so that she could go around one side of a puddle while Fieran skirted the other side. "Especially when it's pouring rain, and you are working late to fix one of the steam engines because it is due to leave in the morning."

A pang shot through her at the memories of her home at Tarenhiel's western rail terminal. Were her parents and brother managing to keep everything running just fine now that the war had begun? They wouldn't say otherwise in their letters.

How she missed her muka, her dacha, and her brother Mak. She had only gotten one packet of letters since arriving at Dar Goranth, due to the mail service being so slow.

She shoved that aside. There was no use in dwelling on homesickness now.

"My magic just incinerates the rain." Fieran stuck his hand out from under the protection of her dome. A single bolt of his power lashed into the rain with a sizzle. Rain instantly puffed into steam while his magic flared through the raindrops and along the ground.

"Your magic incinerates pretty much everything." Pip nudged him, then grimaced as her boot sank into a puddle all the way to her ankle. At least the army-issue boots went nearly to her knees, so her feet were still mostly dry.

"All too true." Fieran pointed toward one of the small rises to one side of the airfield. It wasn't as flooded as the rest of the surrounding ground. "That looks like a good spot."

They trudged across the sloppy ground until they reached the hill. The ground still squelched beneath their boots, but at least there weren't any more standing puddles.

Pip expanded her shield so that it formed a large dome over the entire hill. She created another smaller shield around herself. "All right. Ready."

Fieran halted at the top of the hill and drew in a deep breath. Then his magic burst from him, crackling with nearly uncontrolled power.

Perhaps he'd needed this even more than she had realized. He'd done better here at Dar Goranth to take the time for practice with his magic, but the days of rain and the emotions of the last few days must have played havoc with his control.

His magic struck hers, but instead of incinerating her power, his magic coursed over hers, the two powers blending and strengthening.

Pip poured more of her magic into the shield. This was going to take more power than she'd expected.

With one last glance at her, Fieran held out his hands, as if he held a pair of swords, and unleashed even more of his magic.

Blue bolts burst around him, all but obscuring him from sight. He whirled and struck, as if decimating invisible enemies.

Pip kept her breathing steady as her magic held back the magic of the ancient kings. This wasn't even the full force of Fieran's power. Even now, he was holding back. She wouldn't have even realized that if she hadn't seen him use his magic during the Battle over Bridgetown.

She wasn't sure how long Fieran fought invisible enemies. By the time he halted and let his magic dissipate into harmless sparks that quickly dissolved into the air, Pip was sweating and breathing harder than he was.

Fieran met her gaze, then dropped his hands, the battle light snuffing from his bright blue eyes. "Sorry. I shouldn't have let so much of my magic loose."

"It's all right." Pip swiped a sweaty strand of her hair behind her pointed ear. "It was good practice for me too. Each time we practice together, I'm able to hold back more of your magic."

"Still, I'll try to be more aware of not pressing quite so close to your limits next time." Fieran strode toward her, his shirt showing a few patches of sweat that stuck the fabric tighter to his chest.

Pip swallowed and focused her gaze squarely on his face. In her defense, his chest was a bit more eye level for her than his face. Well, more like his abs were face level for her, but she was *not* going to think about his abs. Which were undoubtedly well-defined beneath his shirt.

Nope. Not doing it. Focus on something else. Not his abs. Not his muscles.

Pip cleared her throat. "I wonder if it would be

possible to create a shield for Dar Goranth by combining our magic."

There. Something scientific and logical. Not at all charged like the moment before.

"Like the Wall?" Fieran fell into step with her. "I think my uncles and my dacha considered making several smaller Walls around principal cities. But it was eventually discarded because the Wall can make taking certain goods in and out rather tricky. A good thing along the border, but not as convenient inside of Escarland or Tarenhiel."

"Yes, sort of. But I was thinking one that could be turned on and off rather than just going off when triggered." Pip gestured between the two of them, her heart rate calming with the more comfortable discussion of inventions and magic. "A large wire infused with my magic could be set up or buried around Dar Goranth. The wire could then be hooked up to a bank of magical power cells with your family's magic. When there was an attack, a switch could be flipped to turn it on. If I got the shield right, the shield could direct your magic—or your dacha's or your sisters' depending on the power cell—as an extra layer conducted through it."

"Hmm. That could work." Fieran's eyes glazed slightly, and he tromped right through a mud puddle as if he wasn't paying enough attention to avoid it. "It wouldn't be as strong as the Wall or able to actively ward off bombs like I can do in person."

"No, it wouldn't. Nor could it withstand heavy bombing like what the Mongavarians did to Bridgetown." Pip resisted a shiver at the memories. "But it would be able to take a few hits. If a shield like that could buy a military base enough time to fight back or protect a city long enough for the nearest military base to send help, then surely it would be worth it."

"It's a good idea." Fieran sighed and shook his head as they neared the hangar mouth. "We won't be able to implement it until after this storm breaks. And then…"

"And then we'll probably be under attack, and it will be too late regardless." If only she'd had the idea weeks ago when they'd first arrived instead of just now. But she and Fieran hadn't had the chance to practice their magic together as he'd been busy drilling his pilots and she'd been spending long hours building—then repairing—aeroplanes. "Maybe it's something to bring up once the attack is over. For next time."

Assuming they all survived this first attack, when it came.

"Yes." Fieran shot her a weary smile as they stepped out of the rain into the hangar once again. "You'll make me rather redundant."

"I highly doubt that." Even if she could implement a shield for Dar Goranth, the base would still need a warrior to defend it.

Would the military transfer Fieran elsewhere, if he was no longer needed to actively defend Dar Goranth? Worse, what if they decided she needed to remain to supervise her shield?

It almost made her want to keep the idea to herself. Even though there was no guarantee that she and Fieran would continue to be transferred to the same bases. Perhaps they'd stay at Dar Goranth for the entire war. Or they'd both be transferred elsewhere. Maybe they'd die in the coming attack.

There was no certainty in war.

Once she and Fieran were inside, she released her

shield outside to avoid dumping rainwater on their heads.

Fieran grimaced down at his boots. His boots were wet, and his trousers muddy all the way past his knees. "I'd better change into my Not-Knot boots before the fighting bouts begin. I'm bound to be challenged at least once before the night is out, and I don't want to start the fight looking like something a mountain lion dragged in."

"Will people really challenge you?" Pip's stomach twisted.

"Yes." The smile dropped from Fieran's face, his tone grim. "I'm my father's son. There's going to be more than a few warriors who will want to test their mettle against me."

Great. Yet another thing to worry about.

PIP SAT WEDGED between Fieran and Aylia along one of the upper tiers of benches in the fighting arena. Unlike the movie night, all the seats were available, and they were even more packed.

It seemed as if every troll on base—and a good number of those from the docked warships and airships—had swarmed the place. A whole contingent of dwarves had plunked themselves in a section in the back while Lt. Rothilion and some of the other elven pilots besides Aylia had actually put in an appearance.

The only semi-cleared space in the whole seat area was the front box where Queen Melantha and Prince Sontar sat. The entire arena of spectators stood and saluted when the troll queen entered, and the trolls had sent up such a howling cheer that Pip had promptly tucked in the moss earplugs Fieran had suggested she take along.

Down in the arena, two trolls bashed at each other with axes. While the blades were dulled, the two of them were bound to have some nasty bruises by the time the fight was over.

Fieran hadn't put his arm behind her like he had during the moving picture, but they were wedged so tightly against each other that they were touching from hip to knee and at their shoulders.

Not that she minded, exactly. But she was far more aware of every time he moved than she was of the fights taking place below. And Fieran moved a lot. He never sat still for more than a second or two at a time.

To distract herself, she turned to him. He bent over to put his ear closer to her level, and she all but shouted into his also thoroughly moss-plugged ear. "These fights are pretty brutal."

Fieran turned to face her, also all but yelling to be heard. "Yes. But I've been told they are better than they used to be. My dacha and uncles tell stories of what the fighting bouts were like back in the day. Fully bladed weapons and lots of bloodshed. But Uncle Rharreth and Aunt Melantha have worked hard to tone down the fights into something somewhat safer that still fulfills the purpose of proving honor in troll society."

"Seems like they're just an excuse to get entertainment out of brutality." Pip shuddered as the one troll went down after getting clubbed on the head. When he stayed down, the other troll was declared the victor.

"There's a little of that." Fieran paused as the injured troll was helped up the stands. "Well, maybe a lot of that. It's saying something about what these fighting bouts used to be if this is an improvement on safety and levels of violence."

Queen Melantha stood as the losing troll was brought to her. Her fingers glowed faintly green as she pressed them to the injured troll's head.

"Still doesn't seem wise to go beat each other up right before a major battle." Pip shook her head. That troll probably had a concussion. Not something to be just brushed aside lightly.

"No, but that's troll culture for you." Fieran tipped his head toward his aunt, who appeared to be waving to Prince Sontar to add his own magic into the mix, likely so that the troll queen could train him as she healed. "Back in the day, there were no elf healers. Participants weren't even allowed to seek medical attention until the fighting bouts were over. Convincing the troll warriors that seeking medical help right away was not a sign of weakness was one of the first things my aunt campaigned for. Or so I've been told. I was only a baby back then."

The injured troll blinked and the pale cast to his gray skin eased. He stood and raised an arm, showing he was all right.

All the gathered troll warriors cheered, acknowledging a warrior who had lost bravely.

Pip winced at the noise. Even her good, magically enhanced elven earplugs weren't fully cutting it.

The winning troll fought one more round before he declined to challenge anyone else, instead making his way back to the stands amid raucous cheers, stomping feet, and applause.

"The limits on how many rounds a winner has to fight and the ability to bow out of a fight and still retain honor was another thing Uncle Rharreth and Aunt Melantha changed." Fieran's warm breath tickled her ear. "Apparently my dacha was forced to fight an inordinate number of rounds at my Uncle Julien's wedding, until Uncle Julien finally defeated him. Well, my dacha says Uncle Julien defeated him. Uncle Julien claims Dacha purposefully threw that fight and let him win."

"Sounds like your large family gatherings are rather interesting." Pip glanced at Fieran, though her gaze was drawn to the two dwarves who were now making their way into the center of the arena, both toting large war hammers and the round bucklers favored by dwarven warriors.

"They are." Fieran shrugged before his gaze, too, swung to the arena. "Looks like dwarves aren't opposed to a bit of violent entertainment."

The two dwarves were swinging their hammers at each other with such force that it was a wonder neither of them had crushed bone or split open a skull yet.

Pip gripped the edge of the stone bench, swinging her legs. "I was raised among elves, so I share more of their sensibilities than dwarven ones. But from visits to my grandparents, well, let's just say dwarves enjoy a good brawl as much as trolls do."

Of the two dwarves, the one with a little more red in his beard defeated the one with elaborate warrior braids. Both the winner and the loser trekked up to Queen Melantha to have various injuries healed.

As the winner also bowed out, the troll announcer stepped into the center of the arena and called out a name from the list of those who had signed up before the fighting bouts as challengers.

"Did he just..." Pip glanced from the announcer to Fieran. With all the noise and the troll's accent, she wasn't sure if she'd heard what she thought she heard.

Fieran heaved a sigh, his hands fisting at his side.

"Yes, he did. Apparently, Lt. Rothilion signed up to challenge someone. One guess who that will be."

Across the arena, Lt. Rothilion stood and glided down the stairs toward the arena.

Pip clenched her fists, tensing as Lt. Rothilion halted in the center of the arena and stared right at where she and Fieran were sitting.

Despite the noise, Lt. Rothilion's contemptuous tone pierced the hubbub. "I challenge Lt. Fieran Laesornysh."

# CHAPTER SIXTEEN

Fieran pushed to his feet, flexing his fingers as he wished he had his own practice swords for this fight. He'd left those back at Treehaven when he joined the army.

Pip lightly punched his arm. "You can take him."

On his other side, Merrik nudged his arm with less force than Pip had. "Do not let him rile you. If you keep your head and actually focus on the fight, you can win."

"Do you think so?" Fieran rolled his shoulders. He couldn't delay long, otherwise the nearby troll warriors would drag him to the arena, thinking him reluctant to fight. "I've never seen Lt. Rothilion fight."

"Nor have I." Merrik's mouth tipped in a hint of a smile. "But you have been trained by Uncle Farrendel, the best swordmaster in all of Tarenhiel."

"And Dacha always kicks my butt and makes me look like a toddler waving my sword around." Fieran grimaced as he faced the arena, where Lt. Rothilion was already inspecting the rack to pick out his blunted weapons for the bout.

"Because you do not focus." Merrik lifted his eyebrows.

"I think it's more that Dacha is the great warrior Laesornysh. No one has a chance against him." Fieran shared one last look with Merrik and Pip. Well, he'd delayed enough. Time to face the fight and hope he didn't disgrace himself and his Dacha's training.

After working his way down the stands and into the arena, Fieran went straight to the weapons rack, sorting through it until he found a matched set of slim swords. They were more clunky than the finely crafted dwarven blades he had back home, but they would have to do.

Lt. Rothilion held a leaf-shaped shield in the style the elven warriors had carried generations ago along with a slim sword that was heavier and longer than Fieran's two blades.

That would give Lt. Rothilion a slightly longer reach, and that shield would be just as much a weapon as the sword.

Fieran wasn't as well-versed in fighting someone with a sword and shield combination instead of two swords. Though he had practiced occasionally with Uncle Julien, who fought in that style.

The troll warrior overseeing the fights glanced between them. "Are you satisfied with your weapons?"

"Yes, these are satisfactory." Lt. Rothilion hefted the sword, as if testing its weight.

"They're fine." Fieran experimented with a fighting stance. His hard-soled army boots weren't the soft, flexible boots he was used to fighting in, nor did these swords feel right in his hands.

Hopefully Lt. Rothilion felt as off with his borrowed weapons as Fieran did.

The troll warrior stepped aside as two others pushed

the weapons racks through a small door in the side of the arena, getting them out of the way. As soon as the door was shut, the troll warrior held up his hand.

Fieran tensed and focused on Lt. Rothilion, sinking into the familiar sword stance he'd been taught when he was barely big enough to hold the wooden sword his dacha had given him.

Across from him, Lt. Rothilion mirrored his stance, though with a sword and shield instead of two swords.

The troll warrior let his hand fall, signaling the beginning of the fight.

Perhaps it would have been wiser to circle for a few minutes, testing each other's guard and movements.

But Fieran wasn't the type to fight on the defensive.

He leapt forward, stabbing with his upper sword and going low with the other. Lt. Rothilion blocked both strikes easily, but he'd been forced to drop his shield slightly to block the lower blow. Fieran curved his upper strike into a swing, disengaging from Lt. Rothilion's sword to take a swing at his head.

Lt. Rothilion ducked as he danced backward, trying to put space between him and Fieran so that he could make better use of his shield and sword.

The elf lieutenant was fast, but he wasn't as fast or as light on his feet as Dacha. This might be easier than Fieran thought.

Lt. Rothilion sprang forward, smashing his shield into Fieran so hard and quickly that Fieran nearly toppled over. He stumbled backwards, even as he barely got his sword up in time to block a downward chop aimed at his head.

All right, not so easy. This wasn't the time for daydreaming or getting cocky.

He couldn't lose this fight. Not only would Lt.

Rothilion never let him hear the end of it, but his dacha's honor was at stake. Fieran might be willing to take the harassment, but he wouldn't let Lt. Rothilion besmirch Dacha's name…again.

Focus, that was what Merrik had told him to do. How many times had Dacha told him that same thing during morning practices?

Fieran let a hint of his magic flood his veins, though he didn't release it. These fighting bouts were to be fought without magic. That was the rule.

But there was nothing in the rules against letting his magic fuel him.

With his magic coursing through his body, Fieran threw himself into an attack. He dodged Lt. Rothilion's sword, one of his own swords grazing Lt. Rothilion's cheek. The blade was too dull to do anything but skim the lieutenant's cheek and tweak a section of his hair out of the way.

But the lieutenant would have felt the cold kiss of steel, and nothing would incite his wrath more than the affront to his long warrior hair.

With fury blazing in his eyes, Lt. Rothilion surged forward, swinging his sword with an abandon that wasn't quite sloppy but wasn't fully controlled either.

Fieran matched him blow for blow, his magic surging through him with a fire that blurred his swords and burned through his blood in a way he'd rarely felt, even in his practices with Dacha.

Perhaps Fieran had never wanted to win one of those fights as he wanted to win this one.

Lt. Rothilion bashed his shield toward Fieran, trying to dart in with his sword. But Fieran was faster, parrying each strike or dancing away from it.

Fieran leapt back a few steps. Time to finish this.

With something almost like a growl, Lt. Rothilion hurled himself forward, and Fieran matched the movement. Instead of taking the lieutenant's shield with his sword, Fieran leapt and planted a foot on the shield, using the lieutenant's own momentum to give him an extra boost into the air.

Fieran wasn't quite as agile in the air as his dacha, but he still spun, kicking Lt. Rothilion's sword out of his hand. As Lt. Rothilion stumbled, Fieran came down on the lieutenant's back, taking him to the ground.

Lt. Rothilion grunted as his chin smacked into the sand, sticking out his arm to keep from taking the edge of his shield across his face. But the edge of the shield struck the ground instead, and Fieran might have heard something pop in the lieutenant's shoulder. Lt. Rothilion gave a louder grunt edged with pain.

Fieran pressed the edge of one of his swords to Lt. Rothilion's neck. "Do you yield?"

"I yield." Lt. Rothilion's voice was strained, but he otherwise did not make any other sound of pain.

Fieran stepped off Lt. Rothilion's back, finally letting his magic settle deep in his chest again.

Lt. Rothilion climbed to his feet, his shield arm hanging awkwardly at his side. He used his good arm to slide the shield free before dropping it on the ground. The lieutenant halted next to Fieran, the anger replaced with his cold arrogance once again. "At least your damasha taught you well."

It should have been a compliment—perhaps even respectful with the more formal elvish word for *father*—but something in Lt. Rothilion's tone still held a hint of insult.

Fieran just grinned back, though the expression lacked its usual warmth. "He is Laesornysh."

As Lt. Rothilion stalked toward the stairs that would take him to Aunt Melantha for healing, the two troll attendants brought out the weapons racks again and retrieved Lt. Rothilion's sword and shield.

The troll warrior approached Fieran. "Do you wish to issue a challenge of your own?"

With his magic still burning hot within him despite the magic practice with Pip earlier in the day and the fight with Lt. Rothilion, Fieran itched for another fight. But who would he want to challenge? He'd already fought the only person he actually wanted to beat up.

As his gaze swept over the benches, his gaze flicked from Pip, who was grinning and clapping, to Merrik, who was smiling, to the rest of the flyboys. Stickyfingers, Lije, and Pretty Face were all standing and cheering for him.

Only Tiny seemed less than enthusiastic. Not that he seemed disappointed in Fieran. More his gaze was darting to where a row of other trolls sat, the ones who had hassled Tiny earlier.

Well, Fieran might not want to fight anyone else, but Tiny had a few scores to settle.

"Yes, I'd like to issue another challenge. But I'd like it to be a group fight." Fieran adjusted his grip on the swords.

The troll warrior raised his voice, making the announcement of a challenge and a group fight.

Merrik's brow scrunched as he began to climb to his feet.

As much as Fieran would love to fight with Merrik at his side, Fieran swung his gaze farther down the bench. "My first ally is Donkyn Sairdron."

Tiny's jaw dropped. It took him a rather long moment to finally push his way to his feet and make his way down the stands. Once he halted at Fieran's side, he peered up at him. "What are you doing? I'm no warrior. I passed the army's hand-to-hand combat just fine, but I'm not good enough to stand against a troll warrior."

"That's why this is a group fight." Fieran grinned, then slightly tipped his head toward the group of trolls, who were now pointing and snickering. "How many of those do you want to beat up? I think the rules allow up to a ten-on-ten fight."

Tiny grimaced, then mumbled, "There are five of them that have been targeting me specifically. Six, if you want to count the one who sometimes joins them."

"Five or six then." Fieran faced the crowd again, raising his voice. "My other allies will be Merrik Loiatir…"

Merrik sighed and pushed to his feet yet again, working his way down the stands. Something that seemed more difficult than it had a few minutes ago. With the lull in the fighting while this group fight was organized, many of those in the stands were taking a moment to get up, grab refreshments, or run to the nearest latrines.

Fieran swept a glance around the tiers of seats again, hoping to spot the ones he was looking for in the milling crowd.

There, sitting among a cluster of trolls and humans dressed in naval uniforms, he found who he was looking for.

Fieran's smirk had an edge. This was going to be fun. "And Rokyd, Lucien, and Sathrah Ardon."

His cousins grinned and shot to their feet, hurrying down the stands and into the arena to join Fieran and Tiny.

Lucien slammed his fists together. "Who do we need to beat up, cousin?"

"A bunch of trolls who have been harassing my friend, here." Fieran gestured to Tiny.

Sathrah cracked her knuckles, glee dancing in her eyes. "Ah, in that case, we'll gladly bust a few heads."

Rokyd slapped Tiny's back. "Tiny, isn't it? Who are we fighting?"

Tiny rattled off the names of the six trolls who had been harassing him for not being a true troll.

As the six trolls made their way from the stands, Rokyd, Lucien, and Sathrah picked out their weapons. Merrik selected the same shield and sword combo that Lt. Rothilion had used, a faint curl to his mouth showing how little he liked it.

"Um, I'm more a hand-to-hand combat person." Tiny flexed his fingers into fists. His arms and chest were as brawny as any troll, even if he stood over a foot shorter than the warriors coming toward them.

"Grab a large shield and maybe a war hammer." Fieran eyed the trolls, who shoved their way to the weapons racks to claim a collection of axes and huge swords. "Those trolls will hit harder than Merrik and I can take, so we'll need you to block their blows. We'll fight in threes. Rokyd, Lucien, and Sathrah will fight together, and Merrik, you, and I will fight as a team."

"Got it." Tiny selected a shield so large and heavy that Fieran would have struggled to hold it. But Tiny toted it like it was nothing.

The six of them lined up on one side of the arena. Tiny planted his shield while Fieran and Merrik stood behind him, ready to dart out in strikes. Beside them, Rokyd held a two-handed ax, standing in the fore. At his right, Lucien held a shield and a sword, prepared to use his shield to protect himself and Rokyd. To the left, Sathrah twirled a long halberd, the gleam to her eyes and the glint in her smile the scariest thing Fieran had seen all day.

The trolls who had been harassing Tiny leered at them. "Looks like the half-breed found a few friends."

"That's right." Rokyd swung his ax as easily as a child might a toy. "The half-breeds against the…" He finished with a crude and insulting word that Fieran guessed he'd learned from his ma. His da—Uncle Julien—didn't often resort to harsher language.

One of the trolls in the back of the group frowned as he gestured at Rokyd. "You're not a half-breed."

"We were raised by a troll mother and a human father, so close enough." Rokyd grinned, a light in his eyes turning a touch feral as well.

Well, this should be interesting.

The troll warrior moderating the fights quickly went through the rules for a group battle. Once each contestant had yielded, they were to move to the side so they were out of the way, and they were not allowed to assist those still fighting. The team with the last warrior standing would be declared the overall winner.

As soon as the troll warrior dropped his hand, Fieran's cousins rushed forward, slicing into the cluster of troll warriors opposing them.

Two of the trolls managed to break away to attack Fieran, Merrik, and Tiny. As one of them swung his heavy ax, Tiny stepped forward and blocked the blow.

Fieran didn't even have to glance at Merrik. As if they'd rehearsed, Fieran went right while Merrik went left.

Time to take some names and kick some butt.

"NOTHING WORSE THAN A BRUISE." Aunt Melantha gripped Fieran's chin, her fingers glowing faintly green as she tipped his face back and forth, inspecting his injury. "You were fortunate you did not lose any teeth or break your nose. It is generally considered unwise to take an ax, even a blunted one, to the face."

"I miscalculated his reach." Fieran winced. Talking *hurt*. One side of his jaw was so swollen he could see it when he looked down.

At least Tiny had done his job and stepped in while Fieran had been recovering his wits so he hadn't been forced to yield.

Instead, it was the six trolls who had yielded. Fieran couldn't even claim most of the credit for that, despite taking out one of them. His cousins were a terror when they fought together. But what else could one expect from someone raised by Uncle Julien and Aunt Vriska?

The healing magic seeping into him soothed the ache in his jaw, and Fieran finally felt like he could see straight. "Linshi, Aunt Melantha."

She shook her head, then moved on to inspecting Rokyd for bruises. She'd already healed the six trolls who had lost the fight. Their injuries had been more dire.

Farther up the stands, Tiny made his way back to his seat, but he kept being waylaid by troll warriors wanting to slap him on the back for his win.

As they made their way out of Aunt Melantha's box to return to their seats, Sathrah pounded Fieran's back hard enough to make him stumble forward. "Good fight. Invite us again if you need anyone else beaten up."

"Always." Fieran straightened, trying to pretend he wasn't trying to roll out his shoulders. At least Aunt Melantha's magic still coursing through him should take care of that bruise as well.

Lucien crossed his arms, making his biceps stand out. "The next time we're all in a fight together, it will be the Mongavarians we are giving a pounding."

"I can't think of anyone else I'd rather have there with me." Rokyd grinned, glancing around to include Lucien, Sathrah, Fieran, Merrik, and Fieran's flyboys a few rows up.

"Well, I don't know. I think I'd rather have Da and Ma here." Lucien smirked and punched Rokyd's arm before jabbing a thumb at Fieran. "And maybe Uncle Farrendel."

"Besides them." Rokyd punched Lucien right back.

Fieran nodded, a thickness in his throat that he had to swallow back. His dacha wasn't here. When the Mongavarians attacked, Fieran would be the only warrior with the magic of the ancient kings here to stop them.

# CHAPTER SEVENTEEN

Fieran pressed against the wall in the command room to one side of Level 1 of Dar Goranth. The place was so packed with ship captains, commodores, admirals, and ranking officers that Fieran couldn't move from his spot along the wall without bumping into someone. He could barely see the topographical chart laid out on the large table dominating the center of the room.

Worse, Lt. Rothilion leaned against the wall only a few feet away, having also been shoved into this far back corner. If Merrik had been here at Fieran's side, Fieran would have at least been able to whisper comments to keep things interesting. As it was, he and the elf lieutenant ignored each other with icy silence.

"Scout planes from the Persatra Aerodrome reported the last position of the Mongavarian Fleet as here, racing toward Dar Goranth at the edge of the storm." The top admiral on the base pointed to a spot on the map. A female troll aide helpfully stepped forward, placing mini warships on the map, each one flying a tiny Mongavarian flag. "They have twenty-nine battleships, nine battlecruisers, fifteen light cruisers, and a flotilla of smaller surface ships. Their airborne fleet has fifteen large, heavily armed and armored airships and three smaller, scout airships."

Fieran mentally ran the calculations through his head. The fleets would be fairly evenly matched, though the weight of surface ships slightly tipped toward the Mongavarians since the Alliance had only twenty-two battleships, seven battlecruisers, twelve light cruisers, and lots of smaller warships of various tonnage. But the Alliance had twenty-two heavily armed airships, not to mention Fieran's squadron of aeroplanes.

And Fieran himself. He would count for a lot.

Of the surface ships, over sixty percent were Kostarian ships while the rest were Escarlish. Most were stationed out of Dar Goranth but the rest had been drawn out of the fleets stationed in other ports along the coast.

Even that was a bit deceiving. Escarland might have slightly less than forty percent of the surface ships mustered there—and most of those were the smaller ships—but a large number of the seamen on the Kostarian ships were Escarlish seamen on loan from the Escarlish Navy to the Kostarian Navy. Escarland might not field the same number of ships, but they provided much of the manpower.

Of the airships, all three kingdoms fielded roughly the same number, though Tarenhiel had the majority by a slight margin.

As the command meeting went on, the troll admiral divided up the fleet. Half of the fleet, named Battlegroup Anvil, would lure the Mongavarian fleet into the iceberg-filled waters between Brenzuk, Urixidor, and Drogenvroh Islands.

The other half of the Alliance Fleet, dubbed Battlegroup Hammer, would be hidden on the far side of Drogenvroh Island. Rokyd's and Lucien's ship the KS *Vanguard* was included in this battlegroup. Once the Mongavarians had entered, they would sail out and engage the enemy from the rear, pinning them between the two halves of the fleet in the narrow strait, where the larger Mongavarian fleet wouldn't have the room to properly maneuver, thus negating some of their superior numbers.

As the admiral explained this, his aide rushed about, quickly placing the various ships in their designated battle positions.

Secretaries and aides. The war effort wouldn't succeed without them.

The Alliance airships—Battlegroup Sky—would, of course, take on the Mongavarian airships and do their best to keep the airships out over the open sea rather than over the island or the battling fleets, both of which could be targets for bombing. Sathrah, on the KAS *Dominion,* would be a part of this battlegroup.

The troll secretary hurried forward again, placing miniature airships held aloft on wires and weighted stands in position on the map.

"Lt. Rothilion, Lt. Laesornysh, assist the airships at your discretion." The admiral peered in their direction, and the various generals and captains shifted awkwardly to make a clear sightline to them. "Laesornysh, the reports from the Battle over Bridgetown mention that you are capable of bringing down airships?"

"Yes, sir." Fieran pointedly ignored the way Lt. Rothilion grew even more stiff and chilly.

"Focus on eliminating the airships as early in the battle as you can without endangering yourself or your squadron in the crossfire between the enemy airships and ours." The admiral tapped the map. "That will free our airships to bomb what remains of the Mongavarian fleet."

"Yes, sir," Fieran said again. Sadly, the aide didn't move forward with any little aeroplanes to add to the battle map. Apparently the squadron was considered too inconsequential in the grand scheme of things to bother marking. A sign of the persistent disregard of the effectiveness of aeroplanes.

Or the aeroplanes would simply be too fast during the battle to bother moving as reports flowed in.

Either way, Fieran would ensure that his Flight proved their worth during the battle.

PIP STOOD at the top of the ladder to inspect the upper wing on Fieran's aeroplane. Both wings had been fully replaced, and she checked every single bolt and connection. If there was a loose bolt, Fieran's aeroplane could tumble from the sky.

After all this time, Fieran's aeroplane still lacked artwork. The gray flyer seemed strangely bland and boring compared to the rest of Flight B, so unfitting for Fieran, who was anything but bland and boring.

She couldn't miss anything in her inspection. Any mistake on her part would kill Fieran or one of the other flyboys.

More, they would be going into battle tomorrow. Already, the rain outside the hangar had slackened from a drumming to a more gentle patter. By the time dawn broke, the storm would too.

To one side, a troll communications officer fiddled with a telephone that he was installing next to the radio. As the high frequency aeroplane radios didn't connect with the low frequency radios in the communications room, a troll officer would be stationed here during the battle to pass messages back and forth.

"Hey." Fieran's voice came from below.

Pip peered down, finding Fieran leaning against the tail of his aeroplane and looking far too relaxed for someone who would go into battle in the morning. "Hey, yourself."

Ugh, her voice didn't come out nearly as nonchalant as his.

"It's late. You should get some sleep." His gaze sharpened on her, his eyebrows quirking upward.

"I need to finish inspecting the aeroplanes." She internally winced as she heard the near desperation in her own voice. "Besides, you're the one who needs sleep more than I do."

He was going to war in the morning. She would be here, safe and sound, listening to it all go down on the radio and helpless to do anything. Some of her flyboys might be killed, and even keeping their aeroplanes in top condition wouldn't prevent that.

Fieran gave her a slightly sterner look, holding out an arm as if for a hug. "Come on. You've inspected all the aeroplanes three times today already. They are pristine."

Pip gripped the edge of the wing as she stepped down from the tippy top of the ladder. Once she was a few rungs down, she released the wing and descended the ladder more quickly. As her feet touched the ground, she turned to Fieran.

She wasn't sure if that arm was truly an invitation or just a gesture for her to come down, but she needed a hug and her brother Mak wasn't here. Stepping closer, Pip wrapped her arms around Fieran's waist and rested her head against his chest, much as she'd done in the aftermath of the Battle over Bridgetown.

Whatever he'd meant, he wrapped his arms around her readily enough, without stiffening or flinching or drawing back as if the hug was unwelcome.

The gesture was simply the comforting hug of brother and sister. Surely. She didn't mean anything by it, despite the way her heart thumped harder. Her proximity to Fieran told her far too much about the strength of his muscles while the whiff of his minty soap clinging to him sent her head spinning.

Surely he didn't mean anything more than the offered comfort, despite his solid warmth and the way he held her as if she belonged in his arms.

"The sneak attack on Bridgetown was awful." Pip closed her eyes, not caring that she was talking into Fieran's shirt. "But knowing an attack is coming is awful too. We have time to dread it."

For a long moment, Fieran just held her, not speaking. Which was concerning. If even Fieran was at a loss for words, things were dire indeed.

"And just…just keep my aeroplanes pristine, all right?" She couldn't help the way she hugged him tighter. "None of this coming back with a wing half-ripped off."

He huffed a breath into her hair. "I'll do my best. And you be careful too. If the enemy airships get past us, they'll bomb Dar Goranth, and I know you'll use your magic to stop them."

Of course she would. It would mean that she wouldn't exactly be as out of the line of fire as either of them would like. But she couldn't just sit by and watch while the base was bombed.

Fieran's hand lightly ran up and down her back, sending tingles down her spine. The longer she stood there, held in his arms, the more her breath caught in her throat.

"Fieran..." Pip tipped her face up, only to find that Fieran had bent his head closer to hers.

His gaze flicked over her face as if drinking her in. His hand paused on her back, his fingers splaying as if he was preparing to pull her closer yet. He leaned still closer, as if he was iron and she was the magnet.

Pip tangled her fingers in the warmth of his uniform shirt, standing on her tiptoes. She'd never been kissed before, but this...this felt like a moment for kissing.

"I think I might like you." The confession tripped out of her unbidden, breathy in the shrinking space between them.

Fieran stilled, then blinked. After a long, agonized moment, his hands shifted from her back to grip her shoulders. "I like you too."

Those words would have been something to treasure, if he hadn't already been gently putting space between them, his grip on her shoulders light but firm as if he was consciously placing a barrier between them.

His gaze dropped from hers. "But we can't. I can't."

"Oh." Pip took another step back, and Fieran let his hands drop back to his sides. She resisted the urge to shiver at the loss of his warmth. "I'm sorry. I shouldn't have...I misinterpreted..."

Great. Now her voice was choking up, tears burning hot in her eyes. No way was she going to burst into sobs in front of him.

She should have just taken the comforting hug and not crossed that line of friendship. Things had been just fine. And now she'd gone and ruined it by admitting her feelings.

"No, no, it isn't...I didn't mind...I...this isn't coming

out right." Fieran hissed a breath between his teeth as he gestured vaguely with his hands. "If we weren't at war, if we weren't serving in basically the same unit, then I'd ask you out on a date in a heartbeat. But I can't trust myself."

Pip hugged her arms over her stomach, her chest in such tight knots she could barely breathe. She didn't understand, and everything in her wanted to flee before Fieran said anything to make this moment even worse. "I trust you. You wouldn't do anything wrong."

"No, I wouldn't." Fieran waved helplessly again, his gaze flicking to her before lifting to stare at the distance over her head. "But I'd do something stupid. I'm impulsive. I proved that with the whole penguin sliding thing. It's easy to curb my impulsiveness when it comes to moral lines. If something is morally wrong, then there's a good reason not to do it. But other things that aren't wrong by themselves? That's harder. And if we were… together, I'd be tempted to sneak off to spend time with you. Or I'd be distracted at a crucial moment. Or something like that. I need to keep my focus right now."

"Oh. I see." She didn't like it. She wasn't sure if she was flattered or offended to be reduced to a *distraction.*

But she also understood. They would be facing battle tomorrow. Now wasn't the time to start dating or courting or change the status of their relationship from friendship in any way. Fieran was putting the safety of his flyboys ahead of his own personal feelings. She would have to do the same.

She drew in a shaky breath and plastered on a smile, even if it felt as painful as a palm sliced open on a sharp piece of metal. "So…friends."

"Yes. Friends." Fieran's answering smile didn't reach his eyes either.

Pip spun on her heel. "You were right. I should get some sleep."

She hurried off as quickly as possible, not looking back or looking around. She didn't want anyone else to see her tears.

# CHAPTER EIGHTEEN

Fog hung heavy over the harbor and ocean when the squadron took off. A light drizzle still misted down from the heavy clouds hanging low in the sky, but otherwise the storm had fully worn itself out.

The control column was cold even through Fieran's gloves as he wheeled his aeroplane higher into the sky, his toes jammed into the holds on the rudder bar. The mist fogged his goggles, and he had to lift a corner of his silk scarf to wipe them off.

But worst of all was the aching cold deep in his chest.

*I like you*. Those words had haunted him all night. For one moment after the words had dropped from Pip's lips, his heart had raced, his head had been light, and he'd thought he could finally stop pretending he and Pip were just friends.

Then he'd remembered Commander Druindar's lecture and the fiasco of his own impulsiveness.

For the good of his men, he'd had to pull back. He couldn't risk their lives by letting himself get caught up in a romance with Pip. As he'd told Pip, he was sure to do something foolish. While the war raged, he and Pip couldn't be anything else but friends.

The radio crackled to life, and Fieran shook himself. The whole point of breaking up with Pip—was it a breakup if they had never actually been together?—was so that he could focus on leading his men.

"Flight A, we will swing southwest." Lt. Rothilion spoke in elvish, so his pilots would understand—as did Fieran, Merrik, and Tiny—but the rest of Flight B would find the incomprehensible orders easy to tune out.

The thirty aeroplanes of Flight A wheeled to the left of Fieran's position, falling into a large formation of aeroplanes gathered in the sky. Each aeroplane in Flight A flew by itself as Lt. Rothilion hadn't adopted the pairs system that Fieran had for his Flight.

"Flight B." Fieran worked to tune out Lt. Rothilion's voice crackling over the radio. "We'll be swinging to the southeast and our primary mission is to prevent as many airships as possible from breaking through to Dar Goranth."

"Not a problem," Pretty Face drawled over the radio, sounding far too relaxed. His aeroplane gleamed with an extra glint. Had he waxed it before the battle? The artwork of himself suggestively lounging shone especially bright.

"Yeah, we have Laesornysh!"

"The Mongavarians won't know what hit them!"

"There won't be any airships left for Flight A or Battlegroup Sky!"

Fieran had to wait a moment for all the cheers to fade from the radio before he could speak again. "We'll all do our duty for our kingdoms this morning. Stick with your wingman. Watch each other's six. Be aware of your surroundings. Visibility is poor this morning between the fog, drizzle, and low clouds. No taking each other out or getting caught in the crossfire of dueling airships."

"Yes, sir!" Various voices spoke over each other amidst the crackle of the radio.

Fieran pointed his aeroplane's nose out to sea with Merrik's aeroplane just to the right and behind him. The low clouds forced Fieran to fly lower than he would have normally, trying to stick in the slightly more open spot in the sky between the clouds above and the fog hanging thick over the ocean below.

Would they even spot the Mongavarian fleet before it was on top of them? Normally, a Mongavarian ship was easy to spot from miles away. Unlike the Alliance ships, which ran on magic, the bulk of the Mongavarian ships burned coal to heat their boilers, resulting in vast plumes of black smoke blasting from their stacks, which acted like a giant finger pointing toward the ship.

Was the fog thick enough to hide an entire fleet steaming at full power? Or would the black pall so discolor the fog that it would still be obvious?

The dark gray mass of Urixidor Island was barely visible below them, its lighthouse shining a light into the gloom. The icebergs and ice floe protecting Dar Goranth were completely hidden by the fog.

Would the Mongavarian fleet follow Battlegroup Anvil into the ice floe? Such a thing was dangerous even in good weather for any ship that didn't have a troll warrior with ice magic stationed on board. But in this soup, the Mongavarians would have to be suicidal or incredibly focused on victory to follow Battlegroup Anvil into the narrow, ice-choked channel between the islands.

Ahead, huge figures of dirigibles loomed out of the gloom, the gray, red, and green circle of the Alliance painted on their sides to make them easily distinguishable from the enemy once the battle commenced.

The airships stretched into a line, ready to go into battle and bristling with guns. The nearest airships flew the flags of Tarenhiel and Escarland. Fieran searched the nearby airships, but he couldn't pick out the KAS *Dominion* among the fleet.

He leaned over the side of his aeroplane, trying to peer through the fog to see the assembled Alliance surface fleet. He caught a few glimpses of gray shapes and white wakes, but that was all he could see. They didn't have funnels or clouds of black smoke pouring from them, so those ships must be Battlegroup Anvil and not the Mongavarian fleet.

Fieran led his squadron above the line of airships. He couldn't see Lt. Rothilion and Flight A in the fog, but he assumed that they must be off to the right somewhere. He could hear the drumming of their engines echoing through the morning.

No, wait...Fieran tilted his head, then lifted a hand away from the control stick to pull his leather cap away from his ear to hear better.

That sound was far too loud for Lt. Rothilion's Flight. The magically powered engines didn't make nearly the amount of noise of gasoline engines or coal-powered steam engines.

Fieran pressed the talk button. "Merrik, do you hear that?"

A pause. Then Merrik's voice came over the radio. "Yes. I think—"

The fog ahead of them parted to reveal the dark gray, massive shapes of the Mongavarian airships slicing through the sky.

"Incoming!" Fieran banked his aeroplane to dive at

the Mongavarian airships. If he could get among them before they engaged the Alliance airships, he would be free to use as much magic as he wished without worrying about taking out any of his own people.

As he neared the enemy airships, he called up his magic, letting it twine around his fingers and burn in his chest with readiness to be unleashed.

Even as he lifted a hand, preparing to strike, something about the nearest enemy airship seemed off. The silhouette was not the same as the one he'd seen in the skies over Bridgetown.

But it had been dark that night. He hadn't been able to see details. The airships simply looked strange because he'd never seen them in daylight.

Or maybe these were newer airships while the ones sent into Escarland had been older models in case their foray turned into a suicide mission.

But the top of many of these airships was oddly flat. Even as Fieran watched, the front wide plate lowered into a better aerodynamic form.

What was going on? Fieran almost didn't want to destroy it so that he would have a chance to figure out.

Oh, well. He could still bring it down. If he did it right, the navy could fish out a dirigible carcass or two and then they could figure out why these Mongavarian airships looked so strange.

Fieran bore down on the leading airship. Their machine gunners opened fire on him and Merrik, but Fieran blasted a shield of his magic, extending it to protect the rest of his squadron following him. The machine gun bullets incinerated in his magic, useless except for giving Fieran an easy trail to follow right back to the airships.

As he'd done in the Battle over Bridgetown, Fieran let

his magic leap from bullet to bullet until he reached the airship. The enemy machine guns went silent as his magic consumed them, metal dripping down the side of the airship a moment before his magic lapped up that too.

Fieran curved his aeroplane around the airship as he unleashed his magic, letting it roar along every metal brace and beam. At one end of the gondola, men jumped out, wearing parachute packs as if they realized their airship was doomed.

The rest of Fieran's squadron zoomed past him, breaking off in pairs to engage the airships.

Fieran's magic ripped the enemy airship apart, briefly outlining the internal workings of the airship.

The inside of the dirigible had odd structures as well. What seemed to be a trolley system ran underneath the metal ramp above with four large metal cages dangling from it. There seemed to be some kind of lift at one end that led to a hatch in the ramp.

What could that apparatus possibly be for? It niggled at something in Fieran, even as the airship gave a groan, the balloons deflating, and it began falling from the sky. This was more than just metal reinforcing the airship's spine or an attempt at armoring something vital.

Those cages had held something. Something that wasn't there now.

Fieran pointed his aeroplane at the next airship. About half of the airships he could see sported the same wide, metal ramp.

A metal ramp that was wide enough for an aeroplane.

Ice ran through Fieran's veins. The schematic sketched in his head, as if he was looking at it with Pip or his dacha.

They hadn't counted on facing enemy aeroplanes today. None of the Mongavarian gasoline-powered aeroplanes had the range to reach Dar Goranth, much less make it there and back.

There had been some experimentation with trying to launch an aeroplane from a ship, but so far no ship was big enough to hold a runway long enough for an aeroplane to gain sufficient speed for a successful takeoff.

But aeroplanes wouldn't need a long runway if launched from an airship. They would just need a long enough runway to get a bit of momentum and control before they plunged off the end. The downward plunge would give the aeroplane enough speed to catch itself and fly.

It would still be dangerous, and Fieran had to give the Mongavarian pilots credit. It took a great deal of bravery to attempt a takeoff like that.

But if those cages had held aeroplanes, where were they?

That roaring engine noise grew even louder. Why did it seem to be reverberating from above and not just from all around him where the airships steamed?

"Incoming! They have—" Fieran didn't manage to get the words out.

"Fieran! Above you!" Merrik shouted over the radio even as he peeled his aeroplane away, pointing the nose upward.

Fieran glanced upward, then spat a crude word. He barely had time to cast a layer of magical protection in front of him and Merrik before a hail of bullets pounded from above. A mass of aeroplanes with the blue and white bars of Mongavaria swooped down like a swarm of wasps, already shooting.

Pretty Face added a crude word into the airwaves. Unlike Fieran, he hadn't had the presence of mind to wait to press the talk button until after he'd vented his expletives. "How did they get here?"

"Does it matter?" Even over the radio, Lije sounded like he was gritting his teeth.

Fieran gripped the control stick with one hand and blasted a dart of his power at an enemy aeroplane as it zoomed past.

His magic missed, but it at least sizzled a hole in one of the enemy dirigibles.

Fieran resisted the urge to let loose a few more crude words.

A Mongavarian aeroplane dove at one of Fieran's flyboys, stitching bullets across the wing toward the cockpit.

Before Fieran could turn in that direction, the flyboy's wingman shot at the Mongavarian pilot. He didn't get him, but he drove him off enough to save his wingman.

A Mongavarian aeroplane dove toward Fieran, the machine gun on its nose blasting. The bullets sizzled as they were incinerated in Fieran's magic, and Fieran followed the line of bullets back to the aeroplane. As soon as his magic touched the volatile gasoline fuel, the aeroplane before him exploded in a fireball.

Aeroplanes darted between the airships, hunters and hunted buzzing faster than the eye could follow. The chatter of guns from both Alliance and Mongavarian aeroplanes burst across the sky. The line of Alliance airships came into range of the enemy and opened fire, adding to the noise and smoke.

The radio waves clogged with voices swearing and shouting, yelling warnings to each other and cheering jubilantly at a good shot.

"Laesornysh, report!" Lt. Rothilion shouted over the

clamor, and only then did Fieran register that it wasn't the first time Lt. Rothilion had called the order.

"The Mongavarians launched aeroplanes off their airships." Fieran threw his aeroplane onto its side to avoid another oncoming aeroplane, keeping a shield of magic around himself that trailed behind to cover Merrik. "I sensed four storage cages for aeroplanes in the airship I took down. Looks like about half of the large Mongavarian airships have those launch ramps."

"There could be twenty-eight to thirty enemy aeroplanes up here." Lt. Rothilion's voice didn't give any indication of his thoughts.

"That means we have them outnumbered only two to one. That is not that bad of odds." Aylia sounded far too cheerful.

No, it wasn't. But their squadron had never faced an aeroplane-on-aeroplane fight before. Yet if their launch off the airships was any indication, these Mongavarian pilots were among the empire's best. They had likely faced battles like this before, facing off against the other Alliance squadrons stationed along the Escarlish border. Their experience could far outweigh a numbers advantage.

"Enemy aeroplanes in sight, sir." Lt. Rothilion's second sounded like he had a pinecone stuffed up his nose even now.

"Flight A, engage." Lt. Rothilion remained as calm and collected as if he was telling his pilots to go fetch him champagne at a soiree.

Fieran maneuvered his aeroplane between two enemy airships. Just as he raised his hand to blast a wave of magic at one of the airships, a Mongavarian aeroplane roared at him, trailed by Stickyfingers, who was peppering the tail of the aeroplane with short bursts from his machine gun. Holleran flew a few yards back and above, targeting the airship next to them.

Fieran pulled back his magic before he hit Stickyfingers and Holleran. In these close quarters, he couldn't just blast his magic at full strength like he had in the Battle over Bridgetown.

Was that the point of the enemy aeroplanes? The aeroplane-launching capabilities of the airships couldn't have been designed and implemented in the month and a half that had passed since the attack on Bridgetown. They'd probably already been in the works for a while since Mongavaria would need a way to launch airborne attacks without a nearby aerodrome.

But the plan of this attack? The way the aeroplanes had hidden until Fieran had been among the airships? That had definitely been planned in response to his abilities. Even if they hadn't had specific confirmation that Fieran would be here, they had planned for his presence just in case.

The chattering of a machine gun tore Fieran out of his thoughts and back into the moment. Right. Middle of battle. Not the time to be dwelling on the Mongavarian strategy. Right now, he needed to focus on his surroundings.

Fieran absently let his magic consume the bullets. All around, the fog and smoke of gunpowder choked the air so thickly he couldn't see more than a few yards at a time. Alliance and Mongavarian airships locked in battle, pounding away at each other. Aeroplanes whipped about. Even as Fieran watched, a Mongavarian aeroplane burst into flames and spiraled toward the sea.

Tiny and Murray circled a Mongavarian airship. Murray tossed his prepared magic, and Tiny blasted out his magic, turning the water into a shard of ice that he used to tear through the airship. In between blasting out magic, the two of them fended off several enemy aeroplanes.

"Merrik, on your six!" Lije's voice came over the radio as he and Pretty Face roared by.

"Merrik, go low!" Fieran yanked his control stick and shoved the rudder with his feet, turning his aeroplane up and to the left. The motion slowed his aeroplane, putting it right in the path of the oncoming aeroplane.

The Mongavarian pilot tried to dive in Merrik's wake, but Fieran blasted out a bolt of his magic, slicing through the aeroplane's propeller, carving into the engine, and melting the two machine guns mounted on the nose. The aeroplane plunged from the sky, headed for a watery grave in the sea.

Fieran turned his aeroplane back to the right and down, falling into place behind and above Merrik. "Sweep under this airship."

Merrik soared into a curve under the airship's gondola, taking them out of the line of fire of an oncoming Alliance airship. The gun emplacement on the bottom of the gondola swung to follow Merrik's flyer.

Fieran aimed at the gun with his own guns, letting off a short burst of machine gun fire to distract the gunners from Merrik.

They swung the gun toward Fieran. Big mistake. Even as they opened fire, Fieran blasted upward and outward with his magic, consuming the bullets, the machine gun, and licking up the underside of the gondola. With a surge of power, he poured his magic over the airship, devouring the metal, the wood, the canvas.

He didn't let himself think about the bodies, the blood and the bones his magic also touched and tore. This was war. Some would survive by parachuting into the ocean. But plenty wouldn't.

Two Mongavarian aeroplanes swooped toward them, machine guns already blasting.

"Focus on the airship." Merrik swerved his aeroplane to face the enemy head-on. His aeroplane shuddered as he let loose with a burst of machine gun fire.

Fieran resisted the urge to tear his magic away from the airship to protect Merrik. He had to trust Merrik had this.

As he and Merrik swept out from under the airship, the airship gave a groan as it began sinking toward the ocean, the balloons and dirigible in tatters.

A terrific boom shattered the air as a column of fire and black smoke blasted into the air from the sea below. Something that almost felt solid blasted into Fieran's aeroplane, shoving him upward and outward with a battering force.

Fieran struggled to breathe as he fought the stick to regain control of his aeroplane.

Merrik's flyer, too, was shoved to the side. One of the Mongavarian aeroplanes tipped on the side before stalling, loosing all lift to the wings. It tumbled into a spin, disappearing into the smoke and fog so Fieran couldn't see if the pilot had regained control.

"What was that?" Lije sounded shaken. At least he was still alive somewhere in this chaos.

"An explosion." Stickyfingers wasn't cackling in glee anymore.

"A ship blew up."

"One of ours?"

"Can't tell."

Fieran leaned over the side of his aeroplane, but he couldn't see any details in the smoke and fire and fog. A few other gray shapes moved about, tongues of orange fire and black smoke blasting from the muzzles of the great guns on the turrets.

Nothing he could do to help the surface navy until he took out the airships first.

"Listen up, here's the plan." Fieran waited a beat for the radio to fall silent—or mostly silent. Flight A continued talking in elvish, but their chatter was quieter and involved less shouting and cursing than Flight B had been exchanging. "I need to focus on taking down these airships. Merrik, Lije, and Pretty Face, converge on me and keep the enemy aeroplanes off my back. The rest of you, forget the airships. Focus on taking down the enemy aeroplanes."

As his men chorused their acknowledgment, Fieran pointed his aeroplane toward the next Mongavarian airship.

# CHAPTER NINETEEN

Pip and the other mechanics—Escarlish, elven, and troll—huddled around the radio at the back of the hangar, listening to Fieran and his squadron as they fought in the skies over the islands.

The troll communications officer occasionally spoke into the phone, relaying the information to the main communications room several rooms below.

Too bad they didn't get any information sent back to them in return. At least in the Battle over Bridgetown, Pip could see what was happening. Now, even if she stood on the cliffs, the battle was happening so far away that it was nothing but the faint sounds of explosions and flashes of orange, when the fog lifted enough to even see that far.

At least she knew her flyboys were still alive. She could hear their voices on the radio, shouting and cursing and warning each other. Over them all, Fieran gave orders with a ring of confidence, even in what must be utter chaos.

Why did the sound of his voice have to hurt so much?

It wasn't like they'd broken up. It wasn't even as if he'd told her he wasn't attracted to her. He liked her too.

He'd just told her *not yet,* for reasons that were completely valid. They needed to put their duties first and any and all relationships second.

An even louder explosion echoed into the hangar, popping against their ears.

"What was that?" One of the mechanics rubbed at his ears. Another raced toward the hangar mouth, peering out.

As he listened to something on the telephone, the troll communications officer washed an even paler gray. After several minutes, he turned toward them. "The KS *Valorous* just exploded."

"What?" One of the troll mechanics pressed a hand to the rock wall as his face turned the same pallor as the communications officer.

Pip braced herself against one of the mechanics' carts. How was that possible? Wasn't the KS *Valorous* one of the dwarf-built ships? How could it explode?

A sharp bang echoed through the hangar. One of the troll mechanics grunted, then collapsed in a pool of red.

"Attack!"

The next thing Pip knew, one of the Escarlish mechanics shoved her to the ground, even as more shots rang out.

Her mind reeled, her body frozen. She couldn't process what was happening.

More shouting. Another body falling. The troll communications officer crouched only a few feet away, shouting into the telephone about an attack.

Her ears ringing, her brain screeching, Pip called up her magic and blasted out a shield, holding it.

Bullets ricocheted off her barrier, and someone on the far side cried out.

The mechanic who had pushed her to the ground cautiously crouched before he reached a hand to her. "Sorry about knocking you over."

"You probably saved my life." Pip grabbed the largest wrench off the mechanics' cart. It made a paltry weapon against guns, but she felt safer with something that could be used as a weapon in her hand.

Baragh knelt by the injured troll, putting pressure on the wound. One of the elven mechanics was also down, but he was alert enough that he was putting pressure on his wound with his hand and a wad of rags he must have grabbed from one of the nearby mechanics' carts. Hopefully Queen Melantha wouldn't mind cleaning grease from a wound.

Past her shield, Mongavarian soldiers—dressed in brown uniforms with blue bands on their arms—streamed into the stairwell. Others stayed in the hangar, shooting up or wrecking whatever they could.

The troll communications officer shouted into the phone. He seemed to have the presence of mind to at least count the number of enemy soldiers passing them. He waited for a moment before he glanced over his shoulder at them. "There's been another attack down below too."

"The Mongavarians must have landed a ship on the north end of the island under the cover of the storm and hiked overland." Baragh gripped his injured mechanic, a grim set to his mouth. For some reason, he was looking at Pip, as if asking her what to do now.

Why would she give orders? Sure, she was the one holding the shield, but it wasn't like she had any more military experience than the others around her. They were all just mechanics, not trained warriors, unless the elf or troll mechanics had a few skills she didn't know about.

If the few troll warriors stationed on the base for security were busy trying to fend off an attack at the docks, how many had been left to protect the commanders and other civilians, like Queen Melantha and the elven healers? Even if those civilians were protected, there wouldn't be any help arriving for Pip and the others.

A second concussive boom tore through the air. Another ship exploding? Alliance or Mongavarian?

The voices on the radio blended together, speaking over each other in a chaos that was nearly impossible to decipher.

What were they supposed to do now? Pip's shield kept her and the others safe, and they could just sit here, waiting out the attack. But the two injured mechanics needed medical attention.

Besides, she couldn't just do *nothing* while those Mongavarian soldiers destroyed their spare aeroplane parts. Fieran and the flyboys would need those.

Pip stood to her full five feet of height, gripping the wrench. "All right, men. We can't just sit by and watch them trash the place. One of you needs to stay here with the radio and the injured. The rest of us are going to throw these Mongavarians out of our aerodrome."

The other mechanics pushed to their feet. The injured elf crawled forward, then took Baragh's place by the injured troll. "I will stay."

Baragh stood, his hands stained red, as he grabbed a wrench of his own. "Let's work our way to the left. We'll block the entrance to the stairs before we attack."

"And take these." One of her mechanics passed out a few sidearms and boxes of ammo. "Sorry, this is all I found in the locker."

Baragh waved a weapon away, pointing to Pip instead.

Stuffing the wrench into her belt, Pip swallowed and took the gun the mechanic offered to her. They'd had to pass basic firearm safety and shooting as part of their army mechanics training. It wasn't quite as rigorous as actual army training, but they were living on an army base. They had to know how to use weapons.

With the handgun gripped in both of her hands, Pip nodded to Baragh.

Baragh led the way, edging along the wall. Pip kept pace with him, expanding her shield as they moved so that she could cover them and the fallen mechanics.

The other mechanics stalked behind her and Baragh, carrying everything from handguns to wrenches to hammers.

The Mongavarian soldiers glanced up, then spun to face them as they moved. They raised their guns but didn't attempt to open fire again. They had learned something from earlier.

Baragh leaned closer to Pip. "Can you just…knock them over?"

"Maybe?" She'd never tried to wield her magic in a fight like this before.

She tried to call up her magic to blast a second shield outward, but she couldn't seem to split her magic that way.

Not wanting to waste time fiddling with her magic, she switched and instead rapidly expanded the shield she was holding. It rammed into the first line of Mongavarian soldiers, bowling them over as if they were twigs.

She quickly lifted her shield over the fallen men. Baragh and the other mechanics rushed forward, knocking the guns from the hands of the stunned soldiers.

"What should we use to tie them up?" One of the elven mechanics glanced around, his hand glowing green. There seemed to be too much stone around him to use his plant magic.

"Here." Pip grabbed a coil of wire off a nearby rolling cart. While the mechanics pinned the men down, she bound their wrists with the wire, using her magic to meld it together instead of tying knots. She then wrapped the end around one of the stone support pillars. Those Mongavarians wouldn't be going anywhere.

The other Mongavarian soldiers aimed their guns at the shield, but they were shifting and glancing around as if they weren't sure what to do now. They couldn't attack Pip and the others while they were shielded, but they didn't seem eager to retreat either. After all, they still outnumbered Pip and the other mechanics.

With the three they'd captured now secure, the mechanics who hadn't been armed claimed those guns, and they moved forward again.

This time when Pip tried to flash her shield outward, the Mongavarians jumped back quickly enough to avoid being knocked over.

Hmm. What should she do now? They were at a bit of a standoff. The Mongavarians couldn't get at them, but they also couldn't attack the Mongavarians. If she dropped her shield, they'd end up in a gun fight for which they weren't trained or prepared enough to win.

A roar came from the stairway.

Pip whirled around, raising the gun with both hands even as she closed her magic in tighter.

A battle formation of dwarves wielding axes and ball-peen hammers raced out of the stairway, led by Yamrarlig.

Well, that would work.

Pip ducked behind a nearby support pillar. "Take cover!"

The mechanics threw themselves into sheltered positions as she dropped the shield. The hazy, blue-gray shimmer across the hangar vanished.

The Mongavarians raised their weapons again, and Baragh and some of the other mechanics shot off a few rounds as covering fire.

Pip gripped the pistol in both hands, drew in a deep breath, and aimed roughly in the direction of one of the Mongavarians. She tightened her finger on the cold metal of the trigger but hesitated. Shielding during a battle was one thing. But actually pulling that trigger and shooting at someone was something else entirely.

Best not to think about it too much. She drew in a deep breath, let it out slowly, and pulled the trigger.

The handgun recoiled in her hand, bucking enough that her shot went high. The Mongavarian yelped and ducked behind a pillar.

At least she'd succeeded in keeping him from firing his gun.

With a roar, the dwarves surged forward. They were on the Mongavarians within seconds, swinging their hammers and taking them down.

Pip stayed where she was behind the pillar, her hands shaking on the gun so much that she couldn't rack the slide back to put another round into the chamber.

Baragh halted next to her, carefully extracting the gun from her hands. "You did well."

Pip swallowed and nodded, her legs and hands still trembling.

The crew leader, Yamrarlig, sauntered back toward her, his hammer resting on his shoulder.

Pip rested her head against the pillar behind her as she glanced up at him. "You arrived just in time."

Yamrarlig patted the handle of his hammer. "The troll warriors had all the fun below, so we thought we'd see about fending off the attack up here. We took out a few of those pesky buggers on our way up here. Cleared the stairwell out."

Good. Then Pip didn't have to worry about the Mongavarians who had gotten past them in the initial chaos.

As Pip straightened, a huge thump shuddered the stone beneath their feet. Another whistling sound filled the air a moment before something slammed into the dirt of the airfield just outside the hangar's mouth.

"What was that?" Pip braced herself against the pillar. Those hadn't been explosions like the bombs the airships had dropped on Fort Linder and Bridgetown.

Baragh's brow furrowed as he moved toward the hangar mouth. "Those were shells from the big guns of a battleship. Some of the Mongavarian ships must have broken through."

With a range of nearly fifteen miles, the Mongavarians wouldn't have to get far into the ice floes to shell Dar Goranth.

Calling up her magic again, Pip jogged for the mouth of the hangar, circling around where the dwarves were securing the Mongavarian soldiers with great alacrity. At the opening, she halted.

Some of the fog had burned off. Flashes, smoke, and gouts of flames marked the furious naval battle at the edge of the ice floes. The main Mongavarian fleet didn't seem to have moved as far into the ice floes as the leaders had hoped. But a contingent of Mongavarian ships had fought their way through and now ranged several miles out with their guns facing the harbor.

Above the ships, several airships with the blue and white stripes of Mongavaria headed in their direction as well.

Pip clenched her fists, her heart pounding.

Whatever the battle plan, it had gone horribly wrong somewhere. Dar Goranth would soon be under heavy bombardment, and Fieran wasn't here to stop it.

As Fieran bore down on another airship, the sun broke through the clouds, burning away some of the fog below.

Ships arrayed on the ocean below, blasting away at each other. Even as he watched, another ship listed to the side before rolling over and heading for the bottom.

More ships seemed to be dueling farther out. Fieran couldn't get a good look between the lingering fog and the smoke and the airships all around, but it appeared the flank of the Mongavarian battle line had intercepted Battlegroup Hammer, preventing them from pinching the Mongavarians between them as planned.

He had no more time for gawking at the rest of the battle. The airship's gunners opened fire on him, though they were simply wasting their bullets. Fieran's magic ate the bullets before they got anywhere close to him.

A swarm of Mongavarian aeroplanes dove around the nearest airship, bearing down on Fieran.

"I got the one on the left!" Stickyfingers was already letting loose a burst of gunfire even as he and Holleran swooped in from the left.

"The ones on the right are ours." Pretty Face and Lije roared from somewhere above Fieran.

Fieran tried to ignore the other aerial battles going on around him. He tucked his aeroplane close to the airship so that no one would dart in between before he let his magic rage. It burned through his veins, licking over the airship, consuming the canvas, melting the metal.

With a groan, the metal ramp collapsed, falling through the air balloons and tearing apart what was left of the dirigible. The airship's wreckage plunged from the sky, trailing black, acrid smoke.

Even as that airship fell, two more Mongavarian airships converged on Fieran, their machine guns blasting away as they flew one above the other.

Fieran headed straight for the lower airship, his magic dancing over his aeroplane's wings and before his eyes. When he was nearly upon the airship, he shoved the rudder, pulling hard on the stick. His aeroplane banked hard, the force pressing his rear end hard into the barely padded seat.

Straining to hold the stick with one hand, he held out the other and unleashed his magic. Bolts of blue magic burned through the canvas and the air balloons.

Gripping the stick with both hands again, Fieran tugged the stick and rudder hard over. He darted his aeroplane between the two airships before he climbed upward on the other side.

This time, he gripped the stick with his right hand as he blasted outward with his left hand.

The aeroplanes had been a tactical surprise, but those metal ramps and cages to launch the aeroplanes proved to be quite destructive once he destroyed the rest of airship's structure.

A few yards away, two Alliance airships—the KAS

*Dominion* and the Tarenhieli airship *Flying Rose*—pounded away at a Mongavarian airship between them.

Another one of those concussive explosions boomed, this time from that second line of surface ships farther out.

Other ships burned, columns of black smoke rising into the sky. The wreckage of airships dotted the waves, flames dancing as they, too, burned.

"Lt. Laesornysh." A flyboy's voice came over the radio. "They got Grady."

Fieran flexed his fingers on the control stick, his magic burning hotter in his veins.

Grady, who wasn't the shiniest tool in the toolbox. Grady, who had taken to the penguin sliding so much.

He hadn't made it.

Another Mongavarian aeroplane swooped at Fieran, and he blasted out a bolt of magic. His magic ignited the gasoline, and the aeroplane exploded, what was left of the wings and tail spiraling toward the sea far below.

Time to end this before any more of his men didn't make it.

# CHAPTER TWENTY

Pip braced herself at the top of the cliff and poured her magic into her shield, expanding it farther and farther. Could she cover the airfield, hangar, and the harbor below?

Another shell hurtled from the sea and slammed into her shield. She grunted at the force, her shield snapping back several feet toward her as she strained to keep it from shattering.

One of the airships glided closer, and she gritted her teeth. She was strong, but there was no way she could hold back both a bombing and a naval bombardment. She wasn't even sure she could hold back even one of those things.

She held her shield at her limits, protecting the hangar and cliff face, but leaving the rest of the harbor vulnerable.

Several more shells slammed into her shield while others fell into the buildings below, blowing out walls and crumbling roofs.

She cried out at the pressure, nearly falling to her knees.

Then a tromping sound came from behind her. A line of dwarves appeared beside her. They pounded their hammers and axes against the ground, creating a rhythm.

Yamrarlig nodded to her. "We stand with you."

Dwarven magic gathered, funneling into her shield. Pip caught her breath at the iron taste of the magic, so strong and sharp. With the dwarven magic flooding into her shield, Pip pushed it farther, stretching it to better cover the rest of the harbor.

More shells pounded into her shield, a succession of blows that rang in her head and stole the breath from her chest.

She blinked past the blur to her vision as one of the airships drifted over the harbor, the big door opening in the bottom of the gondola.

It was still too much. She couldn't hold the shield, and once that second airship arrived, her shield would shatter.

Baragh halted next to her. "What can we do to help?"

Nothing. No one had magic strong enough to help except Fieran, and he was far away over the main battle. The clouds in the distance glowed blue, marking his progress as he destroyed the enemy airships.

If she asked Baragh to call for Fieran on the radio, he would come. He would abandon his post to rescue her.

But that was just the kind of stupid thing he was worried about doing. And she could never ask him to leave his flyboys undefended to rescue her. She would have to rescue herself.

Bombs exploded against her shield, her senses fraying. Her shield crumbled inward by nearly twenty feet, exposing several of the docks to the bombardment. She couldn't hold out much longer.

If her shield failed more, the underground bunker where the cordite was stored for restocking the ships would be exposed. It should be safe, buried under stone reinforced with magic as it was, but if it exploded as so many of the ships in the battle had, it would take out a good portion of the harbor.

At least the magical power cells were stored separately. If those went off too…

Pip stilled, her mind racing. The magical power cells. Fieran might not be here, but his magic still was. Not to mention his sisters' and dacha's magic.

"Baragh, I need you to fetch the magical power cells." Pip braced herself as another three rounds slammed into her shield. It buckled another few feet. "Send someone down to the shipyard and fetch the ones there too. Press them against the shield and open them up. The magic of the ancient kings will reinforce my shield."

Baragh hesitated. "The ships will need those power cells after the battle. Without power, the fleet will be crippled."

"And if we don't do this, there won't be a harbor to come back to." Pip cried out as another bomb struck her shield. "Besides, we have a Laesornysh here. Between the two of us, I'm sure we can rig something up to refill whatever power cells we drain now."

"Right." Baragh spun on his heel and raced back toward the hangar.

More explosions pummeled her shield. Pip blinked, finding herself on her knees. Around her, the dwarves stepped up their pounding rhythm, but their magic was slackening. It wasn't meant to be used like this, as a shield of pure magic.

That second airship reached them, the large door in the bottom opening up.

Pip drew in a deep breath and gathered the dregs of her magic. She would hold this shield or die trying.

A stream of large, cylindrical objects poured from the airship overhead, hurtling toward Pip's head. She squeezed her eyes shut, preparing for the explosions, the shattering of her shield, then the death that would follow.

A familiar crackle filled her senses even as that same power flooded over her magic.

Pip peeled her eyes open as a wash of blue bolts crackled over her shield, starting from the far side just behind the hangar. When she glanced in that direction, all the elven and human mechanics had magical power cells in their hands as they quickly touched the wires to her shield and turned the knob to let the power flow.

The bombs thundered against her shield. A few deflected, but the rest exploded with such force that even with the magic of the ancient kings threaded through her magic, the force still pummeled her chest and pounded painfully in her head.

More power burst across her shield, even stronger than the amounts contained in the power cells used in the aeroplanes. At the edge of her shield below, several trolls hefted the larger magical power cells that fueled the battleships, pressing the wires against her shield as the magic poured out. Baragh must have used the telephone to call to someone below for them to respond so quickly.

Pip remained on her knees near the edge of the cliff as she drew in a deep breath. A different kind of burn filled her chest as she struggled to hold her shield while it conducted so much of the magic of the ancient kings. She was used to Fieran's magic—it felt like him, somehow—but this magic wasn't all his. Some of it felt pretty similar, while one thread of it thrummed over her shield with even more, almost incomprehensible power.

Beside her, the dwarves stopped chanting, yanking their magic back. Or what was left of it. It seemed their magic had been mostly burned away by the magic of the ancient kings.

More bombs fell. Shells shrieked. But none of them so much as shuddered through her shield, much less shattered it.

Through the smoke, another two airships glided at full speed, heading for the harbor. But these had the green, gray, and red circles of the Alliance painted on their sides. They opened fire as soon as they were in range, pummeling the enemy airships.

With a *whump*, one of the enemy airships exploded, flaming debris raining down to be consumed against her shield.

Before the harbor, an Alliance battleship and battlecruiser closed on the Mongavarian ships. Plumes of black smoke speared the sky as the Mongavarian ships steamed away, even as the Alliance ships opened fire.

Pip sank back to sit on the grass with a sigh. She couldn't release her shield just yet, but this battle seemed to be nearly over.

FIERAN'S MAGIC burned through his veins, his sight blurred blue. As he righted his aeroplane out of a spin, he had to blink away a wave of lightheadedness, followed by the dull ache of exhaustion pressing at his eyes.

Still, when he reached for his magic, there was still more of it crackling deep in his chest. Ever more. He'd yet to find the end. Only the end of his stamina and his magical reach, it would seem.

As his magic consumed another enemy airship, sending it plunging toward the ocean far below, he glanced around.

Acrid smoke and the heavy cloud bank still choked the sky, limiting visibility. Yet the only airships he could see belonged to the Alliance.

"Anyone see any enemies left?" Fieran peered around as he weaved his aeroplane between the airships. Based on his rough count, they hadn't shot down all of the enemy airships, though they'd pretty much wiped out the aeroplanes.

"No."

"Nope."

"I think they must have made a run for it." This last was Aylia. During the fight, Flights A and B had worked their way toward each other until now their aeroplanes mingled among the Alliance airships. "Their ships made a coordinated retreat a few minutes ago."

"Then we won." Fieran glanced to the south, but he couldn't see the retreating—disappeared—Mongavarians.

Why didn't it feel like a victory? Yes, they had driven the Mongavarians away from Dar Goranth, which had been their primary goal. But if the Mongavarians managed to retreat in force, then they hadn't succeeded in destroying their fleet.

Burning flotsam and ships coated the ocean below as far as Fieran could see. He couldn't tell what carnage belonged to the Mongavarians and what to the Alliance. But the fleet below seemed thin, and Fieran had seen a few Alliance airships go down in the chaos.

Perhaps the celebration of victory was something that belonged to civilians.

"Laesornysh, channel 2." Lt. Rothilion's voice was clipped and official over the radio.

If the elf lieutenant had more orders for their squadron, he would most likely give it over the wider channel. That meant he wanted to tear into Fieran for some reason.

What could Lt. Rothilion want to berate Fieran about now? Fieran had done what he was supposed to in the battle. Surely there was nothing Lt. Rothilion could get his knickers in a twist over.

With a sigh, Fieran flipped the switch to channel 2. "All right, Rothilion. What do you want?"

There was a longer pause than he'd been expecting. When Lt. Rothilion spoke, his voice was far more ragged than it had been a few minutes ago. "I want you to take care of my pilots."

"Pardon?" Fieran flew his aeroplane between the airships, searching for Lt. Rothilion's flyer. Something was seriously wrong.

Even without knowing what was going on, Merrik mirrored Fieran, keeping his aeroplane tucked behind Fieran's.

"I will not be able to…to keep flying for much longer." Lt. Rothilion's voice was growing more pain-filled by the moment. "The squadron will be yours. Take care of them."

There. Fieran drew up alongside Lt. Rothilion's aeroplane. He was flying level, his aeroplane in seemingly good condition.

Except for the line of bullet holes along the fuselage. Even with the hint of green elven magic reinforcing the wooden frame, those bullets had punched right through into the cockpit. Even if only one or two of those bullets hit Lt. Rothilion, he would be in a bad way.

Already, Lt. Rothilion's head lolled against the back of the cockpit, as if he couldn't hold his head up much longer. Within a few more minutes, he would pass out, and his aeroplane would plunge from the sky into the sea.

And Fieran would have to watch him die.

Lt. Rothilion was a pain in the rear end, but he was still a part of Fieran's squadron. After all the death and loss that day, he just couldn't stomach having to watch yet another person die.

He was going to save him. No matter what it took. Or how crazy the idea currently spinning through his head.

"Rothilion, hold on for a few minutes longer." Fieran didn't wait for his reply. He flipped back to the main channel even as he matched his aeroplane's speed to Lt. Rothilion's. "Erendriel, take over Flight A. Swing to the southwest and make sure the enemy is fully gone. Pretty Face, you're in temporary charge of Flight B. Swing to the southeast and do the same thing. Let Erendriel know if you see anything because I'll be on channel 2. Merrik, switch to channel 2."

Fieran switched back to channel 2. "Still with us, Rothilion?"

"What are you planning, Laesornysh?" Even dying, Lt. Rothilion's voice still had an edge to it.

"Something crazy, I am sure." Merrik's voice held a grim note. He might not have heard what Lt. Rothilion said on channel 2 originally, but as he flew just behind Fieran, he would be able to see the bullet holes as well as Fieran could. "What are you thinking, Fieran?"

"Can you grow vines down from your aeroplane without weakening it too much?" Fieran flexed his fingers on the control stick. "If you fly over Lt. Rothilion's aeroplane, could you grab it?"

"That is a crazy idea." Lt. Rothilion sounded stronger in his scorn. "You will get both of us killed."

Fieran ignored him. "Merrik, can you do it?"

Merrik didn't reply right away. He wouldn't say yes unless he thought he could manage it. He wasn't as reckless as Fieran. Just somewhat reckless if he thought the cause was good enough.

"Yes, I think I can." Merrik spoke slowly, as if he was still hesitant even as he said yes. "Lt. Rothilion, I will need you to reach out with your magic to get a better hold."

Lt. Rothilion didn't answer right away, the pause long enough that Fieran swung his aeroplane closer to see if the lieutenant had passed out.

He hadn't. He tilted his head toward Fieran, as if trying to meet his eyes. His voice was growing quieter, more strained. He didn't have long. "If I do this, promise me, Laesornysh, that if it becomes clear that you cannot pull this off, that you will make the choice. I do not trust Lt. Loiatir to do it."

Merrik made a noise over the radio, as if he thought about interrupting and arguing but then realized it would be futile.

Lt. Rothilion continued speaking as if he hadn't heard. "Now that he has committed to saving my life, he will do it or die trying. But I know that if it comes to it, you will choose his life over mine."

A chill went down Fieran's spine at what Lt. Rothilion was asking. It would be up to Fieran to make the call if this wasn't going to work. If it was time to let Lt. Rothilion die, that would be Fieran's decision.

"I understand." Fieran let the weight of that sink into his gut.

Merrik's aeroplane was already glowing green with

his magic. Vines extended down from the fuselage, and Fieran could only guess what part of the flyer Merrik was taking the wood from.

"When you are ready, Lt. Rothilion." Merrik maneuvered his aeroplane so that he was flying above and just behind the lieutenant's flyer.

Lt. Rothilion's aeroplane glowed even more green than it had before. "All right, Lt. Loiatir." Lt. Rothilion sounded like he was breathing heavily, as if using his magic was a strain after all the blood loss.

Merrik swooped forward and lower until only a few feet separated the wheels of his aeroplane from Lt. Rothilion's upper wing. The vines trailed over Lt. Rothilion's flyer before they snagged, new vines growing up and gripping Merrik's vines.

Merrik's aeroplane lurched as it was tugged back by the weight of Lt. Rothilion's aeroplane. After a moment, Merrik eased his aeroplane's speed to better match Lt. Rothilion's.

It was masterful flying, and Merrik made it look easy.

Fieran took up a station as the rear wingman as Merrik and Lt. Rothilion's tandem aeroplanes set out northward.

Over the course of the battle, the fight must have drifted even more south than Fieran had realized. The islands were nothing but a smudge on the horizon with Dar Goranth completely out of sight.

A long flight. Too long, perhaps? Would Lt. Rothilion live long enough?

Fieran pressed the talk button. "Ground crew, come in."

He waited for several long moments, but there was no reply.

Perhaps they were only monitoring channel 1. He switched back and tried again. "Ground crew, come in."

Still no answer.

What was going on? Surely Pip and the other mechanics had been glued to the radio during the battle. They wouldn't have left.

Was Fieran out of range? Or had something happened to the radio?

Or, worse, had something happened to Pip and the mechanics? Had Dar Goranth been attacked while he had been busy elsewhere? What if they had been bombed? Pip would have done her best to hold out against an attack, but her magic couldn't hold out against a large attack.

Fieran kept switching between the channels, calling out to Dar Goranth. His stomach sank with every moment that passed without an answer from Pip or anyone else at Dar Goranth.

As he changed back to channel 2, Lt. Rothilion's breathy voice broke through before Fieran could call out again. "Laesornysh?"

"I'm here." Fieran dipped his aeroplane lower and to the side to get a better look at Lt. Rothilion.

Lt. Rothilion was slumped over, his shoulders heaving as he gasped for breath. The skin visible between his scarf and his goggles was even more silvery pale than normal.

"I will not...be able to fly...much longer..." Lt. Rothilion's whisper barely carried over the radio.

In the cockpit, the elf lieutenant lifted a shaky hand and tugged off his goggles. In the event of a crash landing, one took off the goggles so that the glass lens didn't crack and gouge out one's eyes. Lt. Rothilion was preparing now, knowing he wouldn't be awake for whatever landing would come.

"Stay with us, Rothilion." Fieran gripped the control

stick, helpless to do anything for the lieutenant but watch and talk. Ahead, the lighthouses marking the channel between the islands rose as white glints against the dark smudge of land. "We're almost there. Just a few more minutes. Hang on a few more minutes, all right?"

"Take care…my pilots…" Lt. Rothilion's breathy voice faded into nothing.

"Rothilion?" Fieran waited a moment. What was the elf's first name again? "Saranthyr?"

No answer. In the cockpit, Rothilion's head lolled, his eyes closed. Based on the way his body flopped loosely as the two aeroplanes were jostled by turbulence, he wasn't conscious.

Was he even alive? There was no way to know until they got him on the ground.

"Fieran." Merrik sounded like he was speaking between gritted teeth. Another buffeting puff of wind tossed Merrik's and Rothilion's aeroplanes up before slamming them a few feet down. "He does not seem to be flying his aeroplane any longer."

"He passed out." Fieran returned to his station behind the two aeroplanes.

"I do not think I can keep us aloft without him steering." Merrik's gritted tone showed how reluctant he was to admit that. "His aeroplane is just a weight hanging off mine, interfering with the lift. It will fight me, especially as we come in to land."

"Can you steer his aeroplane with your magic?" Fieran glanced from the aeroplanes to the islands edging closer.

Too slowly for both Merrik and Rothilion.

"No." Merrik bit off the word as both his and Rothilion's aeroplanes were torn sideways in a gust of wind. "It is all I can do with my magic to hold on to his aeroplane.

Besides, the elevator, rudder, and aileron mechanisms are all metal. I would have to grow new mechanisms to manipulate them."

Ah, right. That would be difficult, especially since Merrik already had enough on his hands and his magic trying to keep the two aeroplanes aloft.

"Hang on a moment. Let me try something." Fieran eased his aeroplane even closer until his nose was only feet from Rothilion's tail. He poured magic from his fingers, holding it in tight control so that his magic danced over the skin of his aeroplane without burning any of the canvas.

Now for the hard part. Fieran peeled a bolt of his magic off his own aeroplane and lashed it out toward Lt. Rothilion's aeroplane.

The magic singed the canvas of the flyer's tail, but it was enough contact for Fieran to unleash more of his magic over the other aeroplane.

Fieran gritted his teeth as he struggled to pour enough magic over the flyers while also not incinerating either of them. Harder than it sounded, considering both aeroplanes were made from light wood and canvas covered in highly flammable resin and paint.

Bits of Lt. Rothilion's aeroplane went up in smoke. Fieran drew back his magic, trying to concentrate it only on the rudder and ailerons.

"What are you doing?" Merrik must have been peering around the side of his cockpit because he sounded about one breath away from saying a crude word or two. "Not sure that is helping."

"It will. Just another moment." Fieran resisted the urge to squeeze his eyes shut to better concentrate. He still had his own aeroplane to fly.

He worked to spin his magic around the rudder and

ailerons. The canvas covering the metal frame went up in a puff.

But when Fieran pushed upward with his magic, the ailerons moved.

"Fieran," Merrik growled into the radio. He must be fighting the extra drag on his aeroplane.

"Got control of Rothilion's aeroplane." Fieran gripped the stick, his toes in the rudder, and tried to visualize those same movements in the other aeroplane.

"Yeah, I noticed," Merrik shot right back. "Now do not take down both of us. You need to match whatever I do."

Right. Fieran shouldn't match his own movements, but Merrik's. Those two aeroplanes needed to fly as one—even if Merrik was piloting one and Fieran was essentially piloting the other. While piloting his own flyer. Easy-peasy.

Another gust whipped up from the ocean, swirling against the islands and the land.

Fieran's aeroplane jumped, fighting him. He let his muscle memory worry about his flyer while he concentrated on tweaking the ailerons and rudder of the other aeroplane.

"Rudder right. Down on the stick. Not that much right!" Merrik somehow retained control of his tandem aeroplane, his magic flaring brighter green along the connection between the two flyers.

Fieran tried to follow Merrik's verbal directions, his gaze flicking over Merrik's aeroplane to note the position of the ailerons and rudder before focusing on Lt. Rothilion's aeroplane.

Merrik dropped them lower as they swept in between Brenzuk and Urixidor Islands.

Fieran kept the propeller of his aeroplane dangerously

close behind Merrik and Lt. Rothilion. This close, if Merrik lost control, all three of them would get taken out.

As the southern coast of Drogenvroh Island rose before them, Fieran gripped the talk button. "Ground crew, come in."

Just crackling static met his ears for one heartbeat, then two. As he drew in a deep breath to try again, a voice called back, "Ground crew here. Sorry about any delays. We were dealing with a situation here."

By the tone of the voice, Fieran guessed the situation had been resolved. He would have to ask about the full story later. Right now, he needed to save Lt. Rothilion's life.

"This is Lt. Laesornysh." Fieran fought to keep both the control stick and Lt. Rothilion's flyer steady. "Lt. Loiatir and I are coming in hot with a gravely injured Lt. Rothilion. He won't be able to stop his own aeroplane, so someone needs to fetch Pip and have her standing by. An elf healer standing by wouldn't hurt."

"Not sure if we can get one of the healers. They're a bit…busy at the moment." Those words held weight. Perhaps the man was referring to that unexplained situation. "I'll fetch Pip."

Fieran breathed out a strained sigh of relief. At least the ground crew at the airfield would be ready.

Because this landing was going to be rather tricky to pull off without killing all three of them.

## CHAPTER TWENTY-ONE

As they swept over the southern tip of the island, the swirling winds grew worse. The aeroplanes danced on the wind, the dead weight—hopefully that was a metaphor and not literal—of Lt. Rothilion's aeroplane jerking Merrik's aeroplane around.

Fieran fought with his own aeroplane and with his magic to fly the other aeroplane. Merrik shouted orders into the radio, and Fieran worked to follow them the best he could.

As they neared, there appeared to be something burning in the harbor and a few extra craters in the hills surrounding the airfield that hadn't been there before. But Fieran couldn't take more than a moment to note them.

"Any ideas of how we are going to land?" Merrik sounded even more strained. "Lt. Rothilion bound his magic so tightly to mine that I do not think I can retract my vines."

A good question. Fieran dropped his aeroplane slightly lower so that he had a better view of the wheels on Lt. Rothilion's aeroplane. "I'll talk you through touching down. Once his wheels are close to the ground, I'll slice the vines with my magic. Then both of us will pour on the speed and climb back into the sky while Pip stops his aeroplane."

"Understood." Merrik maneuvered the aeroplanes so that they faced the airfield.

The land rushed up to meet them. Far too fast. But if Merrik slowed too much, he'd never keep control of his two aeroplanes. The aerodynamics were already off.

"About a hundred feet. Seventy-five feet." Fieran called out how many feet Merrik had to go before Lt. Rothilion's wheels touched down. "Fifty feet. Shoot."

"Shoot, what?" Merrik gritted out. "Fieran."

"Just a minor problem. Give me a moment." Fieran glanced from the wheels to the ground. Right now he could see them because he was flying lower than Merrik's and Lt. Rothilion's aeroplanes.

But once they neared the ground, he wouldn't be able to do that. Not without landing first. Even then, his aeroplane's nose blocked his view of the ground.

Time to try something crazy. Well, crazier than what they were already doing.

Fieran backed off for a moment, then he gave the engine more power as he lifted higher into the air. Once he had enough clearance over the ground, he checked that his lap belt was secure and drew in a deep breath. He'd done this once before...by accident. Now to do it on purpose.

He cranked the rudder and control stick hard over while goosing the power. His aeroplane flipped onto its side, hanging there for a moment, before it tipped all the way over so that he was flying upside down. The lap belt tightened around his hips, the only thing keeping him from falling out.

At least with the magical power cell, he didn't have to worry about dousing his aeroplane with fuel.

The cambered wings weren't exactly designed for upside-down flight. He had plenty of power to maintain speed, but he'd have to match Merrik's coming-in-for-a-landing speed.

Fieran tried to swing back lower, but the aeroplane pitched upward. After correcting, he took another deep breath before he pushed the stick the other way. Of course, while flying upside down, all the motions would be reversed. He would have to push the rudder and the stick in the opposite direction he normally would.

"Fieran, what in the Alliance are you doing?" Merrik must have glanced over his shoulder.

"Don't worry about me. Just concentrate on flying." Fieran maneuvered his aeroplane behind Lt. Rothilion's aeroplane once again. This close to the ground and in the wake of the other aeroplanes, the lift felt...light. Not as solid beneath his inverted wings. "Ten feet to go."

Any strong puff of wind would shove him downward. If he crashed, his wings would crumble, and he'd be crushed.

Best not to think about it.

"Do not kill yourself." Merrik's words were more an order than advice.

"Lt. Rothilion made me promise not to get you killed. He didn't say anything about me." Fieran worked the stick and rudder. His aeroplane was barely floating above the ground. "Eight feet."

To one side of the airfield, several figures lined up outside of the hangar, but Fieran couldn't glance in that direction long enough to see if Pip was among them.

"You are crazy." Merrik sounded like he might punch Fieran if they all survived.

"You already knew that." Fieran forced the lighthearted tone between clenched teeth. "Six feet."

The grass blurred below, so close beneath Fieran's upper wing that it felt like he'd scrape the ground at any moment. If he got too much closer, he'd be able to reach out and touch it.

The wheels of Lt. Rothilion's aeroplane inched closer to the dirt. The wing stabilizers on Fieran's aeroplane shook with the tension of flying upside down. If one of those broke, he was done for.

Fieran kept his eyes glued there, his mind aching as it was pulled in so many directions trying to fly his inverted aeroplane and Lt. Rothilion's right-side-up aeroplane. "At one foot, I'll cut the vines. Get ready."

Fieran could barely hear Merrik's acknowledgment as he continued to speak, counting down in feet. "Four feet. Three. Two. One."

At one, he raised his hand and sliced a bolt of magic between Merrik's aeroplane and Lt. Rothilion's, severing the vines.

Lt. Rothilion's aeroplane dropped to the ground even as Merrik's aeroplane roared upward.

In that instant, Fieran realized the second thing he'd overlooked. Flying inverted as he was, he couldn't peel away as quickly as planned. And Lt. Rothilion's aeroplane was slowing far too quickly right in front of him.

Fieran pushed the control stick to try to rise into the sky. But with the inverted wings, the lift was all wrong. His aeroplane crawled upward. Too slowly. At this rate, his upper wing would crash into Lt. Rothilion's.

His heart throbbing in his throat, Fieran counted the seconds to impact. Five. Four. Three.

He cranked his aeroplane hard over as he blasted his magic between his aeroplane and Lt. Rothilion's. The blast wave shoved against his wings, tipping his aeroplane onto its side and upwards as he skimmed past Lt. Rothilion's flyer with only inches to spare.

His aeroplane flipped the rest of the way right side up and climbed back into the sky.

PIP'S HEART hammered as she stretched out her already exhausted magic and created a shield around Lt. Rothilion's aeroplane. She moved her shield along with the aeroplane, slowing it rather than letting it slam into the barrier.

What had Fieran been thinking? Her heart had nearly stopped when she'd seen him come in like that, flying inverted so low to the ground. Not to mention Merrik's aeroplane attached to Lt. Rothilion's. All three of them could have easily ended up dead if so much as a gust of wind had struck them wrong.

She slowed Lt. Rothilion's aeroplane, holding it there as the still spinning propeller tried to keep pushing it forward.

As soon as the aeroplane stopped, the ground crew raced forward, along with a medic carrying a stretcher. Not one of the elf healers, but he was as good as they were going to get at the moment.

Pip raced alongside them, running full tilt to keep up on her shorter legs. As they neared the aeroplane, she shrank her shield so that it was only gripping the aeroplane's wheels and preventing it from rolling forward.

She scrambled up the side of the aeroplane, reached into the cockpit, and switched off the engine.

Only then did she glance at Lt. Rothilion where he slumped in his seat. And promptly wished she hadn't.

There was so much blood. Staining his shirt and the vines he'd wrapped around his torso to apply pressure to his wounds. Pooled on his seat and puddled on the floor. His skin was so white it was porcelain. Was he still alive? He certainly didn't look it.

The troll medic joined her on the wing and pressed his fingers to Lt. Rothilion's neck. He waited for a moment before he shouted over his shoulder, "He's still alive. We need to get him out of this flyer and to sick bay."

The medic reached past all the blood to unbuckle Lt. Rothilion's lap belt. Several of the ground crew hopped on the other wing and the three of them lifted the unconscious elf lieutenant from the aeroplane. The wing struts creaked at all the added weight, but Pip ignored the sound. She'd help the elf mechanics fix whatever they broke trying to save Lt. Rothilion's life.

As Lt. Rothilion was settled on the stretcher, fresh blood stained the vines and pooled on the canvas. How much more blood could the elf lieutenant stand to lose?

Pip pressed her hand to the lieutenant's stomach and cast another shield around his middle. She wasn't sure how much it would help, but she had to try something. She didn't even like Lt. Rothilion, but he was still one of their own.

As the medic and one of the ground crew carried the stretcher, Pip trotted alongside, holding her shield in place. She barely paid attention as they hurried across the airfield, through the hangar, and into the lift. One of the troll ground crew who had come with them cranked the lever as quickly as possible to lower them, though the levels passed with interminable slowness.

Pip couldn't bring herself to look at Lt. Rothilion on the stretcher, even as she sensed his warm blood against her shield. Her stomach was already lurching. There was a reason she'd become a mechanic and not a medic, and it didn't all have to do with her magic.

This was all too much like trying to find the wounded after the bombing of Bridgetown. The stench of blood. The churning in her stomach. The frantic rush to save a life.

The lift jerked to a halt, and the troll flung the cage doors open.

They hurried out into chaos. Stretchers filled the area around the lift while other wounded trolls and humans packed into the space. In the sick bay, Queen Melantha's voice could be heard, strident and commanding, as she shouted orders.

The medic and troll carrying Lt. Rothilion's stretcher shoved their way through the chaos. Pip hurried to keep up, tripping over one of the stretchers on the ground and nearly stepping on the poor man's hand.

As they stepped into sick bay, an elf halted them. "You need to wait—"

"This pilot has been severely wounded. He needs to be seen right away." The medic nodded his head toward Lt. Rothilion.

The elf must have finally glanced at Lt. Rothilion for his eyes widened, and he motioned. "Yes, take him this way." The elf led the way down the hall before darting into one of the large wards, calling, "Queen Melantha!"

Fieran's aunt looked up from the troll she'd been healing. She nodded, said something to the troll, before she hurried in their direction.

Pip could tell when she was no longer needed. She dropped her shield and quietly drifted out of sick bay. As much as she wanted to stay to see if Lt. Rothilion would be all right, she would just be in the way.

She picked her way through the wounded, giving the

injured men and women a tight smile. Wounded aeroplanes were much easier to deal with than hurt people.

Bypassing the lift, she headed for the stairs. She'd leave the lift for those carrying in the wounded from the harbor. Some of those who had been hurt on the airships and warships must also be coming in as well, considering the numbers packed in there.

On the first stair, she halted at the sight of a large figure huddled on the landing. His shoulders shook, a noise almost like a whimper coming from him.

Pip stepped closer before she recognized him. "Sontar?"

Fieran's cousin started, his head shooting up. He froze, as if he was paralyzed with the need to both run and curl into as small a ball as possible.

"I'm Pip. I'm a friend of your cousin Fieran." Pip eased slightly closer, not wanting to scare him. "Are you all right?"

"Fine," Sontar mumbled as he turned his face away from her once again, his shoulders hunching, his long white hair straggling around his head, as if he was trying to hide.

"You don't look fine." Pip eased into a seat near him but not crowding him. "Do you think it would help to talk about it?"

For a long moment, he remained silent. She couldn't blame him. She was a stranger only loosely linked to him through Fieran.

But sometimes strangers made the best people to talk to.

Sontar let out a shuddering breath, his voice still a mumble that she could barely discern. "Blood and guts make me feel sick."

"Me too." Pip resisted a shudder, trying not to breathe

too deeply. Even here in the stairwell, the stench of blood and gore filtered to them.

"Yeah, but I have healing magic." Sontar clenched his fists, but that couldn't hide his shaking fingers. "I'm supposed to be a healer. The first troll healer. Yet I can't stand to be in there."

"It's a lot right now, even for a trained healer." Pip bit off the words before she added that Sontar was young. He had only barely come into his magic. He was still just a kid, really.

"But I'm a troll." Sontar's fetal position loosened slightly. Perhaps talking was helping. His speech was growing stronger, less mumbled. "Trolls are supposed to have strong stomachs and face things like this with bravado."

Pip nodded. "I understand. I'm half-dwarf."

There wasn't much room for someone more sensitive in traditional dwarven or troll culture.

"I should go back in there." Sontar gave a shudder, that tremble starting in his fingers again.

"No, you don't have to." Pip focused on him, waiting until Sontar flicked his gaze to her briefly. "I'm sure your ma would agree. You aren't ready or trained enough for something like this."

"Ma told me to leave." Sontar curled inward again, as if under weight of shame.

"Then your duty is to obey your mother." Pip stood, gestured upward, and held out her hand. "Why don't you come with me to the hangar? I know you don't have enough training to use your magic without a trained healer present, but you can still help me look after the flyboys when they land. They will probably pull long hours yet, and they will need coffee, food, and rest when they land. That's still a healer's job."

Sontar hesitated a moment before he took her hand. He was so large and she was so tiny, so she didn't so much help him up as pretend to do so while he levered himself upright. Even when upright, he still stood hunched, as if trying to make himself look smaller.

Pip started up the stairs, headed back for the hangar. She needed to be ready when the rest of her flyboys landed.

This would be a long day for all of them.

# CHAPTER TWENTY-TWO

As Fieran's aeroplane clawed its way back into the sky in Merrik's wake, the radio crackled again.

"Lt. Laesornysh." Commander Druindar's voice rang clear despite the static. "I saw what you and Lt. Loiatir did. That was quite the feat of flying."

"Yes, sir." Fieran couldn't think of anything else to say. That wasn't overconfidence. It *had* been quite the feat on both his and Merrik's part. "Your orders?"

There was a pause, as if Commander Druindar sighed but the sound didn't carry over the radio. "The surface warships took quite the beating during the battle. Battlegroup Hammer got the worst of it. The Mongavarian fleet didn't follow Battlegroup Anvil into the ice floes as far as expected, and when Battlegroup Hammer came out of hiding, the Mongavarian flank had the room to turn and face them."

This wasn't exactly orders, but Fieran appreciated the summary of what had happened with the surface fleet. He hadn't been able to keep track of that battle, busy as he had been in the air. By the time he'd taken out the enemy aeroplanes and airships, the battle on the sea had already been over. He'd never had a chance to dive down and help the warships as planned.

As he spoke with Commander Druindar, Fieran eased his aeroplane in a circle over Dar Goranth, getting a better look at the fires and bombing craters. The wreckage of a Mongavarian airship lay on the point, burning.

Commander Druindar's tone turned even more grim. "We lost at least fourteen ships, including one of the battleships. The elven airships have been tasked with aiding the surface fleet in recovering the dead and wounded, but it will be a long process. The surface ships fought a running battle as the Mongavarian fleet disengaged, and the dead and wounded could be scattered over miles of ocean."

Fourteen ships. That struck like a punch. That number was far too high, considering their confidence in the dwarven-built ships. Granted, not all of the ships were dwarven-made. But surely that battleship had been.

What had gone wrong? Even with the surprise attack not working as planned, Fieran had heard those massive explosions. What had caused the Alliance ships to implode like that?

Fieran had to clear his throat twice before he managed, "Which ships?"

"These are just the ones we know at the moment." Commander Druindar listed off the ships, hesitating before the last two. "ES *Warren* and KS *Vanguard* were last seen chasing the fleeing Mongavarian fleet. We lost contact with them twenty minutes ago. They are presumed lost as well."

The *Vanguard*. Rokyd's and Lucien's ship.

Did Sathrah know yet? Fieran had glimpsed the *Dominion* still afloat in the sky after the battle, though the outer dirigible had a few tears and the gondola had taken a pounding. Was Sathrah still alive? Just because her airship was still alive didn't mean she was.

"I'd like your squadron to aid the airships in finding any survivors." Commander Druindar's voice deepened. "Your aeroplanes will cover more ocean more quickly than the airships. Keep a watch in case the Mongavarians return while we're distracted."

This would be the time to attack while Dar Goranth was still shaking off the last attack.

Hopefully the Mongavarians had been too badly beaten to return. While it seemed the surface fleet hadn't been as damaged as hoped, they had lost a large chunk of their airborne fleet. If they returned, Fieran would wipe out the rest of it.

And once he did, their surface fleet would be in trouble. Surely that would be enough of a deterrent that they wouldn't return anytime soon.

"Understood, sir." Fieran peeled his aeroplane away to head back over the debris-scattered ocean. Merrik kept his station guarding Fieran's six even now. He'd pulled the vines back—they would be quite the wind resistance—but his aeroplane still glowed green.

"And Laesornysh?" Commander Druindar's tone left no room for argument. "Set up a rotation so you and your pilots can rest. That includes you. That's an order."

"Yes, sir." Fieran bit back his sigh. It would be tempting to push himself, trying to find his cousins.

But they were all in for a day. They would need food and rest. Not to mention their aeroplanes would need new magical power cells eventually.

Though, Commander Druindar had never given any orders regarding when Fieran landed for rest. If he put himself last in the rotation, well, he was currently the commanding officer of the squadron. That was his prerogative.

Pip groaned at the hand shaking her awake. She blinked wearily up at the person, finding Tiny's face only a foot above hers where she lay on a cot someone had dragged up from one of the rooms and placed in one corner of the hangar.

Tiny straightened and tilted his head. "Fieran's back."

That got her to her feet. She stretched, scrubbing at her eyes to wake up, before she looked around.

It was sometime in the middle of the night. She'd been busy all day and into the night, fixing damaged aeroplanes as they came in, before she'd finally curled up on the cot. She must have only gotten a handful of hours of sleep.

At the mouth of the hangar, Fieran and Merrik wearily trudged inside. They paused to briefly talk to Lije, Pretty Face, and Murray, who were on their way outside to take off for another shift in the sky. Tiny hurried to join them, tugging on his flight cap as he went.

To one side, Sontar was manning a coffee, tea, donut, and medical care station. He'd proved invaluable here in the hangar, seeing to it that all the incoming flyboys were given a coffee and donut upon landing. He'd also assessed all their injuries, binding up the minor wounds and sending the others to sick bay.

"Mind if I take the cot?" One of her mechanics pressed a hand against the wall, dark smudges underneath his eyes. He hadn't had a chance to sleep yet.

"Of course. I'll be up for a while." Pip stepped away

from the cot as the mechanic collapsed onto it. The poor man was snoring within moments.

Fieran extracted himself from his flyboys, Merrik at his side. Sontar met them partway across the hangar, handing each of them a mug and a donut.

Pip wasn't sure how, but Fieran managed a smile for his cousin, the expression digging weary lines into his face and not quite reaching his eyes. Still, seeing that smile sent something like hope through her. If Fieran could smile after the day they'd had, then surely everything would be all right, eventually.

Even though Pip hadn't left the hangar since returning with Sontar, the rumors had flown around Dar Goranth. They were saying it was estimated that there were over ten thousand casualties with perhaps as many as six or seven thousand dead, most of those sailors on the surface ships. Many of the ships that had blown up had few survivors.

The airships with elven healers on board had been turned into mobile healing units, docking at the sick bay level to transfer the worst of the wounded to recover on land. Any surface ships with elven healers had also been turned into hospital ships.

But worst was the ships picking up the dead. The stories floating around Dar Goranth told of ships coming into the harbor with the dead mounded on the decks. There was not enough canvas in all of Dar Goranth to properly shroud the dead, even with many of the trolls in the local villages donating their spare canvas. Teams were trying to identify all the dead before they were quickly buried on a hill farther along the coast of Drogenvroh Island.

At least the Alliance sailors were being given that much. The dead Mongavarians were buried at sea, nameless and friendless, even if they were afforded as much dignity as possible.

That was what Pip had heard, anyway. She hadn't looked out the hangar mouth to see for herself. She hadn't wanted to. Just that one trip to sick bay had been enough.

Instead, she had focused on fixing the aeroplanes, swapping out their depleted magical power cells for the last of the full ones, and getting her boys back in the sky as safely and quickly as possible so they could continue the search for survivors.

Fieran patted Sontar on the back before he turned toward Pip. Their gazes met for a moment. There was so much in his blue eyes. An aching pain. A longing. A weariness that went beyond just his body's exhaustion. The Fieran she was looking at now was older than the one who had gone up hours ago.

Merrik said something to Fieran in a low voice before he strode past him, headed for the stairs.

After another heartbeat longer, Fieran headed in her direction. As he neared, she swallowed and tried to put a little levity into her voice, though it rang hollow on a day like this. "You finally brought back my aeroplane. Took you long enough."

"Yeah." Fieran gave a little shrug, a tilt of his head indicating where the crew was wheeling in his aeroplane. "It's in one piece. There might be a few bullet holes, but that's it."

"I saw the stunt you pulled." Pip poked him in the chest. "That was reckless."

He didn't need dating her as a motivation to do reckless stuff. But perhaps he had been right in not pursuing anything more right now, if that was the kind of stuff he pulled on a regular basis. If he would do something like that for a nemesis, then what would he do for a girl he liked?

"It was." Fieran shifted, peeking at her with more hesitation than the normal confidence he wore so well. "Do you think…can friends still hug?"

"I think so." Pip stepped forward and wrapped her arms around his waist. She wasn't going to deny him. He looked in need of a hug.

Fieran embraced her in return, his arms strong around her. He reeked of acrid smoke and gasoline fumes, as if he'd flown through an explosion. His face was smeared with soot and gunpowder, except around his eyes where the goggles had protected him. But he was alive and unhurt. That was all that mattered.

She sighed and leaned into him. Perhaps she'd needed a hug too.

"We haven't found my cousins yet," Fieran murmured into her hair. "We found the oil slick for the ES *Warren* and the airships picked up a handful of survivors. But there's been no sign of the KS *Vanguard*."

"You'll find them." Empty words, but Pip said them anyway. They both knew that even once the *Vanguard* was found, there was no guarantee Rokyd or Lucien would have survived. Their odds weren't good, and their bodies might never be found.

Fieran just nodded, his arms tightening around her for a moment.

As much as Pip wanted to stay there, hugging Fieran, both of them had duties weighing heavily on them. With an iron force of will, she stepped out of the hug, letting her arms drop. "You need to get some sleep. I'll have your aeroplane ready to go when you wake."

"Thanks." Fieran lifted a hand, as if to stroke her cheek. But he changed the gesture at the last moment to lightly bump her shoulder with his fist in a friendly, far-too-brotherly gesture.

But that was the way it had to be. She didn't like it, but she understood.

Fieran turned on his heel and strode away.

Pip turned too, heading for her tool cart. She had work to do.

FIERAN TRUDGED DOWN THE STAIRS. At the next level down, he paused, listening to the quiet talk of a few of the elven pilots as they took showers or wandered in something of a daze along the corridor. The whole squadron was hurting, but Flight A had taken the worst of it. Flight B had lost Grady and Miller. But Flight A had lost six pilots, and their leader currently lay in sick bay, gravely injured.

After a moment, Fieran got his legs moving again. He climbed down the stairs, passing the level with his rooms. He wasn't ready to face his men yet, and there was something he needed to do before he could rest.

At Level 3, he halted in the stairwell for a moment, nearly staggering back a step at the sight, the smell. So many wounded.

When he could finally force his shaking legs to move, he approached the nearest troll nurse. She was giving one of the wounded men a sip of water and glanced up at his approach. "Can I help you?"

"I'm looking for Lt. Saranthyr Rothilion. He was brought in earlier today." Fieran tried to force a smile. "I'm the second-in-command of his squadron."

"He's resting in there." The troll nurse pointed toward the other side of sick bay, across the way from most of the bustle. "Don't disturb anyone and don't stay long."

"I understand." Fieran nodded to her before he picked his way to the ward that must have been turned into a recovery room for the worst of the wounded.

Inside the ward, rows of cots lined the room, some with curtains drawn around them for privacy, some with the curtains pulled back. A few nurses moved among the wounded, but this room was far quieter than outside.

Fieran paused to ask another nurse, who pointed him toward one of the beds at the far end of the room. Fieran walked down the aisle between the beds.

Lt. Rothilion lay under a sheet, still and pale as his long blond hair straggled across the pillow. A far cry from the normally stuffy and put together elf noble.

At Fieran's approach, Lt. Rothilion's eyes flickered open, and he blinked several times as if he was trying to wake up…or he couldn't believe what he was seeing.

Fieran sank onto the chair next to the cot. "How are you feeling, Rothilion?"

Lt. Rothilion gave a huff that was more frustrated groan than laugh. "About what you would expect."

That was a bit of an unnecessary question, but Fieran didn't know what else to say or ask. It wasn't like he and the elf lieutenant had been close before he'd been wounded.

"I've never been shot, so I wouldn't know what to expect." Flippant probably wasn't the best route to go, but Fieran wasn't going to manage consoling very well.

"Of course not." Lt. Rothilion's voice held a trace of that old bitterness. "Not with your magic."

There wasn't a good answer to that. Fieran did have a rather big advantage when going into battle. He could incinerate bullets.

Lt. Rothilion's eyes dropped closed on a weary sigh, and for a moment he seemed to drift back to sleep. Then he murmured, without opening his eyes, "And my pilots? How many were lost?"

"Six." Fieran hesitated, hoping Lt. Rothilion wouldn't ask.

"And Flight B?"

Fieran couldn't lie. "Two."

Lt. Rothilion grimaced as he turned his face away. "It is my fault. I saw how hard you trained your men. I noticed how effective pairing off your men was. Yet I was so convinced of the superiority of elves that I thought it would be admitting weakness to implement those same measures for my own pilots. And that arrogance got my pilots killed."

"My pilots had the advantage of my magic." Fieran wasn't sure why he was reassuring Lt. Rothilion. Any other time and he would have relished having Lt. Rothilion basically tell him that he was right.

But Rothilion wouldn't have said any of this if he hadn't been dosed up on healing magic and out of it from blood loss.

"Perhaps. But you were not at the side of all your pilots during the entire battle. They held their own, and they did it well." Lt. Rothilion heaved another sigh, seeming smaller and more sunken on the cot. "It is my fault that my pilots did not fare as well."

It was also the elven pilots' first battle while Fieran's flyboys had faced battle before. Not against other aeroplanes, but they had been shot at before.

But Rothilion was in no shape mentally or physically to hear any more reassurances.

"Don't dwell on it now." Fieran squeezed Rothilion's shoulder and pushed to his feet. "I will leave you to your rest."

Rothilion didn't respond. Fieran would have thought

he'd fallen back asleep, but the elf lieutenant was too tense to be sleeping.

Fieran slipped out of sick bay once again. He halted at the base of the stairs, gathering his strength to drag himself back up the twenty flights of stairs back to his room. He might just curl up in the landing and fall asleep here.

A noise echoed up the stairs from the landing below, followed by what he thought was a familiar voice.

But surely not. They couldn't have gotten here this fast, could they?

Fieran crept down the stairs, then peered around the corner at the next landing down.

Uncle Julien leaned his back against the wall as he held Aunt Vriska in his arms. Her face was hidden against his shoulder, one of her hands fisted in his shirt, the other wreathed with gray magic as she slowly pounded her fist against the stone wall. Her shoulders shook, but Fieran couldn't hear any sobs, just a tight note in her voice as she murmured, "Our boys, Julien. Our boys."

"I know." Uncle Julien's voice was choked, tears glinting in his eyes and on his cheek above his red-brown beard.

Fieran withdrew around the corner, easing away. He shouldn't intrude.

When he turned to creep back up the stairs, he jumped, barely biting back his exclamation before he made a noise that would give away his presence to Uncle Julien and Aunt Vriska.

Sathrah slumped against the wall at the top of the stairs on the next landing up, her light brown hair straggling long over her shoulders. She hadn't been there when he'd walked down a moment ago.

Fieran tiptoed up the stairs, then leaned against the wall next to Sathrah.

"They arrived a few minutes ago." Sathrah's voice was little more than a whisper, her tone resigned and lifeless. "They were already on their way when word came of the attack. They had to be here. Famous generals and all that. They did not know they would be here for…for…"

Fieran swallowed. He opened his mouth, but he just couldn't choke out any words.

Sathrah hugged her arms over her stomach, looking more hunched and small than he'd ever seen her. "I can't lose them, Fieran. I can't…not again."

A lump clogged Fieran's throat. He couldn't imagine losing any of his siblings. But Sathrah had lost her entire family once before. How terrified must she be, facing the possibility that she might lose all her siblings yet again?

Fieran cleared his throat, his voice still coming out rough. "We'll find them, Sathrah."

"You can't promise that." Sathrah glared, tears glittering in her eyes. "Their bodies might already be at the bottom of the ocean."

An all too likely possibility. But Fieran held Sathrah's gaze as he said again, "I will find them."

It might be a promise he couldn't keep. But he made it anyway.

# CHAPTER TWENTY-THREE

Fieran flew his aeroplane over the ocean, leaning back and forth over the sides of his cockpit to take in as much of the ocean as he could. A clear blue sky arched overhead, the rising sun warm against his cheek. A beautiful day for a grim task.

Merrik flew several yards to the right and behind Fieran. Farther to the right, Lije and Pretty Face held station with other flyboys ranging to Fieran's left. Nearly half the squadron, both elves and humans, had turned out.

Four airships came into view, two of them standing guard high in the sky while the other two hovered only feet above the water as they searched the debris field and oil slick for any survivors. So far, all they had retrieved were the dead.

They'd found the remains of the *Vanguard* in the early hours of the morning, but it hadn't been light enough until now for the aeroplanes to do a proper search.

In the twenty-four hours since the battle, how far would any survivors have drifted?

"Let's make a swing to cover the ocean between where the ship went down and the shore." Fieran spoke into the radio as he turned his aeroplane in that direction. "Keep your eyes peeled. A head bobbing in the water won't be easy to spot."

Cold as the water was, it was highly unlikely that anyone would still be alive after twenty-four hours in the water.

But there were many trolls on the ship, and if they had ice magic, they might have been able to survive the dousing. Maybe.

Fieran scanned the ocean as he flew over. So much empty water. How would they ever find any survivors who drifted away from the wreck site?

"I've got a body here." One of the flyboys on the far end of their formation radioed in.

"Alive?" Fieran's heart jumped in his throat.

"No, definitely dead. He's floating face down." The flyboy paused before adding, "He's an Escarlish seaman. Brown hair, pale skin."

Not either of Fieran's cousins. But still someone's son. Someone's brother. Maybe someone's husband. Perhaps a father.

"Hold station over the body until one of the airships can retrieve him." Fieran switched to channel 2 and called in the body and the location to Dar Goranth. The troll stationed by the radio in the hangar would pass the message along to the communications room, which would get the word to the airships.

Such a clunky system. Hopefully Louise and Uncle Lance were hard at work figuring out how to integrate the long-wave and short-wave radios. Things would be a lot simpler once Fieran could coordinate with the airships himself.

Thinking of Louise brought up memories of family. Of family gatherings with the whole extended family. Uncle Julien joking with Dacha. Aunt Vriska debating with Uncle Edmund about strategy. Rokyd and Lucien as part of the whole gang of cousins.

They couldn't be gone. Surely not. Fieran couldn't imagine those family gatherings without them there.

Still he flew and searched. His flyboys reported more bodies. He had to make more radio calls.

Then there was nothing. Just endless, empty waves heaving up and down in inky depths.

Fieran flew for an hour, then two, searching. They were far from the wreck site now, the Kostarian shoreline more distinct.

"We should turn back." Merrik's voice came over the radio, low and aching with far too much compassion.

"Not yet. Just a little bit longer." Fieran couldn't turn back. Turning back would mean giving up.

A glint caught the corner of his eye. Fieran peered in that direction, but he couldn't spot what he thought he'd seen.

Still, he eased the rudder and the control stick, turning his aeroplane in that direction.

Merrik matched his turn, not questioning him again just yet.

After a minute or so of flight, there was another glint. Something white sparkled on the waves up ahead, farther south and closer to shore than Fieran would have expected.

Was that a chunk of one of the guarding icebergs? What was it doing way out here? Could the storm have pushed it this far out?

As he neared, Fieran dove his aeroplane closer, then

slowed as much as he could to get a good look at the object.

It wasn't an iceberg. It was a raft made of ice, complete with ice oars. A troll halted in rowing, shading his eyes with a hand to peer upward. Another figure was sprawled partially on top of him, as if they had been huddling together to stay warm.

"It's Rokyd! Merrik, that's Rokyd!" Fieran all but shouted into the radio. "And that must be Lucien with him. They're alive."

"Yes." Merrik's voice held a breath of relief that carried even over the radio.

Gripping the control column with one hand, Fieran reached over the side of the cockpit and called up his magic. He unleashed a shower of sparks and sent bolts of magic through the sky.

The troll on the ice raft waved back, then slumped, not bothering to pick up the oars again.

With Rokyd now assured of which pilot circled overhead, Fieran pressed the talk button again. "Ground crew, come in."

There was no response but static. Not even the chatter of the other members of the squadron.

Shoot. Fieran and Merrik must have flown so far that they were out of range of both the rest of the squadron and the radio at Dar Goranth.

"I will fly back into range." Merrik peeled off, headed back the way they'd come.

"Thanks." Fieran continued circling to mark the location for the airships and keep Rokyd and Lucien company while they waited for help to arrive.

FIERAN SPRINTED down the flights of stairs as quickly as he could without falling. Surely landing his aeroplane couldn't have taken as long as docking an airship and offloading the wounded.

Never had Fieran been so relieved to see an airship than when the KAS *Dominion* appeared on the horizon as he circled over Rokyd and Lucien's boat. Lucien hadn't stirred the entire time Fieran had been circling overhead. How bad off was he?

Fieran skidded out of the stairway into sick bay. On the far side, Uncle Julien and Aunt Vriska paced in the small, cleared space before the double doors that led to the airship dock jutting from the side of the cliff.

Before Fieran could cross the room to them, the large double doors were flung open. Two troll airmen hurried through the doors, carrying a stretcher between them. Lucien lay on the stretcher, still unmoving. An elf trotted alongside, her hand on Lucien's shoulder as her fingers glowed green with healing magic.

Behind them, Sathrah supported Rokyd. He was lacking a shirt and had bandages wrapped over his torso and arms. His trousers were shredded, showing burns and bloody cuts.

Rushing forward, Uncle Julien took Rokyd's other arm, supporting him, while Aunt Vriska clenched her fists, glancing between Rokyd and Lucien as if she really wanted to punch a Mongavarian or two. The faint line of a scar showed starkly on one of the fingers of her right hand.

Aunt Melantha strode from the main hospital ward, her gaze sweeping over Rokyd and Lucien with a cool assessment that someone who didn't know her might mistake for detachment. She paused beside Aunt Vriska for a moment, speaking with a firm, almost fierce note. "I will take good care of your boys, Vriska."

Aunt Vriska nodded, her fists still clenched. "You had better."

From Aunt Vriska, the worry for her sons came out sounding rather pugilistic. Sathrah got it from somewhere, after all.

Aunt Melantha shouted more orders to her healers, nurses, and medics as she led the way into sick bay, as commanding as a general on a battlefield.

Fieran slumped against the wall next to the stairwell. He didn't want to get in the way of the healers. Nor was this a moment for a cousin to be intruding.

Sliding down the wall, Fieran settled in as comfortably as he could to wait.

FIERAN WOKE at the sound of footsteps, then someone lowering himself to sit next to him. Fieran cracked his eyes open, then straightened. "Uncle Julien."

Uncle Julien wearily leaned his head against the wall. "I see you have gained the essential army skill of sleeping anytime, anywhere."

Fieran would have joked right back, but now didn't seem the time. "How are Rokyd and Lucien?"

"They'll be fine." Uncle Julien spoke the words on a weary sigh. "Both of them sustained burns, and Lucien suffered hypothermia. When the *Vanguard* exploded, Rokyd shielded the two of them as best he could with his magic, and they were blown into the water."

"I'm glad they'll be all right." Fieran sagged more heavily against the wall, his muscles aching after the long hours of flying in the past two days.

It was over. Truly over. There would be another long day, another battle, sometime in the future, but for now, he could rest.

"Thank you for finding them." Uncle Julien met Fieran's gaze, something in his brown eyes haggard.

"I just happened to be the aeroplane patrolling that area." Fieran shrugged, dropping his gaze to his hands. "It looked like Rokyd was doing his best to rescue both of them all on his own."

Once Rokyd realized help wouldn't be coming any time soon, he must have made that raft with his magic and set out for the coast. Between how far south the *Vanguard* had been and how the currents flowed in that area, the coast would have been a better option than Dar Goranth.

"Yes, Rokyd made a valiant effort to save Lucien." Uncle Julien's voice held pride, the first hint of a smile twitching beneath his thick beard. The smile faded a moment later. "But that stretch of coast is isolated. Lucien would have died long before Rokyd got him to an elven healer."

Fieran swallowed. He couldn't imagine being in Rokyd's place. No help coming, his brother dying in his arms, and his only option to row toward a shoreline that likely wouldn't even have the help his brother needed. What mental anguish he must have endured during the long night of rowing.

"I heard you made a valiant showing of your own during the battle." The warmth returned to Uncle Julien's voice.

"I'm a Laesornysh." Fieran shrugged, not sure how to reply to the praise. He liked praise well enough, but somehow it was easier to take from strangers and peers than from his uncle. "I'm not sure my efforts were enough. If I could have taken out the enemy aeroplanes and airships sooner, perhaps I could have prevented some of the losses among the surface fleet. I could have done more."

"Don't torture yourself with what-ifs. There's no point to it." Uncle Julien kept his voice low, though still firm. "This is a modern, mechanized war the likes of which we have never fought before. There is no victory. Just being defeated less than the other side."

If even Uncle Julien had that perspective, then that was…discouraging.

"*Did* we lose less than the other side?" Fieran gestured toward the packed sick bay.

Uncle Julien's gaze, too, fixed on the wounded men and women waiting for treatment. "Dar Goranth didn't fall, so the enemy didn't achieve their objective. Thanks to you, their air fleet suffered significant losses. In that regard, we won. While we succeeded in sinking twelve of their surface ships, we also didn't achieve our objective in making a noticeable dent in Mongavaria's seagoing fleet. We lost more ships and men than they did. Mongavaria will probably claim this as a victory as well."

Disheartening thought.

"Why did we lose so many ships? Do you know?" Fieran searched Uncle Julien's face. While Uncle Julien was a general in the army, not an admiral in the navy, he was high enough ranked that he would likely be told that information.

"Some of the losses were the smaller ships built without dwarven magic. Those the Mongavarians sank the same way we sank theirs—by putting enough holes in them." Uncle Julien heaved an even more weary breath. "But as for the others, it seems there were many among the troll captains who grew too confident in the protections of the dwarven-made ships. To prioritize a more rapid rate of fire, the blast doors were left open, and shells and cordite were stacked together. The dwarven-made ships are well-built, but there are still ways for enemy shells to penetrate from the upper decks. And when they did…"

A fire, then a catastrophic explosion.

Fieran scrubbed a hand over his face. "How do we win a war when even a victory feels like defeat?"

Uncle Julien paused, not continuing until Fieran dragged up his gaze to meet his. "All you can do is your duty."

Fieran tried to let that settle into his chest, the way those similar words from his dacha had after the Battle over Bridgetown.

Did his dacha wrestle with this guilt each time he fought? With their powerful magic, perhaps it was inevitable to feel they could have done more. A curse of being Laesornysh.

But if carrying this weight was what it took to protect the Alliance, his family, his friends, and his flyboys, then Fieran would carry it gladly.

# CHAPTER
# TWENTY-FOUR

Pip tightened the last bolt holding the ginormous cable to the junction box. After one last tug to make sure it was snug but not reefed too tight, she stuck the wrench in her belt. "All right, how is the power cell looking?"

"All set." Fieran extricated himself from the power station attached to the junction box. Four large power cells—the size normally used for powering the surface warships—were wired into the junction box, much as they would be in an engine.

"Then we're ready for the first test." Pip dusted off her hands.

Fieran grinned, then led the way from the solid stone bunker that housed the power station and junction box.

At the top of the stairs to the surface, a troll warrior stood guard, and Pip nodded to him as she climbed out of the bunker. She stood at the edge of a cliff overlooking the harbor along one of the points that stretched to either side of Dar Goranth.

In the past two weeks since the battle, most of the

wreckage had been cleaned up and repairs were already underway to the buildings. With so much to do, Pip had been surprised the base's commanding officer had fast-tracked her idea.

Then again, the attack was probably the reason he'd responded to her idea with such eagerness.

The troll warrior swung the massive stone door shut, sealing everything safely inside. He then returned to his post in a sheltered spot next to the bunker.

Fieran waited a few steps away along the rocky headland, half-turned back to her.

Pip picked her way over the rocks, falling into step beside him. "I hope this works."

"It will. You designed it." Fieran's grin remained bright on his face and in his blue eyes.

It was good to see him grinning again after the weight he'd carried in the aftermath of the battle.

"You helped a lot with that. I couldn't have done it without your knowledge of magical power cells." Pip dropped her gaze, not quite able to hold his gaze with that extra warm way he was looking at her.

They'd been able to rig something to refill the power cells she'd drained during the battle easily enough. Her magic and the way it conducted his magic prevented the usual problems of incineration and explosions that normally made filling power cells a tricky thing without the proper setup.

Working on that had led to pursuing this idea and, thankfully, helped her and Fieran regain some of the camaraderie they'd had before all that little confession, almost kiss awkwardness.

Just friends. That was what they'd agreed. That still didn't stop her heart from beating harder around him or banish all thoughts of being held in his arms.

After the war. That sounded like such a long way off.

After strolling along the harbor—stopping briefly to wave at the dwarves hard at work in the dry docks to repair the ships damaged in the battle—they stepped into Level 1.

Commander Druindar and Captain Gradrah met them just inside. Captain Gradrah rested her gaze on Pip. "Mechanic Detmuk-Inawenys, is the shield ready for testing?"

"Yes, ma'am." Pip stood as straight as she could. She still felt far too tiny surrounded by Fieran and the two troll officers.

Captain Gradrah nodded, then spun smartly on her heel. She marched toward a room that had been a storage closet to one side of the communications room. It had been turned into the breaker room for the base shield she'd just finished installing.

Commander Druindar, Fieran, and Pip followed. They left the double doors open, giving a view into the harbor.

At the tiny room, they found a whole bunch of the other troll commanding officers. Everyone was so packed in that Pip couldn't even see the large lever-style breaker she had installed in the control panel.

The troll officer she'd worked with in the past week, training him how to operate the system, called out over the hubbub, "Test One commencing."

The bystanders quieted. Pip shifted from foot to foot. It was even more nerve-wracking, standing there unable to see anything but the broad shoulders of uniformed trolls.

Fieran leaned closer to her. "Do I need to fetch you a box? A ladder? Hoist you on my shoulders like I do my little brother Tryndar?"

"No. Absolutely not." Pip rolled her eyes as she gave him a light shove.

She only caught a glimpse of his smirk before she turned her back to him. That put her nose only a few inches from some troll officer's back.

Perhaps she should have asked him for a box after all. At least here in the back she'd have a good look at the shield outside when it went up.

The troll must have flipped one of the switches because a loud claxon rang out through the base.

Claxons had been installed all over the base and the harbor, giving warning to everyone that the shield was about to go up. Since this shield wasn't as controlled as a shield wielded directly by a person, there was a good chance someone would be hurt if they were standing over the shield when it activated.

For this test, the entire base had been warned, and all ships ordered to stay in the harbor.

Even with those precautions, the troll let the claxon ring for ten minutes—perhaps even fifteen—to make sure everyone was well away when the barrier went up for the first time.

The trolls remained perfectly still and composed as they waited. Pip couldn't help but shift from foot to foot. Next to her, Fieran crossed his arms, then uncrossed them. He tapped his fingers on his arm, then paced back and forth.

If she'd done everything right, once the troll flipped the switch, a signal would be sent through underground wires to that junction box. Magic would flood from the power cells into the gigantic wire that had been buried in a circle following the lay of the land, going around the harbor, up the cliffs, around the airfield, and back down again to encircle the dry docks. That wire had been reinforced with her magic so that the magic of the ancient kings would flow as designed and not just incinerate the wire.

The hardest part had been tweaking the wire and her magic to make sure the magic was directed into a full dome instead of simply going straight into the sky.

Had she done everything right? What if this just caused a massive explosion? Would the troll commanders reprimand her for wasting valuable time and resources on a project like this instead of something more practical for the war effort?

Finally, the troll called out, "Barrier going up." His words were followed by a loud clank as he lifted the lever and shoved it into place, completing the circuit.

Pip spun to face the doors. With a crackle, a dome of magic shot into the air, covering all of Dar Goranth with a shield.

Pip held her breath, waiting one heartbeat. Two. The dome remained, solid and powerful. No explosions. No power lashing out of control in unintentional ways.

"Very good. Switch it off."

The clank rang again, and the dome disappeared.

Pip released a breath in a whoosh. It had worked. It had really worked.

"You did it." Fieran reached for her as if to pull her into a hug, hesitated, gave a little cough, and instead stuck out his hand. "Congratulations, Pip. You've made me obsolete."

Pip took his hand and shook, though she would rather have had that hug. "Not so obsolete. My shield will only give a little extra protection. It won't stand up to a large-scale bombing. Just buy enough time for airships or aeroplanes to drive away attackers."

It wasn't a solution for every base and city across the

Alliance. For one thing, she could only stretch a dome like that so far before her magic wouldn't be enough to handle it. She could rig something like this for a compact base like Dar Goranth, but most military bases and cities in Escarland were far too large to be protected this way. Nor would this work well for Tarenhiel with its extensive tree cover that would get in the way.

Not to mention the shield drew a lot of magical power every time it was switched on. While Fieran and his family had great reserves of power, no one wanted to risk them draining themselves too much when they were needed in so many facets of the war and infrastructure.

Besides, the raw materials to make magical power cells were limited, due to needing high grade metals and very specific resources. On top of that, there were the logistics of shipping out the magical power cells to keep everyone supplied.

This might not be a widespread solution, but it would be a boon for Dar Goranth, the most important Alliance base that wasn't protected by the Wall.

"It's a great achievement, Pip." Fieran stepped slightly closer, as if he was still thinking about that aborted hug. "Don't minimize it."

It was the kind of thing to put on a resume, if she applied to the Alliance Magical Power Company after the war. Not that her magic wouldn't be enough on its own.

She shoved that thought away. As much as she wanted to dream about the future after the war—a future involving Fieran in some way, even just to figure out if they could have a future—now wasn't the time. They had a long war ahead of them yet.

Before she could respond, Pip was swarmed by the troll commanders. She felt like a pinball being knocked between the various officers as they shook her hand and pounded her back. By the time they finished and drifted away, she was stumbling and a bit dizzy.

"You all right?" Fieran steadied her elbow, though he dropped his hand only a moment later.

"I'm fine. Trolls are very bombastic with their congratulations." Pip rolled her shoulders and drew in a deep breath to steady herself. Once she felt steadier on her feet, she faced Fieran again. "Now that the shield test is over, don't you have a medal ceremony to prepare for?"

Fieran heaved a sigh, looking rather glum for someone about to receive a medal. "Yeah. I probably should have already started. Formal uniforms take a long time to prepare. You have to measure every little thing on it to get it exactly right."

"Ah, yes. Fiddly little details. Your favorite thing." Pip nudged him, giving him a slight nudge toward the stairs. "Get going. I'll see you there."

She wanted to do one last check of the shield, the junction box, and all the wiring, now that the shield had been turned on once. If any of it showed any signs of incineration or burning or blackening, then she would need to fix the issue before it became a big problem the next time the barrier was raised.

But after her last checks, she'd hurry up to her room for a quick shower and a change into her best set of coveralls. She wasn't going to miss watching the medal ceremony.

Or the sight of Fieran in his dress uniform.

On the airfield in front of the hangar, Fieran stood at one end of the double line of flyboys, the tight collar of his uniform itching at his neck. The dress uniform with dark brown jacket and lighter brown trousers was tailored so stiffly and tightly that he wasn't sure he could actually sit down in it.

Merrik stood beside him, standing so still and seeming unbothered in his dress uniform. The rest of the flyboys lined up in two lines, looking official and solemn.

There was a small space, then the elven pilots also lined up in two lines, dressed in deep green uniforms. Lt. Rothilion stood at the far end of his front row, still a bit pale but on his feet.

Before the hangar, rows of chairs and benches had been set up, and they were currently filled with various spectators, including Rokyd, Lucien, and Sathrah. Rokyd and Lucien were both still recovering here at Dar Goranth, but they were well enough to attend.

The mechanics had the front row, and Fieran resisted the urge to break the military formation to wave at Pip.

In front of the formation of pilots, a bunch of troll officers stood at military attention, including Captain Gradrah and Commander Druindar. Aunt Melantha, Sontar, Uncle Julien, and Aunt Vriska stood with them, along with an elf official Fieran didn't recognize. He must have shown up pretty recently, given he still had a bit of a green, seasick look to him.

The base commander finished his speech, then nodded to Captain Gradrah.

Captain Gradrah stepped forward and unfolded a piece of paper. "For wounds received in combat, the following have been awarded the Tarenhieli Bronze Maple."

As Captain Gradrah read off the names of the elven pilots who had been wounded in the battle, the elf official handed the medals to Aunt Melantha, who pinned the medals on the uniforms of the elves who stepped forward, including Lt. Rothilion.

Once the elven pilots had received their medals, Captain Gradrah read off her paper again. "For wounds received in combat, the following have been awarded the Escarlish Royal Heart."

This time when Captain Gradrah read off the names, Uncle Julien stepped forward and pinned the medals on the uniforms of the flyboys who had been wounded in the battle.

Something almost painful swelled in Fieran's chest. This was the recognition his men deserved. They'd been denied it after the Battle over Bridgetown. Everyone had been reeling after the attack, and Fieran's actions had overshadowed those of his men.

Once those medals were distributed, Captain Gradrah spoke again. "Mechanic Pippak Detmuk-Inawenys, please stand and step forward."

Pip's face drained of color, her mouth falling open.

Fieran couldn't fully hide his grin now. Hadn't she realized that *she* would be honored today too?

After another heartbeat, her fellow mechanics chivvied her into standing. She took a step forward, straightening her shoulders and pulling herself together.

That feeling was welling in his chest again. That was his girl.

The thought popped the swelling pride like a dirigible balloon scoured with his magic. She wasn't his girl. All because he'd been too scared of doing something rash to pursue anything with her.

He still wasn't sure if he'd done the right thing in pulling away from her that night. A part of him—the rash part or the smart part, he wasn't sure—still thought he should have kissed her.

"Pippak Detmuk-Inawenys, in the Battle for Dar Goranth, you threw yourself into the line of duty, even though you are a civilian. By your actions in defending Dar Goranth with your magic, you saved many lives and preserved the integrity of this base. For these actions above and beyond the call of duty, you have been awarded the Stone of Courage, the highest honor a civilian can be awarded by Kostaria."

Fieran's aunts Vriska and Melantha strode to Pip. Aunt Vriska held out the medal, and Aunt Melantha took it from her before looping the medal's ribbon over Pip's head. Since Pip was so short, the medal fell all the way to the belt of her coveralls.

Fieran itched to run over and congratulate Pip then and there.

Once Pip had retaken her seat and Fieran's aunts returned to their spots up front, Captain Gradrah read off, "Second Lieutenant Merrik Loiatir, step forward."

Merrik took a step out of line, his head high, his shoulders back. A slight breeze tossed his chestnut hair, which reached his collar.

"Second Lieutenant Merrik Loiatir, in the aftermath of the Battle for Dar Goranth, you demonstrated remarkable skill of magic and flight to preserve the life of a fellow pilot at great risk to yourself. For these actions above and beyond the call of duty, you have been awarded the Tarenhieli Silver Beech and the Escarlish Royal Valor, the second-highest medals awarded to an elven warrior or an Escarlish soldier."

The elf official handed the elven medal to Aunt Melantha, who pinned the medal on Merrik's uniform.

Once she stepped back, Uncle Julien pinned the Escarlish medal on Merrik's uniform. But Uncle Julien didn't immediately step back. Instead, he pulled out a set of silver shoulder bars and a matching set of wings. When Uncle Julien spoke, he raised his voice loudly enough for those gathered to hear. "It is also my pleasure to announce that you have been promoted to First Lieutenant in the Escarlish Flying Corps."

It was all Fieran could do to resist clapping Merrik on the back when Merrik returned to his spot in line.

Then Captain Gradrah's voice rang over the airfield again. "First Lieutenant Fieran Laesornysh, step forward."

Fieran worked to keep his face straight as he did as ordered. He'd had an inkling he would get a medal at this ceremony today, but it still felt surreal to hear his name called. In some ways, he didn't feel he deserved a medal. Saving Lt. Rothilion hadn't been so much a brave act as one of rash desperation not to lose another man on his watch.

But perhaps all medals were awarded for things that didn't feel so much like courage in the moment. It was just doing what needed doing.

"First Lieutenant Fieran Laesornysh, during the Battle for Dar Goranth, you used your magic with great effect to eliminate much of the Mongavarian air fleet, thereby sparing many lives among your fellow pilots, the Alliance naval fleets, and in Dar Goranth. You also demonstrated great skill with your aeroplane and your magic to save the life of a fellow pilot at no small risk to yourself. For these actions above and beyond the call of duty, you have been awarded the Kostarian Stone of Duty, the Tarenhieli Silver Beech, and the Escarlish Royal Valor."

Aunt Vriska and Aunt Melantha stepped forward. The moment was so solemn that Fieran didn't even have to fight a smile as his aunts pinned first the Kostarian medal, then the elven medal on his uniform.

The Kostarian medal was made of steel with stone embedded into it. The stone was formed in the shape of the ancient rune for the word *duty*. The Tarenhieli medal was crafted of silver with the shape of a beech tree embossed on it.

Both of his aunts gave him a slight nod they hadn't given the others before they stepped back into place.

When Uncle Julien replaced them, he met Fieran's gaze with a hint of a smile half-hidden by his beard. He pinned the Escarlish medal, a plain brass medal featuring a stylized sword and crown, onto Fieran's uniform.

Like with Merrik, he didn't step back. Instead, he pulled out silver shoulder bars from his pocket. "It's also my pleasure to announce your promotion to Captain in the Escarlish Flying Corps."

Captain. Fieran's ears rang as Uncle Julien added the bars to each of the shoulders of his uniform.

Fieran barely heard the rest of the ceremony nor the dismissal. He didn't have time to give Merrik a thump on the back before he was swarmed by family. Uncle Julien, Aunt Vriska, Aunt Melantha, Sortar, Rokyd, Lucien, and Sathrah all gathered around him, shaking his hand, telling him congratulations, or thumping his back hard enough to make him stumble.

As the chaos began to break up, Uncle Julien pressed a folded set of papers into Fieran's hand. "Your orders, Captain Laesornysh."

Fieran didn't have a chance to open and read the papers before Uncle Julien nodded and strolled away.

As his family dispersed, Fieran finally glanced around. All his flyboys had vanished, as had all of the elven pilots. Strange, that. He would have expected a few to stay. But even Merrik was gone.

Only Pip remained. She joined him, tapping one of the medals. "These look good."

"Yours does too." Fieran grinned back. "Now let's head for the hangar. I think the flyboys are up to something. Unless you were tasked with delaying me?"

"No. Well, yes. But your family already did a good enough job of that." Pip's smile took on a mischievous tilt.

Fieran kept his stroll easy so that he didn't force Pip to trot to keep up. As they stepped into the hangar, Fieran stopped short.

All the flyboys were lined up, blocking his way and his view of much of the rest of the space.

Lije stepped forward. "We've been thinking. Our squadron is so new that it doesn't have a name."

Stickyfingers waved his hand. "Every unit needs a name."

"Not to mention, you have been sadly negligent on picking out art for your aeroplane." Pretty Face sauntered forward a step.

"So we took it upon ourselves to pick a name and paint your aeroplane." Murray gestured over his shoulder.

The pilots stepped apart, leaving an opening between them to reveal a canvas-covered aeroplane. Next to the aeroplane, Tiny gripped the canvas and yanked it off, revealing the artwork.

A pointed elven ear had been painted on the side of Fieran's aeroplane. Waves of red that looked like they could be hair turned into flames at the tips. Blue bolts twined among the red hair-flames while tiny images appeared among the blue magic and red hair-flames. An upside-down aeroplane. An airship wreathed in blue magic. Two elven swords.

It was bold. A bit gaudy. And very perfect.

But more than that, Fieran finally got a glimpse of the aeroplanes beyond his. All of them had pointed, elven-style ears painted over or incorporated into whatever design had already been there. Even Pretty Face's lounging self-portrait now sported pointed elven ears.

"We are the Half-Breed Squadron," Lije stated, grinning from ear to ear. "After all, our captain is half-elf, half-human, and that's what makes him our Laesornysh."

On cue, all of them saluted.

In a bit of a daze, Fieran saluted back. The term *half-breed* had been thrown at him—and Merrik and Tiny—as an insult. Yet there was something powerful in embracing it. As he'd told Rothilion. He was a half-breed, and he was proud of it.

"So is our first lieutenant." Lije nudged Merrik, who shifted and ducked his head. "Who else but another half-elf, half-human could watch our captain's back?"

Merrik gave a little cough, the tips of his pointed ears flushing pink, likely with embarrassment at so much attention. "Our chief mechanic is a half-elf, half-dwarf with magic that can channel the power of the ancient kings."

Seeming less uncomfortable with the attention than Merrik, Pip grinned and pointed to Tiny. "And we have a half-troll, half-human who can hurl shards of ice down at airships."

Shifting, Tiny gestured to Lije. "And Lije is part ogre."

Lije rolled his eyes. "A distant ancestor might have been an ogre. Maybe."

"I'm half-criminal," Stickyfingers announced, a hand patting the pocket where he must have his lockpicks stored. He nudged Pretty Face. "And Pretty Face is on the path to becoming a halfway decent guy."

The others crowded forward, all announcing ways that they were half. One had half a pinky finger. Several joked that some of the others had half a brain.

"What about us?" The voice quieted the hubbub a moment before Lt. Rothilion limped forward, leading the elves of Flight A. His tone and expression lacked the supercilious edge, instead remaining more open and almost humble. "Where do we fit into the Half-Breed Squadron?"

Fieran held Lt. Rothilion's gaze. How honest could he be? Would Rothilion take the humor as the olive branch Fieran intended? "You are half as stuffy as you used to be."

Instead of sniffing in offense, Lt. Rothilion's mouth tipped with a wry almost-smile as he nodded to Fieran. They weren't exactly friends yet, but perhaps they could stop being enemies.

"Well, I am half-crazy." Aylia flipped a lock of her hair over her shoulder as she swaggered to a halt. "Obviously."

A few of the other elves piped up, adding their own "halves."

Fieran let them talk, something in him relaxing at the way the elven pilots and his flyboys started mingling more than they ever had before.

Battle had honed and bonded them. Going forward, they would be a much more united squadron, and they would be all the better for it.

That reminded him of the papers Uncle Julien had handed him. Fieran unfolded them, quickly reading what they said.

He must have made a sound or showed something on his face, for Pip, Merrik, Stickyfingers, Lije, Pretty Face, and Tiny were soon gathered around him.

"What's that?" Pretty Face leaned forward, as if he was trying to read over Fieran's shoulder.

"New orders?" Merrik crossed his arms, his voice low. He positioned himself at Fieran's back, still the wingman even here on the ground.

Fieran glanced from Merrik, his oldest friend, to Pip, the girl he liked, to the gathering of friends he'd made during battle. And beyond them, the rest of his flyboys who had followed him so readily here at Dar Goranth. Finally to Lt. Rothilion and the elven pilots who were now under Fieran's command as well.

His duty had grown, weighing more heavily than the medals now pinned to his uniform. He'd come far too close to failing to be a true leader here at Dar Goranth. He'd have to do better at their next duty station.

Clearing his throat, Fieran raised his voice. "Half-Breed Squadron, listen up."

Silence fell, all of the pilots turning toward him.

Huh. That had worked better than he'd thought.

Focus. He was a captain now. He had to be all official and everything.

Fieran held up the papers, something in him lifting even as he said the words. "We've been ordered to Fort Defense."

# DON'T MISS THE NEXT ADVENTURE!

Thanks so much for reading *Stalk the Sky!* I hope Fieran, Merrik, Pip, and all the flyboys brought a few laughs between all the intense moments.

The adventure continues in **Fly to Fury (War of the Alliance Book 3)!**

After their victory in the skies over Dar Goranth, Fieran and his newly-unified squadron travel to Fort Defense to reinforce the squadrons defending the Escarlish-Mongavarian border.

Once there, they discover a harsher war than they have yet experienced.

If you'd like some War of the Alliance bonus content, including a short story of Pip and Fieran's wedding, sign up for my newsletter and download *Soar to Destiny* today!

Sign up for my newsletter now

A downloadable map and Fieran's family trees are available on the Extras page of my website.

If you ever find typos in my books, feel free to message me on social media or send me an email through the Contact Me page of my website.

If you want to learn about all my upcoming releases, sign up for my newsletter, buy signed books directly from

me, and get a full list of my books, head over to www.taragrayce.com.

# Acknowledgments

Thank you to everyone who has been following along with Fieran's adventures! I appreciate all of you who were willing to continue the stories in the Elven Alliance world with me.

A very special BIG thank you to my brother Andy for your service. Second, thank you for once again pre-reading to check my military stuff to make sure it was as accurate as it could be (given this is a steampunk fantasy not intended to be historically accurate). Any mistakes still left are fully mine. Third, thank you yet again for the use of a basic training story. Yes, the whole penguin sliding/mattress surfing down a multi-story staircase only to hurtle into a room with commanding officers happened in real life. While I made some tweaks to fit the story and characters (and to condense it because the real version was even more involved), everything from knocking each other over while trying to salute, the sandcastles, the sandcastle wars, and having to return the sand using only a single spoon all happened. Sometimes real life is even stranger (and funnier) than fiction!

Thank you, as always, to my parents who are always so supportive and excited for each of my books! Thank you to my other brothers Ethan and Josh for always reading my books no matter what genre I write. For my sisters-in-law Alyssa, Abby, and Meghan for everything from book chats to trips to the zoo to thrift store finds.

A special thank you to my nephew Elijah for loving the book (and loving having a character named after him!) For my nephew Danny: I hope you love the books just as much once you read them! For my nieces Adry and Louise: I hope both of you enjoy seeing your names in a book someday!

Thank you to my friends Bri, Paula, and Jill for all the encouragement, support, and years of laughter. I don't know what I'd do without you! For my author friends, but especially Molly, Morgan, Addy, Savannah, Hannah, and Sierra. I know I can always count on you through all the ups and downs of this writing life!

Thanks also to Tessa and Sierra for proofing what you could. Thank you once again to Deborah for a copy edit that was as filled with fangirling as it was with edits (Merrik fangirl club all the way!). Thank you to Bethany for joining the proofreading crew for the first time with this book. Your edits helped SO much in the final polish.

But most of all, I'm grateful to God for all the gifts He's given me. I'm so thankful to be able to live this author dream.